UNDERCOVER ANGEL

LISA LOCKWOOD

Bloomington, IN   Milton Keynes, UK

AuthorHouse™
1663 Liberty Drive, Suite 200
Bloomington, IN 47403
www.authorhouse.com
Phone: 1-800-839-8640

AuthorHouse™ UK Ltd.
500 Avebury Boulevard
Central Milton Keynes, MK9 2BE
www.authorhouse.co.uk
Phone: 08001974150

First published by AuthorHouse 4/9/2008

ISBN: 978-1-4343-0276-2 (sc)
ISBN: 978-1-4343-0277-9 (hc)

Library of Congress Control Number: 2007901971

Printed in the United States of America
Bloomington, Indiana

This book is printed on acid-free paper.

Visit us at www.lisalockwood.com.

DEDICATION

This book is dedicated to a set of the most selfless parents a daughter could want.

Mom, thank you for being such an incredible example of love and strength throughout my life.

Dad, thank you for sacrificing your personal life for so many years to support our family the best way you knew how.

Because of you, I set upon an unconventional path comprised of obstacles and rewards that resulted in more successes than I could have ever dreamed of. I love you both.

ACKNOWLEDGEMENTS

Thank you, God, for being my perpetual source of love and daily blessings.

To my soul mate, Rock Thomas: thank you for making me believe in the existence of heaven on earth through your unwavering love and eternal support.

To Anthony & Sage Robbins, my mentors since 2001: thank you for teaching me the skills to create incredible balance and harmony in my life.

To Susan Barnes, my angel sister: your support has been God-sent.

To Kelly Skillen, my New York City friend: your brain and dedication to *Undercover Angel* has been priceless.

To Mark Yegge: thank you for your friendship, time, faith and selfless feedback over the years.

To Mike Sirota, my extraordinary editor: you left no stone unturned during every phase of the editing process and it was truly a pleasure to work with you.

AUTHOR'S NOTE

This is a work of non-fiction. Due to the perilous nature of my former occupation, names and descriptions of individuals as well as locations have been changed to respect their privacy. I attended and graduated from the Chicago Police Academy, however, was not a member of the Chicago Police Department. I was a police officer, detective and SWAT member in a Chicago suburb for seven years.

While circumstances and conversations depicted herein come from my recollection, some of them are not meant to represent precise time-lines of the events or exact word for word conversations-re-enactments of my life. This work is entirely from my perspective, thus keeping with the true spirit of the events that shaped my life.

CHAPTER 1
BANK ROBBERY

Let's get that bastard! This is what gives cops hard-ons. Small technicality: I was a woman. I grabbed my portable radio and walked stealthily down the precinct's rear staircase, hiding like a common criminal. Ethics were thrown in the gutter in that instant.

As I ignited my nark-car and haphazardly threw up my gumball, the dispatcher continued: "All units responding to the armed robbery at La Salle Bank of Chicago be advised the blue Hyundai Tiburon was last seen traveling northbound on La Salle. It may be headed for I-290."

It's a real pisser when a dispatcher assumes where a criminal might be heading. We only want the facts from the dispatchers; let us coppers do our jobs. Knowing I-290 was an obvious getaway route, as was Lakeshore Drive, I went with my hard-earned gut. Most of the coppers who wanted this guy as bad as me were going to take the dispatcher's hunch as sacred and bog up those streets anyway. *Let 'em, I've got my own plan,* I thought as I headed into the Loop.

I didn't dare pick up my radio; ghost detective was ready to violate Chicago Police Department General Orders by actively getting involved in a pursuit, in plain clothes and in an unmarked police vehicle. A marked unit responding to the call broadcasted, "Unit 1310's got our vehicle and I'm heading north on lower Wacker Drive!" With that, I white knuckled the steering wheel. Hell yeah! I was right, and one block from the dirtbag. Radio transmissions from that point on became a disgrace. Coppers walk on one another competing for air time, leaving the guy who needs it the most in the dust. I cracked a sharp U-ee and punched the gas pedal, praying my Taurus had enough balls to back up the Corvette engine buried inside 1310's Crown Vic.

Just then I remembered my vest was still in the trunk, *another violation*, and my only protection was coming from the sorry gumball on the roof. The dispatcher called out, "Anyone in the area to back 'em?" I was, but dared not give away my position. Damn! This was self-imposed masochism. I was close enough to smell the exhaust from Unit 1310 but not properly equipped to say so. The street coppers again fought for air time, vying for the prime back-up position in the pursuit. Thankfully, Unit 1310 was so focused on his robber, he didn't see me and called out, "I just made a right on West Harrison and the Hyundai is picking up speed, anyone nearby?"

I heard a familiar voice respond, "Unit 1603 is five blocks away." It turned out Sgt. Degnan was the street supervisor today. As tough as I'd become, his Irish temper was no match for me. Even with that information, I couldn't pull off from the pursuit. I wasn't going to leave that cop hanging without backup. Now, I hoped a street cop would get to us before Degnan did.

"Unit 1310 is making a right on Canal. The Hyundai just cut off a Camaro and sent it into a 360…I need backup!"

Through the screaming sirens, the radio again squealed and squelched, overburdened by an angry mob of tardy coppers. I saw that the driver of the spinout wasn't injured and continued on with 1310.

State Police intervened and began positioning their units to shut down streets to keep the public out of harm's way. If they could project the robber's direction, they were prepared to throw out stop-sticks to puncture his tires. A peek into my rear-view mirror revealed an angry Irishman three feet away from flying up my ass. I broke from my position and allowed Degnan to jump in behind 1310. Still pumped with adrenaline and operating with tunnel vision, I slid back into the pursuit immediately behind Degnan.

"Unit 1310 has back-up and we're still with the Hyundai making a right on Archer Ave. He seems to be slowing down."

Our three units were inches from one another, stacking up from the robber's sudden lag. Moments later 1310 announced, "Disregard; he's picking up speed and we're now making a left onto Halsted."

It turned out the State Police had horseshoes up their asses. As we headed up Halsted the side streets were blocked off with police units from State and County. It was like cops on parade as Halsted Street opened up, practically vehicle free, to allow for the pursuit to continue uninhibited. Years ago I pictured myself in parades like this, only I was on a float wearing a Miss USA crown and sash. I was a far cry from that now. Although I wore tight jeans, black heeled boots and a low-cut v-necked peach sweater, I was armed with a 40 cal. Glock on my hip and necklace police badge tucked under my chick shirt and buried between my breasts.

I'd been involved in pursuits before, but they were usually short-lived. The bad guys usually ditched their vehicles within the first three minutes of a non-highway pursuit. We were now about five miles into it on commercial streets. This guy was either nuts or had a death wish. A two-man tactical squad appeared behind me and again I surrendered my spot to them. As bad as I wanted to be right in the action when the robber finally made his stop, I knew continuing like this was testosterone driven. I could actually smell the burning rubber from my tires caused by the harsh stops and peelouts from skidding around corners.

"Unit 1310 be advised dispatch, we're heading east on 35th Street."

Every cop knew at this point that the robber was lost; he was headed directly toward the 9th District Police Dept. An illuminated barricade was instantly assembled at Lowe Ave., forcing the robber to turn right on Union. The only thing was, Union was a one-way street and we were going in the opposite direction. In an instant I saw red brake lights blaring from the three squads ahead of me, a high-pitched squeal and a billow of smoke. As police units skidded in varying directions at the intersection of 36th and Union, I could see our robber slammed up like an accordion into a tree and another innocent vehicle crunched from an obvious head-on collision.

I drew my gun and darted from my vehicle toward the robber. In the next moment, I was being drawn down on. Two Cook County Sheriffs barked in unison, "Drop your weapon!" Shit! These guys must think I'm an accomplice.

I lowered my weapon and yanked my badge from under my shirt and bellowed back, "Police!" In the seconds it took to satisfy them, the robber was already cuffed and stuffed into the back seat of 1310's squad. It was his turn to feel like the queen of the parade as coppers peered into the back seat to get a look at the guy that would put them all on the five o'clock news.

Without skipping a beat I bolted to the car crash victim, who was laid out on the pavement bleeding from her nose. I held her hand and spoke to her in a soothing tone until the ambulance arrived. After she was squared away, I saw him. He swaggered over to me, delaying my pending doom. Sgt. Degnan looked me square in the eye and said, "Lisa, Lisa, Lisa."

I saw his disappointment and was speechless.

"How long were you with him?" he said, referring to 1310.

"From the beginning" I said in a whisper.

"You know what you did?"

"Yeah." I sighed.

"I'd have done the same thing."

And just like that, I was in. Welcomed, unofficially, into the boy's club.

CHAPTER 2
MISS ILLINOIS - USA

Alas, the life of parading in crowns and gowns was once my naïve reality. I was born fifth into a family of seven children and we were living at poverty level. Although we were on welfare, and Dad always seemed to be working around the clock, it was never enough. I just graduated high school and enrolled in Daley Community College. This would make me the first member of my family to attend college. I didn't care that it was an hour commute and I had to take three city buses to get there. I continued waitressing full time at a local restaurant with hopes of saving enough money to attend a state university for my second year.

In mid-June, I answered a telephone call from a woman who asked to speak to Lisa Lockwood. "This is she," I responded.

"Hello, Lisa," she said, elated. "This is Veronica Reed, and I am an official with the Miss Illinois-USA Pageant. I'm calling to tell you congratulations. You have been accepted to compete in the pageant."

My heart pounded. Confused, all I could muster was, "Thank you." I continued listening in a haze as she rambled on about sponsors, applications, and deadlines before congratulating me again and hanging up. I raced into the basement where Mom was folding laundry and said, "Mom, I just hung up with someone from the Miss Illinois pageant and she said I've been accepted to compete."

She exclaimed, "Really!" and hugged me tightly into her robust Italian frame.

"Mom, what did you do, how did this happen?"

She smiled wryly and said, "I came across an application, filled it out and sent a picture of you."

This was the greatest surprise of my life.

As an idyllic escape from our meagre lifestyle, our family frequently watched the various pageants on television throughout the year and always rooted for Miss Illinois. I secretly dreamed of competing in a pageant, but thought myself too short. A year earlier, Mom had taken me to a finishing school to inquire about the cost of enrollment. A staff member had bluntly told us that at 5'5" I was not tall enough to be considered for any kind of fashion or modeling work. We naively took that information as sacred and banished any further thoughts of a modeling career. Mom, however, had the final card hidden up her sleeve.

I soon found out that the pageantry business was just that—a business. Each contestant was required to pay a $1500 entry fee, as well as purchase an evening gown, a business suit for arrival and interview day, a swimsuit, and special workout clothing for the opening number rehearsals. They may as well have told me I needed to win the lottery first. We had no idea where I was going to get that kind of money, until we found out that the pageant encouraged soliciting sponsorships to defray the cost.

My resourceful Mom took out an ad in the local newspaper requesting that businesses contact her if they were interested in supporting their "very own" south side girl. The ad worked. The next few months made for a thrilling ride. I joined a health club and practiced walking in high heels. As Mom and I shopped together, I listened to her boast to the store clerks that her daughter was competing in the Miss Illinois pageant. I felt like a celebrity trying on evening gowns and swimsuits. A whole new world was opening up for this dark blonde 110 lb, 5'5" brown-eyed eighteen-year-old girl. The one striking physical quality that I was often recognized for was my prominently high cheekbones. I received these from Dad's gene pool. His parents were a mixture of Swedish, English and Native American Indian (Cherokee).

Mid-fall, Mom and Dad dropped me off at the venue to prepare for the three-day pageant event. I was awestruck as I was shuttled between various registration points with the other 204 contestants from across Illinois. Many of the women exuded refinement and wealth, as indicated by their Louis Vuitton luggage and "to die for" business ensembles. This made me question my acceptance into the pageant.

Beauty, poise and personality were the only requirements for competing; I thought I possessed all of them but was suddenly feeling less than adequate. *Who was I anyway?* I was eighteen, living at home, attending a community college and working as a waitress. *Was this the making of a Miss Illinois winner?*

When I arrived in my hotel room and began unpacking, this gorgeous, classy blonde entered the room. With a flawless smile and whirlwind appeal, she introduced herself as my "roomie Diane," told me my suit was dynamite, and offered to change beds if I preferred to sleep near the window. Feeling clumsy and timid I mustered a mere, "Nnnno, I'm fine." Surely the jig was up. She probably thought I could have used some classes on etiquette to communicate on her level. She asked to see my evening gown and responded with the same "dynamite" exclamation. I admired her confidence and style, and thought I was lucky to have her as a roommate. At bedtime we spent a little time with "getting to know you" questions, and I learned that my refined and flawless roomie was the former Miss Teen-Illinois. *Of course she was.*

We arose ninety minutes before our scheduled group breakfast to primp for our official debut with the pageant officials. Diane's toiletry supplies made the sink look like a department store cosmetic counter. *What was all that stuff?* I had all of two hair products (shampoo and hairspray) and the bare essentials for my face.

At breakfast the cliques were already forming. Diane instantly began hobnobbing with the pageant officials, who welcomed her with hugs. I continued to watch and learn, as my fellow contestants resumed their endless primping. I was an "apply-the-lipstick-once-and-forget-about-it-for-the-rest-of-the-night" kind of girl. These women were constantly whipping out mini-compact mirrors and touching up their canvasses.

At orientation, I spotted a woman who could have easily passed for Christie Brinkley's little sister. She had flawless skin, baby blue eyes, hair that resembled Farrah Fawcett's from her famed poster, and she stood six feet in height. Her stunning beauty mesmerized me; I would have guessed that she was already a professional model for the likes of Cover Girl. I continued scanning the room, comparing myself to other girls, hoping to find less competition. I was so incredibly naive. What did winning Miss Illinois really mean? The only thing I knew for certain were the prizes that the title winner would receive, scholarship money and miscellaneous perks. The scholarship money was the reason I was there.

After orientation we began rehearsing the opening dance number. I had never taken a dance class in my life, and it showed. The experienced women were given the prime spots on stage, performing quick jazzy numbers, while the challenged women—like me—were thrown into two long chorus lines. *Beauty, poise and personality—I think not.* It was becoming increasingly clear who belonged in the winner's circle.

At bedtime, my roomie asked where I had trained to walk a runway. *Trained to walk a runway? Was she joking? Boy, was I out of my league.* I responded, "I never trained, it looks simple enough," trying to convince both of us.

Initially, she stared at me in disbelief, and then her wide eyes softened to a look of reassurance. She must have felt sympathy, because she added, "I'll teach you tomorrow if you like." *How was I supposed to learn all of this stuff in two days, when some women had spent their entire lives preparing for this one opportunity?*

Half of the following day was spent rehearsing our dance number and the other half was spent on oral interviews. The ten interviewers sat behind long tables. Surely these women had interview coaches and had prepped diligently before today. There was nothing I could do now except feign confidence.

When our leg of girls was called into the room, I took note of the demeanor of the girls who'd just finished. They exited tight-lipped and professional. I followed my roomie and looked to her for guidance as we were directed around the table. When the conductor called out the official start time and sounded a buzzer, I seated myself in front of a woman. As she kept her head buried in a file, I was horrified when I noticed Diane still standing behind her chair, waiting to be invited to take a seat. When she was acknowledged, she extended her hand and smartly introduced herself before sitting. Too late for me, I was instantly mortified at my obvious lack of etiquette and forced a smile as my interviewer introduced herself. *Is attending a State University really that important to me?* I pondered as I considered disappearing under the table for the next two days. The interviewer asked, "Are you nervous?" I replied, "Yes…a little." She suggested I take a deep breath and relax. As I put each interviewer under my belt, my confidence soared.

The next day consisted of more tedious rehearsal. Minutes before our first walk I could feel the butterflies fluttering in my stomach. Our dance number started, and the first talented group of girls marched onstage to a roar of applause and high-pitched whistles. I made my grand debut as part of the chorus line halfway through the song. I knew my family must have been eagerly trying to spot me; with no formal dance experience, they couldn't have been too surprised to see me arrive in a line of talentless high kickers.

We hustled off stage in a frenzy, tearing through the dressing room to change into our swimsuits. Again the mirror mob scene was reenacted. Girls assisted other girls with taping their breasts together and fastening their swimsuit bottoms to their bums.

Soon after, the mayhem backstage was repeated. New hairstyles were needed for the evening gown competition. Blow dryers, rollers and curling irons were running full force. Half-naked women with taped breasts pranced about as mini-emergencies erupted.

My evening gown was dazzling: a form-fitting, full-length, black sequined gown with gold, flame-like sequins framing the plunging neckline and shoulders. A pair of black-patent-leather shoes with gold flames complemented the gown. Feeling the weight of the gown on my body as I walked made me feel as rich and as beautiful as Krystle on *Dynasty*. Again, I took the stage and walked with exaggerated poise and elegance, making eye contact with the sea of judges in the first row.

I arose the next morning feeling different. The evening before was thrilling, yet I felt a sense of peace on this new day because I took myself out of the equation. I knew I didn't meet the standards of what *they* were looking for in the winner.

The other ladies, however, appeared exceptionally nervous. The cliques gathered and opinions were offered on who would make the final cut. I, too, had my ten finalists in mind. As all 205 of us filled the rear of the stage, the ten names were called. The usual shrieks of excitement followed, and the remainder of us poured off stage. The dressing room felt like a graveside funeral. As I peered around the room, I felt removed from it all. Women were weeping and consoling one another. I realized why I felt less affected—most of these women had centered their lives on the outcome of this event. I never made any conscious effort to compete; after all, it was Mom who entered me and I spent less than four months preparing for it.

I joined my family members—who all gave me real Italian hugs this time—and rooted for the Christie Brinkley look-alike I'd spotted the first day. My top pick, the gorgeous, six-foot, Purdue University senior became Miss Illinois-USA. She went on to make the top ten finalists for the country in the Miss USA pageant.

That experience made me realize even more than ever that I needed to further my education. *How does one learn to become refined?* I thought travel, education and studies were my ticket to a life of luxury. Attending a community college was good, but I thought there had to be another way, a quicker way for me to leave the nest, have a career and finance my college education. I remembered meeting a girl at the pageant who was a reservist in the U.S. Coast Guard and thought, how could such a feminine girl serve in the military? Surely she must have some masculine qualities. The more I came to know her, the more I realized that she was not much different than me.

Shortly after the pageant, I researched all of the branches of the military and discovered that the Air Force seemed to offer the best package and would finance four years of University. The choice was made; now I just needed to convince Mom that it was the right one.

CHAPTER 3
THE ROOKIE MARRIAGE

At the U.S. Air Force recruiter's office I was met by a well-built black man, who took one look at this smartly dressed (I wore my pageant business suit; it was the only professional thing I owned), petite woman before him and practically dismissed me. With the little grooming and interview etiquette tips I'd picked up from the pageant experience, I believe the sergeant thought he'd been set up for a joke. "Yes, I'm seriously interested in enlisting."

After shaking off his initial shock he said, "Have a seat." He composed himself and supplied me with study materials and test dates. I walked out of the recruiter's door knowing that this was the right thing to do.

Breaking the news to my parents was my next challenge. Mom was appalled.

"Do you realize that you can be sent to fight in a war?" she said as Dad looked on.

"Yes Mom, but the probability of that is pretty low." Continuing, I pleaded, "Mom this is the only way I know how to pay for four years of college, and that's the most important thing to me right now."

I opened some of the Air Force brochures that showed pictures of young, sharply dressed military men and women engaged in different career fields smiling and appearing fit and intelligent. She rifled through some of it, appearing increasingly interested, and asked, "What if you hate it...will they let you out?"

"Well…no Mom, when I enlist, I sign a contract for four years."

Dad surprisingly perked up. "I tried to get in the Air Force before I met your mother."

"What happened?"

"I didn't pass the test."

That was quite the disclosure. Not the fact that he didn't pass; Dad dropped out of high school in the ninth grade. I was astonished that he was interested in becoming a soldier in the very branch I was going to enlist. Mom didn't say much else and Dad, who used up his word quota of the day, continued looking through the paperwork.

The decision was made. Little did I know what a bond this would create between Dad and me. As I studied the ASVAB (Armed Services Vocational Aptitude Battery) study guide to prepare for the entrance exam, I came across a section in the mechanical field for which I knew nothing about. How on earth did they expect an eighteen-year-old girl to know about the inner working of a car's engine? Or have knowledge about the polarity of electricity? Yuck! It was bad enough helping around the house with yard work; the last thing I wanted to do was dive under the hood of some smelly car and get grease under my fingernails changing a broken spark plug. Sitting at the kitchen table, I asked Dad, "What's a spark plug?"

Dad looked at me quizzically, never expecting to hear that sort of question from his delicate daughter, and answered, "It ignites the engine on the car. Why?"

This one question fueled Dad's desire to see that his daughter would pass the exam. He escorted me out to his car and began the tedious job of teaching me the inner workings of an engine. I brought out a note pad and diligently drew diagrams and took notes. At times I could tell I tested his patience.

"Why is everything so greasy under here?"

"Because it's an engine!"

"Can't you clean it, like hose it down or something?"

If looks could kill…

I'm sure at that point he wondered if his efforts were futile. Over the next few days, I asked him to read off the prep questions and test my knowledge. One thing I was gifted in was my ability to learn new information and spew it back in record time. Dad was impressed, and I realized that this was the first time I ever asked him to help me study for anything.

Weeks later I aced the exam and scored high in the mechanical field. So high in fact, my recruiter persuaded me to sign up for a job in that field. He convinced me that the military was short on women in that area and the probability of promotion was high. Later, I realized their main job is to enlist as many naïve kids as possible and fill in the gaps where there are shortages. The last thing they're concerned about is whether or not you're the perfect fit for the job. I saw myself doing something administrative (the area where I scored the highest) but foolishly believed that the recruiter was looking out for my best interests.

Because I still didn't want to get grease under my fingernails I chose what I thought would be the cleanest mechanical job there was: airframe body mechanic. The recruiter explained that I could put in for that job but there was no guarantee I would get it. The only guarantee the military could make was that I would get one of my top three choices for desired regions to be stationed. I was clueless. Mom slowly adapted and was soon bragging about her future Air Force kid the same way she did when I was competing for Miss Illinois.

* * * * *

Due to the popularity of the movie *Top Gun*, there'd been a massive flood of young men and women enlisting in the Air Force. Therefore, I was put on a waiting list, a.k.a. delayed enlistment program. My recruiter would not—or chose not to —tell our group of applicants when we would actually be leaving. I remained in limbo as I waited for the day I would take my first airplane ride to basic training.

Waiting to be called "any day" limited my day-to-day existence. I couldn't enroll for another semester of community college, because I risked being called up for duty before completing the semester. I was growing weary of waitressing and was anxious to begin the rest of my life.

One night while on a date with a man (Jack), I grew wise as he returned from his second trip to men's room in thirty minutes and watching him sniffle incessantly. I suspected he was snorting cocaine. I asked him to take me home. He refused.

"C'mon baby. What's wrong? We're havin' a good time," he whined.

I mingled with some of his friends and watched him get increasingly squirrelly. Again I asked him to take me home. My options were limited. I had no money and no one to call and pick me up at such a late hour. It would have been humiliating to phone my parents for a ride. When I saw Jack start an argument with the bartender for slighting him on a shot of whiskey, I pleaded with him to take me home.

Tony, a man I had harbored a crush on in my teens, happened to be at the same bar and remembered me. When Jack took another trip to the men's room I asked Tony to drive me home. He saw that I was with Jack and asked, "Are you sure?"

When I said yes, we ran for the door. Jack pursued us. Tony explained that he knew Jack was a cokehead and had a volatile temper. Jack drove a Corvette and had no problem catching up to us. Tony was driving like a maniac, cutting other drivers off and heading in the wrong direction on one-way streets. For what felt like an eternal three minutes, Jack followed us. Tony finally cut down an alley and pulled into a loading dock in some industrial park. I had no idea where I was and could barely catch my breath from the ordeal. We waited to ensure that we had lost Jack for good.

We spoke for nearly two hours before Tony dropped me safely at home. As far I was concerned, he was my hero.

He phoned the next day to tell me that Jack threw a brick through the windshield of his mother's car. I felt horrible. Tony used it as an opportunity to ask me out on a date to make it up to him.

Tony was a construction worker who looked and acted like a macho Goodfella. After several dates he confessed that he was Polish and revealed his actual surname, which ended with a "ski." He had jet-black curly hair, a mustache, and a rock-solid physique. He became extremely possessive of me during our courtship, and initially, I was flattered whenever he'd stare a man down for glancing at me. But soon he escalated the ritual by asking, "You gotta problem?"

After nearly coming to blows with his perceived rival, I grew concerned. I was getting a taste of Tony's quick temper, and I wish I had been exposed to Maya Angelou's sage advice: "When someone shows you who they are, believe them." But by then, I'd fallen in love.

* * * * *

Tony and I became inseparable. He insisted I stop waitressing, because he thought too many men were flirting with me, and gave me a weekly allowance to make up for it. Tony was always generous, showering me with gifts and taking me out for dinner nightly. But he knew I was waiting to be called for my four-year enlistment, and would question my decision:

"Are you sure this is what you want to do? Can't you go to a local college? I could help pay for it. What if you get stationed somewhere shitty, it *is* four years, ya know?"

Throughout his inquisitions, I held firm. "I need to do this for me."

Three months into our relationship, he proposed with a stunning twenty-three-stone diamond ring. To my surprise, I said yes. To his surprise, I still refused to change my mind about the Air Force. So he promised to leave his prominent construction position and work for a construction company wherever I was stationed. He made me feel like a princess.

During our early dating days, I noticed that Tony enjoyed a beer or two with his dinner and would often pick up a six-pack for the road. One evening he became so enraged at me for requesting he not smuggle beer into a movie theater, he punched his fist through a wall and broke his hand. I was so frightened by the escalation of his temper that I avoided him for two days. He began wooing me with a barrage of flowers, cards, and phone calls, until I forgave him. He even refrained from drinking for a week. I thought I'd won the battle and continued the relationship.

In January 1989, eleven months after enlisting, I was called to duty. I was the first member of my family to leave for such a lengthy time; three of my sisters lived in apartments near my parents, and the rest of my siblings still lived at home. I felt wrenched inside. I was leaving everyone I loved for six weeks of military training, and I still had no idea if I would be stationed stateside or overseas. After a final series of physical testing, form completion, and swearing in, I signed my name and officially enlisted as Airmen Basic Lockwood of the U.S. Air Force.

Touchdown! With San Antonio soil beneath me, I got a taste of my impending doom. I had never heard so much screaming in my life—even with an Italian mom. From the time our bus of recruits arrived on Lackland Air Force Base until the time I graduated, the training instructors' only mode of communication was many decibels higher than the norm. Watching their faces turn as red as beets, their veins protrude snake-like through their necks, and spit inadvertently launch from their mouths reminded me of the movie *Alien*. I wondered if the criterion for a drill instructor was to adopt the identity of an exploding-headed extraterrestrial.

Regardless, I was afraid. After twenty-four hours of being treated like criminals in a prison camp, they permitted us to make a two-minute call home. When I heard Mom's voice I burst into tears. Sounding like a wounded hyena I sobbed, "I hate it here…it feels like I'm in jail…they're so mean to us."

"Lisa…Lisa," she called out repeatedly, trying to interrupt my rambling, "you wanna come home baby? You can come home…you don't have to stay there."

A drill instructor approached. "Hang up the phone your time is up!"

"I have to go Mom, they're hollering at me to hang up."

I surrendered the phone to the next crying victim in my squad. I was a mess, sobbing uncontrollably as the angry drill instructor ordered me to move into another line. I desperately wanted my Mommy. Trembling and on the verge of hyperventilating, I marched into the next formation and stood alone among hoards of strangers, where I experienced my first encounter with inner courage. It was then I decided that I was doing this thing until the bitter end. I could not return home a quitter.

As the days progressed, I grew stronger. I realized all we needed to do to survive the six weeks was be compliant, subservient, offer no excuses, take responsibility for every act, and do exactly as ordered. There was no favoritism, so that made it a bit easier to cope. I suppose I could thank Dad and his mass punishment methods for that insight.

Dad was quite the disciplinarian, which meant weekly Saturday beatings for all seven of us. The neighbors often heard our screams penetrating the closed basement window of Dad's "House of Justice." There was always a struggle after each strike, as we would squirm and yelp in pain, making involuntary attempts to block the next impending blow with our hands. This would make him angrier; if we moved, we knew to expect an additional strike. Often, due to our blocking movements, Dad's would accidentally hit us on the backs of our hands, forearms, thighs and calves.

Mom would remind Dad to be more careful to strike us only on our behinds because of the welts that remained on our legs and forearms from the belt and electrical cord impressions. It was difficult trying to explain to teachers, neighbors, and schoolmates the origin of our wounds. What was most perplexing was that, every week, no matter what, in Dad's eyes, we all managed to do something that required a beating.

As the days wore on I became inventive with my coping skills. When it was my turn to get yelled at, I focused on the top bridge of their nose and held my breath to avoid their mouth odor. I would sing a song in my mind as a source of distraction until it was over.

When the day came for us to handle our "new best friend," the M-16 semi-automatic rifle, I was stirred. In a flash, things became very clear; *I may have to use this to kill people.* Even when my mother told me I may have to go to war, I blew it off. I completely severed any thoughts about a war. Now, here it was in my face. I held the daunting black weapon and thought: I chose to enlist in the military to receive a college education. *Why had I not considered that this came with the possibility of voluntarily killing people or even getting killed myself? Who was I becoming?* I was snapped back into reality when the instructor began introducing us to the names of all of the rifle's parts. Within a few days we were taught to clean, field strip and reassemble the rifle so well we could do it blindfolded.

During the last few days of our final week of basic training, we were set up with appointments with the career counselor. "I see you are going into the mechanical field," my counselor said.

"Sir, Airman Lockwood reports as ordered sir, that's correct."

"You can drop the formalities...talk to me like a normal person."

"Yes sir!"

"Do you have a driver's license?"

"Yes sir!" I had received it a few weeks before entering the Air Force.

He pecked away at his keyboard, printed out a form, handed it to me and hustled me out the door like he was fanning away a pesky fly.

Those who had already received their duty assignment were told to wait for the rest of our squad to finish. As I approached the women I could see nearly everyone smiling and bragging about their duty assignment; the job they would be doing for the next four years. I looked at my form and couldn't figure out what I was assigned to do. It said something about logistics, and none of the women could help me decipher the codes. Their forms displayed their jobs simply: medical assistant, administration, human resources, dental hygienist, computer intelligence, linguists, etc. I summoned the nerve to approach a training instructor and asked if he knew what my job was. He snatched the form from my hand. Chuckling, he said, "You're a truck driver."

I walked away from him in utter shock. I felt ashamed. I thought I was going to be an airframe body mechanic. I'd told everyone I was going to be an airframe body mechanic. I just learned how to drive a car and barely spent any time on a highway; how was I going to be a truck driver? I don't want to be a truck driver for four years. I didn't even know the Air Force had truck drivers.

After graduation, Tony kept his word and followed me to my new base a month later. Living together was a dream in the beginning—and then new challenges arose. The carpenter's union was not as strong in Boston as it was in Chicago, and work was difficult to find. Although the military paid for our apartment and my meals, we weren't able to save any money. Tony took on side jobs he felt were beneath him in order to supplement our income. He had lost his sense of significance, worked longer hours to earn less pay, and drank more heavily. To earn extra money, he would fly back to Chicago every few weeks to work at his former company.

As I was transitioning into my new career as a heavy equipment operator, it seemed that Sgt. Rustin, my immediate supervisor, had it in for me. Before me, she was the only female assigned to the logistics transportation squadron and for that reason considered me a threat. She was a single parent who looked like Olive Oyl from Popeye, was a heavy smoker, spoke in a guttural voice and snorted when she laughed. Even though I was engaged to Tony, I still received lots of attention from my fellow airmen. No one hid the fact that they wanted to "show Lisa the ropes" and vied to take me out for driving training on the larger equipment. Sgt. Rustin would evaluate my progress after a record was turned in from my various trainers. Even though I received passing marks, she would tell me I was *borderline* and should consider giving up my lunch break to train more. Of course she wanted me to surrender my lunch break; this was where I bonded with my work team at the chow hall.

I consulted with another supervisor (Sgt. Andrew) assigned to my unit and asked him if there was anything I could do to improve my relationship with Rustin. Andrew was amazing. He was like a stick of dynamite: short, powerful and respected. All of his airmen were honored to work under him and often worked overtime without compensation if he requested. He made us feel like family. He confirmed my belief that Rustin was envious of all the attention I was receiving. He sympathized with her single parent and friendless status and asked me to consider inviting her to do things outside of work. This was touchy, however, because of her role as my superior. I decided I would try to kill her with kindness. After several months of this, and feeling like I was making some headway with her, I accidentally stumbled upon her true feelings.

Rustin was standing on the bottom step of a doorway on one of our tour buses facing the driver's seat that was occupied by Sgt. Andrew. Unknown to her, I approached the bus and stood behind her, waiting for her to finish speaking to Andrew, when I heard the following:

"I don't know who she thinks she is, making decisions without my authorization, so I told her if she pulls something like that again it'll be her ass!"

That same day, our squadron colonel requested that I and another airman from the transportation squadron attend an official disciplinary hearing as part of our training. He wanted us to witness the military criminal procedure. I posted the appointment on an official board in the main dispatch center and went about my daily work. When Rustin arrived she noticed that I was scheduled for the hearing and called me into her office.

"Who authorized you to schedule an appointment this afternoon?"

"The squadron colonel."

"Just so you know, I need to approve every appointment you make!"

I was shocked.

"It was my understanding that when a colonel gives us a direct order we obey it. I didn't think I needed your authorization."

"Maybe I didn't explain it to you properly. Yes you are required to obey his order, but I still need to be notified."

Still defensive, I slowly articulated every word of my response: "I wrote it on the board because you weren't here this morning."

"I understand that Lisa, I'm not trying to make this hard for you...just let me know next time you make an appointment."

It was pointless for me to continue. "Thank you for the clarification. Am I excused?"

Now, standing behind her, I listened as Rustin blatantly lied about what she said to me in her office. "Excuse me," I snapped. She nearly jumped out of her skin when she saw that it was me. I continued, "I just wanted to let you know I'm headed to the appointment."

Swallowing hard, she muttered, "Okay."

I rushed off feeling betrayed and hurt. Later, I realized it was obvious that she didn't want to be my friend and would make things up about me to make herself look better. *Where was the sisterhood?* I guessed I was foolish to think we could get along based solely on our gender. I thought I would only have to compete with men in an obviously male-dominated career. Little did I know that the only sisterhood outside of my sibling and best friend relationship was rare in the real world. I needed a new strategy to get through the next few years with Rustin.

After three months, my training on the larger vehicles had ceased. A roster was posted in the dispatch center so all of the airmen knew what their daily duties entailed. More times than not I was assigned to the wash rack. This meant enduring an eight-hour shift washing trucks and buses out in a large enclosed bay area with high-powered hoses and industrial strength soap. Even worse, it also translated to a full day of wearing drenched clothing. It was useless to complain. I'd heard more times than I could count, "The needs of the military come first." There was no concrete way for me to complain of Rustin's treatment without sounding like a whiner. So, instead of complaining, I would find ways to turn the wash rack into a fun rack. I invented competitions among the airmen, like racing to see which team could wash and wax a bus the fastest, which airmen could make it through the day with the driest clothes, etc. We listened to music, laughed, shared stories, and "accidentally" hosed one another to make our days enjoyable. Wash rack duties lasted for a full year. I often thought about the day I received my official career assignment orders in basic training and complained about driving buses. I didn't fathom that it could be worse. Spending a year working at a car wash was beyond my realm of reality.

Tony often mocked my job. "I left my job to move to Boston so you could wash trucks and buses all day?"

"No you didn't leave your job so I could wash trucks and buses...you followed me here so I could get an education from the military. What does it matter to you what I do? I get paid the same amount of money regardless if I'm washing trucks or doing something administrative."

An education wasn't the most important thing to a high school dropout that was earning a decent living, so it was useless trying to get Tony to appreciate the value of it.

Sixteen months into my Air Force career, I received incredible news: Rustin was getting transferred to fleet management. She would still be working in our squadron but would no longer have anything to do with me, or my training. This was a day to celebrate! Quicker than you can say *hallelujah*, I was under a new supervisor and back to training on the heavy motorized equipment. Yes, I was actually excited to learn to drive forklifts, snowplows and tow trucks.

Two years had passed since my engagement to Tony and he demanded to know when we were going to set a wedding date. Upon his return from one of his Chicago trips, he gave me an ultimatum: "Marry me or I'm moving back to Chicago."

Ouch!

I knew in my heart that I wasn't completely satisfied with our relationship—especially with Tony's drinking and temper—but I was afraid to be alone for the next two years. I begrudgingly began making wedding plans. After trying to convince myself and Mom that I truly loved Tony and it was the right thing to do, we drove to Vermont for a quickie wedding at a bed and breakfast.

On the eve of our wedding, Tony and I went out for what should have been a romantic dinner. Why I thought he would change his stripes was a ridiculous dream. We started the meal with a glass of wine that escalated to a few hard liquor cocktails for him. Hours later, back at the B & B, repulsed by his slurred speech and pungent breath, I cunningly requested that we sleep apart to "make tomorrow that much more special." Tony fell for the ruse. I was grateful to be sleeping separately in one of the two elevated beds in our suite. Then, suddenly, sometime after two a.m. I was awakened by the sound of what I thought was running water. Opening my eyes and fighting to focus, I was horrified to discover Tony seated naked on the bed stool, facing my bed and urinating on the skirt with the intensity of a fire hose. Jumping from my bed, I screamed, "What are you doing?"

"This is what you do," was his groggy answer.

"What are you talking about?"

"This is what you do at an inn."

With that, I shook him, realizing he was half asleep and pulled him from the stool to guide him into the bathroom. I then ordered the pathetic drunk into the bedroom with wet towels to wash the mess, praying the innkeepers wouldn't notice or smell the damage in the morning.

Sadly, I didn't have the courage to cancel our wedding. Every bone in my body was telling me not to go through it. *How many red flags did I need to run from this nightmare?* I was so ashamed of the woman I was, that I promised myself that I wouldn't tell anyone. The next day, I suppressed the horrible event and married a man I feared and did not respect.

Things only got worse from there. Tony's anger was out of control. Because of our marriage, he was considered my military dependant and privy to all of the base amenities. Once, he caused a scene at a BX over waiting too long in line and was banned from shopping on the base. Another time, he became so drunk at a function at the NCO club that the police needed to escort him out. They ordered me to drive him home. After a hellacious drive, he insisted on returning to the base to "kick everyone's ass." He struggled with me to get the car keys. A mad chase around the apartment followed, as Tony overturned couches and chairs, and knocked things from their shelves. I had never witnessed such a brutal display of rage.

I ran into our bedroom and dialed 911. Tony wrestled the phone from my hand and hung it up. Minutes later the police arrived, saw the condition of our home—as well as the redness around my wrist—and arrested him.

Like most naïve women involved with abusive men, I didn't follow through and sign complaints. But my objective was not to have Tony sit in jail and have the little money we had depleted by lawyers and court costs. I wanted Tony to go to marriage counseling or, at the very least, recognize that he was an alcoholic and enroll in AA. When he returned the following morning, he saw the condition in which he'd left our home. He quickly began the task of making order out of mayhem, but wouldn't listen to anything I had to say about counseling. As usual, he donned his Don Juan mask and refrained from drinking for two weeks, so I sought counseling at the base. They ran a battery of tests to determine if I was exhibiting behaviors tied to depression. I wasn't. I was soaring at work, taking college courses, and had even been asked to be the Carnival Queen for the base parade. The psychologist said she could recommend nothing short of re-evaluating my marriage with Tony and get him to join me in counseling.

Several months later, I received a frantic phone call from Tony's drinking buddy that they'd gotten into a bad car accident. He wasn't sure of Tony's condition. When the accident occurred, his *buddy* ran from the scene because there was a warrant for his arrest.

In a state of shock, I mechanically grabbed for the car keys and drove to downtown Boston, all the while questioning: *Is this the life I wanted to live? Did I survive all the challenges of my youth to be married to a man that I had to have arrested? A man who spends time with someone who has an arrest warrant? A man who causes a drunk driving accident?*

When I arrived at the hospital emergency room, no one could find him. I overheard an attendant say that they take dead bodies down to the morgue immediately. Feeling my blood boil from the callousness of that response, I shouted, "Can someone please check if he even arrived at *this* hospital?"

As I stood there in a haze, a police officer inquired about the accident on his radio and relayed that Tony had in fact been taken to Tuft's hospital, his condition unknown. I drove through downtown Boston's rush hour traffic to get to there. I stormed into the emergency room, plowed past everyone, and began swishing back curtain after curtain until I found Tony.

There he lay, drenched in blood. His face was unrecognizable—a broken jaw, missing teeth, broken ribs, a broken arm, a concussion, and head abrasions comprised the final tally. His room reeked from the familiar sour odor of alcohol. I couldn't find an uninjured place on his body to touch to let him know that I was there. A cop directed me into the hallway and filled me in on the *highlights* of his accident. An eyewitness informed him that Tony had been driving wildly through traffic at a high rate of speed, cutting off vehicles, until he was forced into another lane by a tractor and skidded head-on into a guardrail, on an overpass. His truck was totaled. I looked through the officer, deeply ashamed, knowing, that the eyewitness was telling the truth.

I spent the next forty-eight hours holding vigil over Tony, as he slipped in and out of consciousness. Sgt Andrew was extraordinary, offering me all the time I needed to care for him. His jaw was wired shut for several weeks. He lost weight from his liquid diet and could barely move.

As Tony recovered, I told him I couldn't live that way any longer and weakly threatened a divorce. He promised he would change; that he'd lost his desire for alcohol. I foolishly believed him. One guilty plea and five thousand dollars in court costs later, Tony was sentenced to an intensive five-day alcohol program. It had been two months since he'd drunk, and I truly thought that he'd benefit from the program. But after the five days, Tony mocked the program, made fun of the other attendees, and claimed he was nothing like them.

Tony assured me not to worry; he still didn't have a desire to drink, but refused to be labeled an alcoholic. I decided I would go along with his delusion. For three-and-a-half months, he stayed away from the booze. Then, one fateful day, his wonderful-arrest-warrant-fleeing-the-scene-of-an-accident-friend came by to *hang out*. I was preparing to ship out for a ninety-day tour of duty in Saudi Arabia and left them behind as I tended to some errands. When I returned home, a surprise going-away party that included alcohol awaited me. In all of the excitement, I overlooked the fact that Tony was slowly consuming beer after beer.

CHAPTER 4
DESERT STORM

Remember when my mother said, "You know this means you may have to go to war one day?" and I candidly told her not to worry? Eighteen months into my four-year tour, the Persian Gulf conflict arose. In 1990, Saddam Hussein invaded Kuwait and in less than four hours he had taken control of the country—as well as 24 percent of the world's oil supply. It seemed as if his next target was Saudi Arabia.

The United States entered the conflict after a call for protection by Saudis. The U.S. set a date, January 15, 1991, by which all Iraqi forces had to leave Kuwait, but Saddam ignored the deadline. This triggered Operation Desert Shield—a systematic build-up of troops in the region—and eventually led to Desert Storm, an all-out attack to liberate Kuwait.

During Operation Desert Storm I remained at Hanscom Air Force Base, assisting with logistical ground support and providing supplies to our troops in Saudi Arabia and Kuwait. I watched as my sergeants and fellow airmen were shipped to the war and wondered if I would be called. When two of my sergeants (Andrew was one) received orders to leave, I was left behind to run ground transportation operations for the entire base, despite having only two years on the job. This was an example of adapting to the needs of the military. With the two main transportation sergeants off somewhere in Riyadh, Saudi Arabia, I was appointed to the position of Chief Transportation Dispatcher. I was given the authority of a ten-year veteran. Our unit was composed of enlisted military along with government civilians. The civilians, all military veterans, were primarily employed to drive the base shuttles and taxis, handle tractor-trailer deliveries and provide limo service for dignitary support. I enjoyed working with these men, who ranged in age from their late 40s to late 50s. Some were responsible for training me on the heavy equipment, and they watched as their young green airman blossomed into a soldier.

As I took the reins, I noticed that some of my civilian comrades began to test their new boss. Sadly, I watched these men turn into children before my eyes.

"Why do I have to do this taxi run? I just did one an hour ago."

"I'm not taking this tractor run, it's not my day for tractor driving."

"I can't do that V.I.P. run, I didn't bring my business suit today."

Initially, I was a pushover and honored their requests (and at times demands) to get out of doing some of the runs. It became extremely frustrating, and I began to realize they were taking advantage of our former co-worker relationship.

After weeks of trying to accommodate their needs and still feeling disrespected, I summoned up the nerve to do my job properly. I forgot I actually had the authority to give these men assignments and even discipline them if necessary. The last thing I wanted was to adopt Rustin's supervisory methods, and it was evident that the men didn't respect me like they did Sgt. Andrew. After all, one day I was their equal and the next day I was their supervisor. This had to be a hard pill to swallow, considering my age (twenty-one) and gender. I remembered what I learned in basic training: "never make or accept an excuse." This went over like a lead balloon. I felt like the Gestapo as I declined excuse after excuse over the next few weeks. The men didn't recognize the new and improved, firm and authoritative Lisa. The grumbling began. They resented my power and made the smallest gestures to ensure I knew it; they snatched keys from my hand, gave me the evil eye and turned their backs on me as I relayed their assignments to them. I felt betrayed. They made it clear that they were OK working with me but not *for* me.

With the knowledge that men and women were sacrificing their lives defending our allies across the world, the last thing I wanted to concern myself with was how these men treated me. I pretended that our safe stateside base was in the middle of Desert Storm and no one was going to get in the way of completing our daily missions. I learned that change is first ridiculed, and then questioned, before it is ultimately accepted. Par for the course, the men mocked my authority, questioned why I was chosen to lead them and tested me, before adapting to their new leader. It took nearly six weeks for them to accept my appointment and a few more weeks for them to socialize with me as they had before.

I efficiently ran our unit as if my life depended on it. Less than a year later, I was nominated for and won the prestigious honor of Airman of the Year Worldwide for the Logistics Squadrons. This honor was largely due to my stateside performance in 1991 during the military conflict.

In July of 1992, after serving three-and-a-half years in the Air Force, and promising my family that I wouldn't be going to Saudi Arabia for Desert Storm, I found myself packing my duffle bag for a ninety-day tour of duty in Southwest Asia. *What had I been thinking, making a promise like that?* I did, however, keep one end of the deal.

Desert Storm had been downgraded to Operation Desert *Calm*. Mom, unfortunately, was no more at ease, regardless of what title the Department of Defense put on the Operation. I was looking forward to my tour. I had been stationed in Bedford, MA, a historical town on the outskirts of Boston for my entire military assignment, and I was ready to go overseas.

I said goodbye to Tony with minimal angst. My feelings for him had diminished, and I felt more independent. As I boarded the plane, I felt a newfound sense of freedom and was proud to be serving my country overseas. I didn't have a clue what was in store for me upon my arrival. I'd heard "war stories" from my colleagues upon their return, but assumed my conditions would be better due to the downgrading of the conflict.

Upon setting foot on Saudi sand, I was hit with a blast of raging heat and blinded by the scorching sun. It was mid-morning, and after sensing my discomfort from the heat, a solemn luggage attendant told me that *this* was considered cool—the afternoon is what I should beware of. A shuttle, driven by an airman from my new base, King Abdul Aziz Air Base in Dhahran, waited curbside to retrieve the new tour. The airman, Randy, was light-hearted and engaging, especially when he discovered I would be assigned to his unit. He proudly described our exquisite facilities on the base. I truly thought he was pulling my leg when he spoke of the condos—*not barracks*—that comprised our living quarters. He said, "They've got marble floors, three private rooms, balconies, Persian rugs, a large kitchen, and two bathrooms." Then he added, "The chow hall serves steak and eggs, cooked to order."

I listened intently, hoping it was true, but trying not to appear excited in case the joke was on me. I asked him about our duties. He chuckled and asked sarcastically, "What duties? We work four days in a row and have two days off. During our work days we do a few tractor trailer deliveries, loading and unloading aircraft, run a couple of shuttles—like what I'm doing now—and take military personnel on Morale Welfare and Recreation (MWR) tours."

I asked where MWR tours traveled, and he described an island called Bahrain, home to top-notch restaurants, swimming pools, and alcoholic beverages. Considering Saudi Arabia's religious Muslim customs, I was surprised to hear that alcohol was available, but he explained that Bahrain is its own kingdom and thereby exempt. I knew this had to make the military personnel very happy.

Randy grew quiet as he neared the entrance to the base, and said we had to show our identification to the Saudi gate guard. We zigzagged our way through an anti-terrorist barricade made up of ten concrete partitions. One of the guards entered the front door of our mini-bus with his assault rifle slung over his shoulder. He walked down the center aisle, snatching each passenger's ID card and maintaining piercing eye contact with his *guests*, carefully matching the photo to the individual. Once satisfied, he exited the bus and returned to his guard shack. Randy explained that the Saudi gate guards are extremely stringent and are not permitted to socialize with American or European allied forces stationed there.

Randy dropped us off at an orientation tent, and again welcomed us to our new home. Inside the tent, we were greeted with bottles of water and a table covered with fruits, breads, and pastries. It was the sort of buffet one would find in a four-star restaurant. I started to believe our driver.

After we had our fill of snacks, a lieutenant colonel rallied the "newbies" to take a seat for orientation. We were introduced to the American base commander and received a load of handouts, which contained pertinent information regarding rules of the base, Muslim customs, and the potential dangers in the desert terrain. The base commander elaborated on the snakes and scorpions we would most certainly encounter. So that we knew exactly what he was talking about, he pointed to several glass tanks in the rear of the tent that contained the live versions of our desert "friends," and encouraged us to pay them a visit upon our departure. As if a slide show wouldn't have provided an adequate depiction!

The base commander shared the history regarding the odd placement of the condominiums, which erupted in the middle of an otherwise austere environment in the city of Al Khobar. In 1979, a community with luxury housing was developed as a way of deterring the Bedouins from their gypsy way of life. But, the multi-million dollar plan was an enormous failure, and the condominiums, shops, and restaurants remained vacant until 1990. The only solution was to turn the community into a military base. When Desert Storm erupted, the base was split in half, with a barbed wire fence separating the Saudis from the allied forces.

Ninety minutes later, armed with goody bags containing chemical warfare gear, snake venom antidote, mini first-aid kits, sun block, sandstorm capes, and countless other essentials, we were dismissed. I was given a key and directed to a cluster of buildings between six and ten stories high. Emerging from the air-conditioned tent, I lugged my gear for nearly a block in the extreme, 110° heat, before entering the foyer of the building I would call home for the next ninety days. A blast of frigid air and a marble floor stood on the other side of hell.

I realized I had the fortune of being situated on the main floor adjacent to the elevators. I walked into the condo and was met by a woman who was packing her things in the living room on a Persian rug. Our tours were set up in ninety-day increments, and the three women I encountered were flying back to their respective bases the next day. One of the women, Debbie, introduced herself and gave me first dibs on the largest bedroom before my new roommates arrived. A shower was an immediate must; Debbie read my mind and offered me two of her towels and a washcloth.

The bathroom was immense and immaculate, boasting marble floors and walls. Noting my amazement, she added, "Isn't it great? As I washed my hair, my head was spinning. From the time I'd left the airplane, my experience in Saudi Arabia had been surreal. This was not what my colleagues had experienced during Desert Storm; here I was in this posh condo with marble floors and Persian rugs. *Was I in the military or on holiday in St. Tropez?*

The next day, my new roommate and I walked the grounds of the base to get acclimated to our environment. As we strolled along the barbed wire fence, we could see Saudi military personnel going about their day. They didn't look in our direction much, and when they did, they seemed to detest our very presence—even though we were allies. I soon discovered this was due to our gender, rather than our nationality. Women have a place in the Muslim-Saudi Arabian culture, and serving in the military is definitely not it!

Later that afternoon, I was led to a hundred-foot cylindrical tower that sat upon a round concrete platform on the Saudi side. I peered through the fence and listened as my new friend, John, who'd been assigned to my unit, explained that I was looking at an execution tower. It had been specifically constructed for the use of killing women who were found guilty of committing adultery. The women would be escorted to the top of the tower and thrown off, as a crowd of onlookers watched and cheered. If the woman did not die from the fall, she would be dragged back to the top for what she would certainly hope would be the last time.

What happened to the old-fashioned scarlet letter? And while we're at it, where's the *male* execution tower for adultery? Silly question, I was told. Of course, men are punished. If the crime of adultery is proven, the offender is beheaded. I joked at the revelation but was, however, incensed at this barbaric system of criminal punishment, as well as the gross disparity between genders. I wondered how this could still be occurring in the world.

At vehicle operations, or the "motor pool," I met my colleagues and supervisors. The airmen shuttle driver, Randy, took me into the equipment yard to get me acquainted with our vehicles. After handing me a bundle of keys he said, "Meet me at the fuel tanks so we can gas up these shuttle buses."

As I entered the shuttle, I noticed it had a standard transmission. I was horrified. Here I was in Saudi Arabia, my only assignment was to drive, and I had never been trained at my home base to drive a stick shift. Stateside, we had the luxury of newer equipment with automatic transmissions. I told Randy that I didn't know how to drive it. Alarmed, he said, "Are you serious? Ninety percent of our equipment is stick-shift."

I felt hot blood rush from my head and pump through my body. Being one of only two women assigned to this squadron, I felt my impending humiliation rise in anticipation of the moment my colleagues learned of my deficiency. But Randy took pity on me.

"Don't worry, I could give you a crash course—it's easy to drive stick."

He was my savior! He went inside the workshop and told the dispatcher, "We'll be gone for a few hours; I'm giving Lisa a tour of the base."

He drove the shuttle out of the motor pool and took me to an inactive flight line, where he hopped from his seat and directed me to drive. Two hours later I was a natural, and no one at motor pool was the wiser.

I soon realized that scorpions in the desert were as common as rats in the inner city. I was grateful for the contrast provided by the black and tan speckled scorpions against beige sand—it lessened the likelihood of a surprise sting. What I couldn't protect against, however, was the sting of Saudi eyes. As I regularly drove tractor-trailers downtown and buses to tour sites, Saudi men frequently cut me off. They harbored such rage toward this woman with the audacity to "drive" on their roads! They would blast their horns, nearly sideswipe my truck, or give me the Saudi version of the middle finger. All I could do was obey the speed limit and keep my focus on the road ahead.

American military men and women were required to wear their uniforms downtown. Additionally, we women were required to keep our hair pinned up tightly and our heads covered at all times. I refrained from making eye contact with Saudi men, walked behind my fellow airmen, and adhered to prayer time customs.

What I found surprising was the trusting nature of the shopkeepers in the downtown area. Trays of gold, silver, and other expensive items were often left out without anyone attending to them. I soon discovered the penalty for theft was to get a hand chopped off. Later that month, I was assigned to take an American tour bus to a place nicknamed "Chop-Chop Square" in Riyadh. The curious U.S. military found it entertaining to spend an afternoon watching as Saudis were judicially punished for crimes ranging from alcohol and sexual offenses to stealing by having their hands publicly lopped of with an axe; or being beheaded for witchcraft and sex crimes. Needless to say, I remained on the bus and listened to the gruesome details from my colleagues for the length of the bus ride home. I was no longer surprised by the trust of the shopkeepers.

Feeling rather proud of myself for my ability to drive a stick shift, I arrogantly volunteered to do a tractor-trailer run downtown with a 32-foot flatbed trailer. I got onto the highway feeling confident. I ignored the usual Saudi road rage and felt euphoric driving such a powerful big rig. I dared a Saudi to cut me off in this monster! I now knew what it felt like to power such a huge machine and earn the respect of mortal drivers. When a 32-foot tractor-trailer changes lanes, everyone moves out of the way.

My trip went without a glitch. I picked up the load, strapped down my cargo, and headed back to the base. But as I arrived at the main entrance, my illusion of confidence came to a thundering halt. I had forgotten about the zigzagging, anti-terrorist barricade that I would need to weave through to get back onto the base. I recalled that, weeks earlier, this had not been an easy task with the 1.5-ton box truck. I came to a dead stop, took a deep breath, and ran a series of options through my mind:

Option #1: I could drive around the entire base and ascertain if all the entrances had the barricades.

Option #2: I could park the truck and beg the Saudi guard to open what looked like a padlocked entrance a few yards adjacent to the main gate.

Option #3: I could swallow my pride, radio the motor pool, and request that a more experienced driver meet me at the gate.

Option #4: I could give it a try myself.

An advocate of common sense, I jumped down from the rig and walked up to the guard shack. The guards noticed me approaching on foot and became alarmed; one of them scurried to meet me. He held his weapon cautiously and demanded, "What you need?"

I handed him my identification and said, "I don't think I could get the truck through the barricade—is there another entrance without a barricade, or could you open the side gate?"

"No!"

"No what? No gate without a barricade or no you can't open the side gate?"

He glared at me and insisted, "This way in only!"

I looked at him in disbelief and said, "Thanks."

I felt fired up and thought, *I'll show 'em*, as I climbed back into my tractor and prepared to fit King Kong through the gerbil maze. I wove through the first barricade with relative ease. But as I started my turn into the next one, I could see in my sideview mirror that I was not going to clear the rear barricade. I was exasperated. There was no way humanly possible to get this rig through such a tight configuration. I noticed chunks scraped from the barricades and black rubber marks staining the concrete—definitely a sign that what I was attempting was no easy task. As I tried to back up and restart a sharper forward cut, I came nearer and nearer to the rear barricade thinking, *I, too, will be leaving a personal mark.*

Vehicles were now piling up behind me, waiting for their turn to get through the maze. I jumped from my rig and asked the driver of the Jeep behind me to spot me as I tried to maneuver out of this mess. For the next twenty minutes, I backed up and pulled forward, rocking back and forth, inching myself between the barricades. All the while, I was stalling out between reverse and first gear. The cars continued to stack up behind me and the gate guard finally had enough. He approached the side of my truck and barked, "Get this out!"

I looked at him with equal rage, and asked, "You wanna try it?"

He shouted, "Let's go, let's go!"

I assured him help was on the way, radioed my dispatcher, and humbly asked for assistance at the main gate. One of the sergeants arrived, laughed at my predicament, and took my seat. I remained outside the tractor and spotted his movement. It took us an additional ten minutes to get through the gate. When I finally climbed into the passenger seat of my rig, he said, "You did pretty good kid."

"What if I told you I just learned how to drive stick shift last month?"

"Then you did great. Be prepared though, they're all laughing at you back at the shop."

It didn't matter, if the sergeant needed ten minutes to get through with years of experience driving a truck, I didn't do so badly. At least I tried. This is something that shaped the way I treated life circumstances from that moment on. I would *always* try.

Ninety days had gone by in a flash. I returned home free of snakebites and scorpion stings and the skill of having learned how to drive standard transmission vehicles. I became enlightened about the Muslim culture. I'd experienced the notorious desert sand storms and 130° heat. Also, I'd been unanimously chosen to be interviewed for an article in the *Air Force Times* because of my optimistic view on serving in Saudi Arabia considering the gender issues.

Several years after that experience (1996), I learned that the condominiums I once called home, the Khobar Towers, had been blown up in a terrorist attack. Nineteen Americans, Saudis and allies were killed, and five hundred were injured—this in a time known as "Desert Calm." The terrorists abandoned a fuel tanker full of explosives, just adjacent to the anti-terrorist barricade, and detonated it a short time later.

I learned, for the first time, that there are places where it was not advantageous to be a woman; Mom was right to worry, and it made perfect sense that the Saudi guards were so cautious and ill tempered.

After completing my four-year tour of duty in Boston I was in a flux. I was asked to re-enlist but had no passion for the transportation industry. There was certainly no future for Tony in Boston, as the Chicago Carpenter's Union was significantly stronger. My goal had been to enter the Air Force to get an education; therefore, moving back to Chicago was the logical solution.

Once home, I entered community college and began working full-time as a private security officer. The more I learned about public safety through my employment and my criminal justice courses, the more interested I became in law enforcement.

While working the security job, I met a police officer who would periodically find a reason to enter my building and engage me in casual small talk.

"What's a nice girl like you doing in a job like this?"

When I explained that the "nice girl" was a Desert Storm Veteran, he became reticent. Even with that information—and knowledge that I was married—"Officer Friendly" was clearly in denial. Time after time, this rogue refused to look beyond my shell and mocked my interest in becoming a police officer. He was more interested in trying to cheat on his wife than answering my litany of police-related questions.

As part of my college course criteria, I was required to devote two hundred hours as an intern at a police department of my choice. I chose the Chicago Police Department for two reasons: I was aware that Chicago gave educational incentives beyond a four-year degree, and I'd have plenty of opportunities for excitement.

CHAPTER 5
911

The police internship sealed my decision to become a police officer. While waiting for the department to test (it's given every two years) for a position on the police force, I thought it wise to get my foot in the door by becoming a 911 dispatcher. Tony was his usual supportive self and mocked me for going to college, bragged that he made more money than me, and found it absurd that I wanted to be a cop. The more I did to enhance my life, the more threatened he was. He'd grown emotionally aware that the more educated and independent I became, the less I would need him. What I needed to do was convince myself to break free from my perceived dependence on him.

My reception as a dispatcher wasn't as welcomed as I thought it would be. The gossip in the radio room (dispatch center) was so cutting that it was difficult to function. I learned from Mark, the only male dispatcher in the department and one of my assigned trainers, that it was common to be given the cold shoulder by the women. I was fresh meat and, as he put it, "It doesn't help that you're thin and attractive." Some of the women either dated, were married to or longed to date the police officers.

Mark and I clicked instantly when we learned that we shared the same sense of humor. He would often have the ladies in stitches with his impersonations of some of his ridiculous 911 calls. Extremely intelligent, he juggled his dispatch job, law school, and a part-time police officer position with apparent ease. On top of this, he was a musician in a local band. Aside from that he was my most challenging trainer. I received a pass status and was deemed to be ready by Mark after the standard three months of training.

I was confident and ready to handle my own dispatch computer system when I was called into a meeting with the dispatch center supervisor. "Have a seat Lisa," she said, wearing a strained smile.

This was the official moment when she would release me from training and assign me to midnight shift. I was thrilled. However, she looked uncomfortable, fidgeting with paperwork as she continued.

"There have been some rumors that have even made it to the Chief, that you are having an affair with Mark."

"What!" I exclaimed incredulously.

"Several people have brought it to my attention that you too have gotten very close during your training and I have to take some action based on that," she said matter-of-factly.

Horrified, I replied, "I have no idea why someone would say something like that, but I can assure you, it's not true!"

"Well…I spoke to the Chief and because of this I decided to put you back in training with another dispatcher to ensure you're equipped to handle the job."

Infuriated at the accusation, I asked, "So let me get this straight: if someone starts a rumor it's assumed to be true and I am punished for it?"

"Lisa," she said, sounding exasperated, "it's the only way for me to prove you weren't given passing grades that you didn't deserve."

I knew that some of the women in dispatch were threatened by me physically, and Mark warned me that appearing at work smiling and confident fed their jealousy. I never fathomed it would reach this level.

I walked out of her office feeling as if I had a dagger lodged into my back, no different than the one Rustin plunged into me in the Air Force. I drove home paralyzed. I told Tony about the accusation and even with the state of our unhealthy relationship, he thought it ludicrous.

"Sue 'em," he offered.

Amused by his solution, I broke a smile. "No. Better yet, I'll show those backstabbers I can do the job and their little stunt will have no effect on me. I vow to show up at work looking even more cheerful than before."

"I still think you could sue 'em," Tony said.

I consulted with Mark, who was equally livid. He said, "I knew they were vicious but did not expect this."

He chose the same solution as I: behave as if we're unaffected.

I kept my word, and on my first day back and thereafter I arrived for work wearing my happy mask. When some of the busybodies asked about my re-training, I simply said, "Ask the dispatch supervisor."

After an additional month of training with one of the senior female dispatchers on the department—who incidentally was one of the few who didn't have a hate-on for me—I was cleared to work independently. I'd won! Temporarily anyway.

"Nine-one-one, do you need police, fire or medical?" I would answer, after the distinct blare of the steadily ringing hotline. Initially, I was surprised to learn that 95 percent of all 911 calls are of a non-emergency nature. It was the other legitimate 5 percent that keeps dispatchers on their toes.

I became accustomed to misdials. Comically enough, some people actually took the time to program 911 into their phones; they thought remembering to press a pre-programmed number would be easier than direct dialing. Last time I checked, when someone is screaming in pain or fear, inevitably someone will call out, "Dial 911! Did anyone call 911?" The convenience of having the one-button access made for a great inconvenience for the police due to all of the accidental grazes over the button.

In my eighteen months as a dispatcher, I honed the skills required to persuade three- to five-year-old children to put Mommy or Daddy on the phone. The second most common misdial was the result of a child playing with phone. In order for us to save on precious manpower, I needed to speak to an adult in the home to determine with certainty that there was no emergency. If the child wouldn't produce Mom or Dad, and left the phone off the hook, a squad had to be sent to the home.

Then there were the ludicrous 911 calls. One time I answered to an irate man's voice: "Send a cop over, now!" he shouted.

"What is your emergency, sir?" I asked.

"I want to file a report and need someone to write my neighbor a ticket."

"What did your neighbor do?"

"He mowed the lawn on my property!"

"Sir, are you telling me he mowed your lawn and you're angry?"

"Not the whole thing; he mowed his lawn and extended over a foot on my property."

I knew this needed to be handled with kid gloves. "Has he done this before?"

"No, last time it was more, but I told him if he does it again, I'm callin' the police."

It was a classic case of the Hatfields and the McCoys. In my wildest dreams, growing up in the city of Chicago, I never imagined that someone would think to call 911 over a few mown blades of grass. We classified this call as a neighbor dispute, and I was obligated to send an officer to resolve the dispute before things escalated. Later, the officer relayed that Mr. 911 caller had a very specific diagonal grass pattern that had been ruined by the straight edge Mr. Willy-Nilly Mower. The officer had spoken to Mr. Willy-Nilly, explained the precision method Mister 911 used to cut his grass, and requested he keep his mowing to his own property. Mr. Willy-Nilly replied, "You gotta be kidding me," before shutting the door in the officer's face.

My most bizarre 911 call came in one night from an Indian man working the counter at a Subway restaurant. "Oh my God!" he screamed into my ear.

"Sir, what is your emergency?" I asked firmly.

"Oh my God, oh my God, send police, send police!" he cried.

I dispatched the street sergeant and two squads to the unknown emergency as the man continued his ranting.

"Sir," I continued, "you need to calm down and tell me the problem so we can help you. What happened?" I assumed it was an armed robbery due to the time of the evening.

"Oh Goddd!" was his moaning reply.

"Are you injured, do you need an ambulance?"

"Send police, send police!" he bellowed.

"Sir, I have three police cars on their way, what happened?" I shouted sharply, irritated at not getting my questions answered.

"They take it!"

"Took what, was there a robbery?"

Through uncontrollable sobbing he cried, "Oh God!"

Back to square one. I was growing frustrated as I relayed to the responding street officers that I could not ascertain the problem. The sergeant sarcastically barked over the air, "We need the nature of the problem! What do we know, dispatch?"

I explained that the caller was highly emotional but would not forfeit any information aside from "someone-taking-something." I continued with the caller:

"Sir, the police are thirty seconds away, can you give me a description of the people you are talking about?"

"Oh God!" he cried over and over until the officers arrived on the scene, and I was disconnected.

The atmosphere in the radio room was thick. My co-dispatcher listened to me handle the call, sitting helplessly on the edge of her seat. One of the clerks who had filtered in to hear the crisis stood frozen at the door. I felt drained and defeated. In an attempt to console me, and appearing equally overwrought, my co-dispatcher said she couldn't have done a better job.

An eternal minute had expired when the sergeant calmly radioed that everything was 10-4 at the location. Now I was able to breathe. But the question remained, what was this man so insanely bonkers about? Moments later, the sergeant and one officer cleared the call, leaving one man behind to handle the paperwork. A dispatcher's chief frustration is releasing a 911 call to the police officers and not receiving an update on the incident. Finally, the case officer explained what the problem had been: a group of teenagers had walked in and left with a six-foot cardboard cutout of a submarine sandwich. Yes! All of that mind-blowing drama for a piece of cardboard.

Then one day, when you least expect it, a call comes in, and it's the real thing. "Nine-one-one do you need police fire or medical?"

"An ambulance," was her calm response.

I sent the ambulance and asked, "What's the problem, Ma'am?"

"Send an ambulance to 334 Main Street, my husband has been shot," she said with a little more conviction in her voice.

I dispatched an ambulance and several police units to the home. But as I looked at my 911 monitor, I noticed the woman was not calling from the address she'd just given. "Ma'am, the police and ambulance are on their way, where are you?"

"At a neighbor's house."

Perplexed, I asked, "How do you know your husband has been shot?"

"I did it," she offered matter-of-factly.

While she was still on the phone line, I radioed the responding officers and directed a unit to the wife's location. The ambulance could not go directly to the home and needed to temporarily "stage" nearby, until the officers determined the environment safe.

Meanwhile my co-dispatcher did an inquiry into prior incidents at the house. We learned it was the Pacella residence. Our officers had responded to their home countless times over the years for alcohol-related domestic disturbances. We also had a red alert indicating that Mr. Pacella owned numerous firearms.

I asked Mrs. Pacella where her husband was shot. She said it had been an accident; the gun had gone off in his mouth, and she wasn't sure if he was still alive. After the officers picked up Mrs. Pacella and determined that she was unarmed, the ambulance attended to a bleeding Mr. Pacella. He had suffered a non-life-threatening gunshot wound through his cheek.

Mrs. Pacella was subsequently arrested for attempted murder. Later in court, Mr. Pacella took full responsibility—convincing the judge that the shooting was self-inflicted—and spared his adoring wife from jail.

Toward the end of my dispatching career, Tony and I had more of a brother/sister relationship. Not by his choice, though. I was mentally beaten down by his lack of interest in my new police endeavors. Because of his drinking, smoking, and lack of support, I ended our sexual relationship. I could barely bring myself to kiss him the last year we were together.

I tried convincing myself that Tony was not so bad. He was a creature of good and bad habits. He worked zealously, grabbing every opportunity to earn overtime or take on side jobs to provide us with a beautiful home and new cars. He also continued to drink daily and hang out with his fellow carpenters at the sort of bars that entertained male patrons with lingerie fashion shows. I actually *condoned* fashion-show Thursdays. I felt palpably guilty for the lack of intimacy in our relationship and secretly hoped that he would have an affair—and leave me.

Over the years, Tony had threatened to kill himself if I ever left and swore he'd never let me go. I was fearful of his temper. But while he became destructive during his drunken episodes, he'd never harmed me physically. Sadly, I looked at that as a plus. After some eight or so months of my intentional frigidity, I was hoping to push Tony to file for a divorce.

One evening I lay napping in our bedroom, preparing for a midnight shift. Tony arrived home drunk and knelt along side the bed. He shook me and grunted, "Hey."

I recognized the putrid stench of alcohol emanating from his mouth and was instantly repulsed. Waking from a deep slumber, hoping I was in a nightmare, I responded, "Huh?"

"Get up!" he slurred, "I brought home dinner."

It was 9:15 p.m., and I thought it obvious I would have already eaten dinner considering my schedule and the hour. "I'm not hungry," was my irritated response.

As I drifted back to sleep, I heard him mumble, "You never eat dinner with me."

The next thing I knew, my blanket was stripped from my body and an excruciating heat permeated the flesh on my bare back. Instinctively, my chest pressed deep into the bed and my shoulder blades arched together, as I cringed and screeched "Aaaaaaah!" In the next instant, I leapt up and realized Tony had dumped the searing contents of a Chinese food container on me.

Without thinking, I raced toward him in nothing but my underpants as brown gravy dripped down my legs. He must have seen the rage in my eyes, because he darted for the bedroom door. I chased him into the kitchen, clueless as to what I was capable of doing next. Feeling superhuman, I lunged toward him.

Forcefully, I plunged my open hands into his chest with all of my might and watched as he lost his balance and crashed backward onto the kitchen table. Tony clumsily skidded onto the floor, dodging the overturned table as the remainder of the Chinese food tumbled onto his chest.

Surveying the damage and fearing retaliation, I raced into the bathroom and locked the door behind me, panting for air. Tony was on my heels, and pummeled the locked door with his fists, pleading with me to open up. As I stood with my back pressed against the door, I caught sight of my reflection in the mirror. I was horrified at the red-faced stranger staring back at me. Then I turned to see the pie-sized crimson burn on my back and burst into uncontrollable tears.

Tony remained outside the bathroom door, bellowing, "I love you Lisa…I'm sorry…please let me in." All I wanted to do was get away from him. I showered as quickly as I could and decided I would repress my shaken, vulnerable state. Cloaking it with an air of seething anger, I tore open the bathroom door and stepped over a startled Tony, who was lying in a pathetically crumpled heap at the foot of the door. There he remained, staring at me, wide-eyed and silent. I shot him one fleeting look with my new daggers, just daring him to follow. I locked myself in the bedroom and threw on my work uniform, pausing for a moment as I ceremoniously affixed my Chicago Police administrative badge to my uniform shirt.

The second I heard Tony enter the shower, I raced from the bedroom and left for work. I knew it ironic that part of my job entailed sending help to victims of domestic batteries; and here I was, "a victim" who decided to keep my battery a secret, as I continued helping strangers that very evening. Unfortunately, despite my show of power against Tony, I still feared his threats. I couldn't bring myself to share this atrocity with my family, or move in with Mom, even if it was only temporary. My image of independence was too important; asking for help was out of the question. So instead, I threatened Tony with a divorce if he didn't join me for relationship counseling. *Sound pathetically familiar?* Tony was more than eager to do anything I wished—for the moment.

The counseling began, and Tony chose to clean up his act, giving up drinking and lingerie Thursdays. But our communication was minimal over the following weeks. After four unsuccessful sessions with the counselor (Tony felt the male counselor favored me), he announced he wasn't returning.

My new goal was to get hired as a Chicago Police Officer so that I could finance my own home and leave Tony forever.

CHAPTER 6
CHICAGO POLICE ACADEMY

The year and a half as a dispatcher flew by and I had proven to be an asset to the department. I was now ready to take the police exam. The physical agility portion was the first stage. One of the physical exams required us to pull a 180-lb. dummy from the window of a mock burning automobile and drag it twenty yards into a safe zone within a prescribed amount of time. I wondered what it felt like dragging dead weight. Before my turn I asked some of the men who were also testing how much they weighed. When I found one close to 180 lbs, I asked him if he would be willing to collapse backward onto me so I could run my own trial. He looked at me like I was crazy. I suppose it was an odd request. Some of the other guys laughed, but one guy said, "I'll do it." I grasped him under his arms, locked my hands across his chest and held him still for a second to feel the impact of the weight. As I did this, other guys began mimicking my trial. All of a sudden, it was a good idea. I dragged the guy about thirty feet, struggling across the grass lot. "Okay," I huffed, "that's good, thanks. Now I know what it feels like." *I'm screwed.*

I started to internally prep myself: okay, I'm going to pretend that the dummy is my father and this is a real life-and-death circumstance. If I don't get him out and to the safety zone fast, he's dead. The timekeeper blew the start whistle; I ran to the car and reached through the window for Dad. First, I had to lean in and throw his forty-pound legs over to the passenger side so I could extricate him in one swoop. As I dug around through the window, maneuvering the dead weight, one leg caught on the stick shift. I retreated from the window, went to plan B and began lifting the whole torso with both of the dummy's arms pinned under my bear hug hold. I banged my head on the top edge of the window and felt as if time was ticking away at warp speed. I sweated like a pig, knowing the men were watching me with disgust. I continued pulling the dummy until it broke free from the window. If it didn't have broken legs from the car accident, it did now. The legs slammed to the ground as I dragged it into the safe zone, panting all the way. The timekeeper stopped his watch and said, "Passed." I dropped the dummy and looked around at the guys waiting their turn. Most avoided eye contact, and the ones that did looked at me with sympathy. They no doubt wondered, "Why is she even bothering?"

To add insult to injury, our next test required us to ascend a staircase carrying a barbell weighing 70 percent of our body weight, in my case about eighty-four pounds. Upon picking it up, my string bean arms felt as if they were being ripped from my shoulders. They soon grew numb as I ascended the staircase. I could barely breathe. One of the overseers noticed this and shot out, "Breathe!" after noticing my face turn beet red. Because the goal of this test was to ascertain strength, not keep time, I knew going in that I needn't rush. I took his advice and began to breathe as I continued up. Once I reached the top and turned around for the climb down, I saw the others again look at me with sympathy. There was no giving up now. I stayed focused and had no recollection of the descent; it was over in a flash. Not until I heard the word, "passed" did I realize it was over. I dropped the barbell to the ground and walked off to the next testing station.

After all was said and done, my test score landed me the number four position on the long list of people who had tested to become police officers. How, you may ask? I aced the written exam. Fortunately for me the physical agility portion of it wasn't based on a point system; you either passed or failed. I managed to pass them all.

Several months later, still a dispatcher, I watched anxiously as the top three on the list were called up to begin their training. I would have to wait for the next rotation of new police officers to be hired when a vacant slot opened. Several days later, though, the department decided to terminate an officer who was struggling in his field training, which opened an additional position. With one day's notice, I was sent downtown to perform another physical agility test that was required to enter the police academy. *Not again.*

Tony was still in denial about my decision to become a police officer. "You know you're gonna have to shoot people? Whattaya gonna do when some 6'5," 300-pound man wants to kick your ass for writing him a ticket? Are you really gonna do this?"

Sometime around that incident I found a cannabis plant in our backyard. I knew he occasionally smoked pot with his friends and opted for the "don't ask don't tell policy," because pot smoking made him a different man, relaxed and non-confrontational. When I discovered the plant in our yard, I went berserk, surprising myself with my foul mouth and show of strength. "I work for the police and you're growing pot on our fucking property! Are you sick? We could go to jail and have our home seized." He knew he'd crossed the line and ripped out the plant.

Even after I'd proven my commitment to the military and enrolled in college, Tony still fantasized that I would succumb to his concept of the ideal wife (drinking beers with him and pumping out babies). But I ignored his remarks, realizing that nothing short of being a playboy model housewife would satisfy him. I had a plan this time; I needed to get through the next sixteen weeks at the Chicago Police Academy, see it materialize into a career and leave.

Physical agility round two; I completed the strength, sit-and-reach, and sit-up portions of the test with ease, but the one-and-a-half mile run worried me. I hadn't run for two years and since three rookies had been ahead of me on the list, I'd naïvely assumed I would have a sixteen-week cushion during which to properly train. I was wrong. On sheer will, I rounded the track fifteen times and passed with thirty seconds to spare. Afterwards, I walked off behind an unoccupied PR trailer and threw up.

I'd done it! I was off to the Chicago Police Academy one week later. Mom was beside herself. I had caused her so much anxiety already with my Desert Storm experience. My actions were always the opposite of what she expected of me. If I didn't know any better, I would have guessed that she and Tony were co-conspirators in a plot to hold me back from a life of independence.

Following in the tradition of my Air Force battle-dress camouflage, the private security uniform, and the oh-so-flattering blue dispatcher polyesters, I now proudly donned the infamous brown khakis and Navy-style cap for the police academy. Talk about self-imposed fashion masochism! Was this the same girl who competed for Miss Illinois? The academy was as severe as the military regarding women who attempted to look like women. Make-up and jewelry were not permitted, nor was hair allowed to hang outside the cap. Of course, given Tony's jealous streak, these rules were right up his alley. "You look great, babe," he said sarcastically as I left for my first day of training.

Unlike the military, the police academy did not require us to live at the training site. Rather, we were required to exhibit the self-discipline to return home, study, and exercise on our own. Personally, I would have preferred a sixteen-week vacation from Tony to focus on my training.

After the massive orientation assembly, we were divided into our classrooms. I quickly noticed that I was one of only two females in our class of fifty. The barking commenced. Orders were shouted and egos were crushed as the games began. I smiled inside, reflecting on military boot camp, knowing exactly what to expect. I wore my most earnest, respectful face and snapped to the orders like a whip. We were hustled into a military formation and given a quick course on marching as we filed out of the gymnasium.

Having settled into alphabetized seats, we watched Officer Brown scowl at the bodies before him. Then he began his customary memorized speech: "If you came here because you want to wear a badge and carry a gun and arrest people, you can march right out that back door and go back where you came from. We're not looking for police men and women who want to be John Wayne and brag to their buddies about how many fights they got into and how many times they got to pull their gun."

There was that gun thing again. This time I knew full well I was choosing a career that may require me to kill or be killed. It was a far cry from the princess life I thought I'd lead. Again it felt like I was bartering for something that would give me freedom—freedom from Tony, that is.

The speech droned on, including points about bribery, human rights violations, abuse of police power, and the infamous code-of-silence. Brown punctuated every sentence with a dramatic pause, as he stared down the nearest random rookie. I felt sorry for the first two rows.

Halfway through the day, Brown asked, "With a show of hands, who's been in the military?" A young man in the front row, Gott, said that he was a reservist in the Navy. "No cadet, I mean the real military." I proudly raised my hand and said, "I served four years active duty in the Air Force." He immediately told the class to look at the two of us, because we were the Class Commanders; specifically, Gott was assigned Commander, and I was his assistant. Initially, I was flattered, but then I thought it through. Because I had served four years active duty, I felt that I was superior to Gott, who was what active duty military referred to as a "weekend warrior." I concluded that Gott had been appointed to lead the class because he was a man. Here we go again; after four years of proving myself capable of doing a "man's job" in the military, it was time to start from scratch.

Brown released our group for lunch, then pulled Gott and me aside for a briefing. "You two are responsible for every person in our squad...this class is a direct reflection on your abilities as leaders...I do not tolerate excuses and expected you to whip these troops into shape! Don't come running to me for help. I didn't choose experienced people to run this group so I could hold your hands, got it?"

"Yes sir," Gott and I responded in unison.

"Don't ever call me sir again, I work for a living!" was Brown's final order before walking off.

Afterward, Gott confessed that he wanted no part of the job, but was afraid to tell Brown. I eased his mind by telling him everything I'd learned during my training. I knew that getting forty-eight men to take orders from a woman would pose a challenge, and explained to Gott that we needed to be firm. Like Brown said, our class would be a reflection of our performances as leaders. Gott barely listened as I spoke. Then he left me to rush off with a group of his friends for lunch, saying, "Yeah, yeah, you're right, sounds good..."

I sat with my new friend, Tom Malloy, one of the four rookies hired from our list. A Rob Lowe look-alike, he was endearing, low-key, and initially kept to himself. He congratulated me on my appointment and chuckled.

"I don't envy you."

"Thanks," I replied, as I explained the situation with Gott.

After lunch, we were required to make a military formation, according to height. Gott and I stood in front of the group and relayed what Brown expected and how we'd like to see the plan carried out. The group grumbled a bit. Whispering emanated from the back row; some trainees were uninterested in anything we said. I had given Gott most of the floor but saw that he was losing respect. He even whined, "C'mon guys, I don't even want this job, don't make it harder."

I saw red. Everything that I had learned about leadership was being thrown into the gutter by Gott's desperate pleading. I said in a firm voice, "Excuse me, officers. You are aware that we were not given a choice about our positions; even so, I have decided to do exactly what Brown expects with the experience I have."

The group became still and I continued: "This is what is called parade rest position." I demonstrated the stance and requested that they assume the position. Gott and the entire formation complied. The training went on in this manner for several minutes. No sooner did I bark out the order of "Atten-hut!" did Brown round the corner and witness our group, attentive and eager to learn.

He looked at Gott and said, "Now lead them into the classroom."

Gott stood flustered as Brown walked past us and waited in the room. I whispered, "Right face, have them do a right face."

Gott yelled out, "Right face," and I directed the group to file in, starting from the back row.

On our ride home, Malloy told me that Gott had looked like an idiot in front of the group, and laughed because Brown had arrived just in time to witness me leading the class. Officer Sharkey, another woman hired from my district whom I'd hoped to befriend, didn't reciprocate my desire. She was assigned to a different class and, despite her military background, was not chosen for a command position. Witnessing me leading our group the first day did not sit well with her. She remarked, "Any monkey can do that job," obviously trying to take away any significance I may have felt. *The elusive sisterhood once again gets trampled before my eyes.* After ripping yet another dagger from my back, I rushed home to Tony to report how great I'd done on the first day.

He listened with minimal interest and said, "That's great. What's for dinner?" I couldn't understand how I could be so strong among the cadets and so weak when it came to leaving Tony.

Moments later, I saw just how much my yellow lab, Tyler, my only source of affection, had missed me: my brand new leather gun belt (the one we had to earn to wear) lay gnawed to oblivion on my office floor. *Welcome home! Whose idea was it anyway to have police cadets return home after a full day of training?*

The next few weeks were a blur. Because our academy class was training through the blistering heat of a Chicago summer, our hours were altered. We started at six a.m. instead of eight, in order to safely run outdoors for the physical agility portion of our training. We were fortunate to be assigned to Officer Tero. He was built like a brick house: 6'2" and 240 pounds of pure muscle. He was the brother of the actor Mr. T, and didn't want any one to remind him of that. Every morning we would hit the streets of Chicago running in formation, up Jackson Blvd. toward the Sears Tower. I ran directly behind Tero and was inspired. He screamed out the last names of certain officers who began to fall behind:

"Move it Pledge, lessgo Sutton, get a move-on Lockwood. Tero don't tolerate slackers!"

I was revisiting the run and barf scene from a few days earlier. Now that I was this group's appointed leader, something had to be done, and fast. Every night after the academy, I pushed myself to do an evening run to get in shape. Tero's voice haunted me. After weeks of running, I caught up to the men. There was something about Tero's energy that got into me; it began to feel like I was running on a moving walkway. Once Tero realized I could hang with the faster runners, he encouraged me to drop back and motivate the stragglers.

Several weeks into the academy, we began our firearms training. Delaying this segment was probably a precaution designed to weed out the cadets who were just interested in getting their hands on a gun. I was learning that there really are John Waynes out there. After hours of classroom training, we graduated to the indoor range. As I stood on the firing line with six other cadets, we were directed to load our guns and charge the weapons with a round. I had never shot a handgun—the Air Force only qualified us on M-16's—and was excited. My range master asked, "Have you ever fired a handgun before?"

"An M-16 in the Air Force," I replied.

"That's not a handgun," he sarcastically shot out.

With that he directed me to "Squeeeeeze the trigger and fire." I did, and nailed the target right through the bulls-eye. He looked at me in disbelief. "I thought you never shot a handgun before."

Equally shocked, I laughed and replied, "I haven't." Skeptically, he ordered me to fire again. This time, he was livid. As he pulled the target closer, we both realized I'd done the unthinkable; I shot through the same hole twice. I couldn't believe my eyes.

He truly thought I had lied to him and called over another range master to examine my target. "She said this is the first time she fired a handgun."

The second guy exclaimed, "She shot before!" and turned to me. "Haven't you?"

I adamantly declared, "This is the first time I have ever fired a handgun!"

The third shot ended up centimeters from the first two and I was stunned. The instructor was speechless. He raised his eyebrows as if to say, "You liar!"

Now I began to perspire. My hands were clammy, and I couldn't concentrate on anything but the enraged range master. I was torn up inside, wanting to do well but afraid that the man beside me thought I was lying. My breathing changed, and my target became blurry. Every subsequent shot ended up scattered around the target—some missed altogether. The range master barked, "Concentrate!" and grew angrier. Then, a bell rang to proclaim the range safe, and I was dismissed. I gathered my things and walked out, feeling beaten.

I guessed that all the range masters were taught to discourage progress, as a mental test—or maybe this one took my progress personally. I contacted my police department and requested additional firearms training after I was finished at the academy. They were supportive and set up skill training sessions immediately.

Our Police Chief, Tim McCarthy, a retired secret-service agent, world renowned for taking a bullet with Jim Brady while protecting President Ronald Reagan, held his cadets to extremely high standards and was a class act. An examination was given every Friday. Chief McCarthy made it clear that he expected nothing less than a 90 percent score on our weekly exams. Additionally, I was given the task of turning in the grades of our group of four. Talk about motivation! I never wanted to be linked to the cadet with the lowest score. Thankfully, we all managed to maintain the Chief's standards, and then some.

Seven weeks into our training, Gott finally told Brown that he wanted to step down from his position as Class Commander. Brown was surprisingly supportive and told me to run the show solo. Once I was in charge, Brown showed up more and lingered behind the scenes observing my progress. Occasionally he would perform a uniform inspection and blame me for any infraction found in the group. I knew not to take it personally and began pre-inspecting my team every day. I had a daily challenge with one particular cadet, who would pass highly interruptive gas while at attention. Little did anyone know how funny I found this. For as long as I could remember, I'd lose it at the sound of someone farting—an idiosyncrasy no doubt passed down to me by my dad.

When I tried to persuade the anonymous officer to claim responsibility, the group would laugh even more, waving their hands and gasping, "Aw, man, that was wrong. Someone ain't right. Who did it?"

I often had to turn away from the group and bite my lip to refrain from laughing. A few times, I was ordered by a passing instructor to control my class.

Finally, one day, it was evident who the emitter was. I looked at him sternly and said, "Ski, please stop doing that."

He looked at me earnestly and said, "I'm sorry, I can't. It's a medical condition; it runs in the family."

The formation roared at his proclamation.

I knew he was lying after witnessing his antics over the past two months, but I couldn't prove it. I naively set myself up and asked, "What's the condition called?"

Without hesitation he snapped, "Irritable bowel syndrome."

With that, I lost complete control of the group. They were laughing hysterically—just as Brown rounded the corner. "What's the problem?" he demanded.

Not wanting Ski to get in trouble, I explained, "It was a gas issue, Officer Brown, and it's been resolved."

One day in firearms training I was instructed to march my class into the room and await our range master, Nash, who would be a few minutes late. The range masters were a different breed of trainers. They were extremely severe and straightforward in their approach to teaching—rightfully so, considering the subject matter. To our surprise, the instructor walked in and overheard our class engaging in quiet conversation. He stormed over to his desk, slammed down his briefcase, and snapped, "Oh, excuse me for interrupting, I'm sure none of you needs to study anything about firearms. I think I'll take a break and wait to teach the next class. It's obvious you don't see the value in firearms training. Who's your Class Commander?"

I stood and said, "I am, Officer Nash."

"You should be ashamed of yourself."

I felt a shot of heat rush to my cheeks and stood speechless.

"Sit down!" he barked, before grabbing his briefcase and storming out the door.

I sat there stunned for a moment along with the class, until I heard a whisper in the back row. *The audacity.* I shouted to the guilty officer, "Give me a To-From at the end of the day on why you shouldn't talk in class." (A To-From was a memo used to discipline an officer. It was their opportunity to formally admit to a mistake.)

With that the room took on the character of a funeral parlor. Ten minutes later, Nash gleefully waltzed into the classroom as if nothing had happened. My guess: he was running late for work, needed time for a coffee break, and used the tiny infraction to his benefit.

As the weeks passed, I felt that our class had developed an incredible amount of camaraderie. We engaged in study groups at a local pub on Thursday nights and got to know one another on a personal level. I tolerated many inspection infractions and never "narked" anyone out, as other Class Commanders had. We worked as a team with some of the students who weren't pulling the grades they needed. They began getting used to "the game" and knew when I needed to be harder on them in highly visual locations, such as public hallways. I was truly coming into my own, feeling more self-confident, trimming back down to 118 pounds and taking the time to care about my appearance again by adding a few blonde highlights in my hair.

Toward the end of the sixteen weeks, I had my group stand in formation outside a class that was being conducted in an open lobby area. Our brother Metro-class had already entered. My group was pressuring me to join the other class, so I asked, "Since when do we enter a class without permission?"

The other class pointed their fingers at us and mocked me for being so stringent. One renegade in my formation said, "Fuck this, I'm goin' in."

"Excuse me," I called out, "unless you've decided to join the other class, you need to get back in formation."

"This is bullshit!" he exclaimed.

The other class began humming "Woooooh," in unison, trying to add fuel to the fire, as he penitently walked back into formation.

Suddenly, one of the most notoriously strict police instructors arrived to substitute our class. He looked at the ones who had already taken their seats and asked, "Where's your Class Commander?"

The other Commander stood up, and before he could even open his mouth, the overweight, gray-haired retired policeman stood right in his face and yelled, "Who the hell do you think you are, disrespecting me in front of one hundred cadets?"

"No excuse, sir," was his response.

"What? You saw your brother class standing in the hallway and thought you were better than them?"

"Nnnno sir, no excuse sir," the Class Commander replied.

"I want a To-From from everyone in your class explaining why you felt the need to break the rules after months of training," he continued. "You know what you need to do." The Commander rapidly ordered his class into formation alongside our group.

The Instructor walked over to me and asked, "Who is your HRI (homeroom instructor)?"

"Officer Brown," I responded.

"I'll be sure to let Brown know what a fine, respectable class he has. Now, come in and have your group take a seat."

As we settled into our seats, I peered around our group and spotted the cadet who didn't want to wait in the hallway with the rest of us. Once we made eye contact he shrugged his shoulders and mouthed the word, *Sorry*.

I smiled and gave him a thumbs-up. As I scanned the room, I began receiving winks and thumbs-up from other members of our group. The instructor decided to torture our brother class a bit longer and said, "I haven't decided if your class is worthy enough to join us." He left them to stand at attention for an additional ten minutes.

In the end, our rookie group of four impressed Chief McCarthy, with our final combined tests results averaging in the low nineties. My entire family, my best friends and Tony (out of obligation) attended my Chicago Police Academy graduation ceremony. I beamed with pride as I began my new career.

It's peculiar how an obscure event can become a catalyst for life-changing decisions. Less than one month out of the academy, I was on my way to work and was rear-ended by a woman speeding in a school zone. The back of my candy-apple red Mitsubishi 3000 GT looked like an accordion. I was dazed by the abrupt slam and reached for my police radio to call for help. The dispatcher could hear the cracking in my voice and sent an ambulance. Within a minute, the ambulance and a swarm of police cars arrived on the scene. As they extracted me from my car, the other driver, who'd sustained no injury, saw my uniform and realized that she had run into a police officer. She began to cry.

As I lay in the back of the ambulance, one of my fellow officers asked if I wanted her to notify my husband.

Without hesitation I said, "No."

She asked again: "It won't be a problem, Lisa; I could have dispatch track him down at work to contact him."

Again, I said, "No thank you."

In my moment of truth, I realized, *My gosh, I was injured and being transported to the hospital, and I didn't even want my husband there.*

After several hours of treatment for a concussion and whiplash, I called Tony and asked him to meet me at the hospital. He was livid and couldn't understand why I hadn't called him earlier. When we arrived home that night I told Tony that in the moments following my crash I decided I wanted to end our marriage. Tony thought I was delirious and said, "We'll talk about it tomorrow."

I told him we would, and went to bed knowing that tomorrow would be the end of our eight years together—and the true beginning of my new life.

CHAPTER 7
FIELD TRAINING - STREET TIME

"Real" street time began. Attired in full uniform, gun belt, vest, and the infamous bus driver cap, I was ready to learn from the best. O'Malley was my first Field Training Officer (FTO). He had an impeccable reputation as a street cop who literally worked the eight hours he was paid for. Our thirty-minute lunches were always spent in our squad car; O'Malley wouldn't even consider calling out of service for something as silly as eating on his watch. O'Malley had high standards and expected the same from me.

Between calls, he would sit with my FTO manual on his lap and ardently review case law, department procedures, criminal offenses, and radio codes. He diligently checked off each column and directed me to initial the points we covered. O'Malley exhibited anal retentiveness, but I went with the program, eager to please him. I was ready to be a police officer and anxious to begin problem solving, even if it meant conforming to his rigid methods.

A few weeks into our training, we received a call to assist an ambulance on a "code." This was our means of communicating that a person was dead. Our job was to determine if there was any foul play. When we arrived, the paramedic team was already on the scene. I watched as O'Malley interviewed the daughter of the recently departed eighty-five-year-old woman. She relayed that her mother had been bedridden for well over a year and received in-home hospice care. No foul play here.

Aside from seeing dead people at funeral services, I'd never been exposed to death in a home setting. I was certain I could handle it. I didn't have any personal ties to the woman and felt rather confident in my uniform. I pretended as if I were a veteran, accustomed to handling death as part of the job.

When O'Malley completed his interview with the daughter, he pointed to the room where the paramedics were. "Why don't you go in and see if they need any help?" he suggested.

"Sure." I briskly headed into the bedroom. Two paramedics stood on either side of the bed, attempting to lift the woman. Her wrinkled face was pasty white, her eyes and mouth frozen wide open; she looked skeletal. I was fixated on her and lost myself in the room. My body began to perspire and heat emanated from under my collar. One of the paramedics startled me with a question: "Is this your first dead body?"

"Yes," I replied. "Is there anything I can do?"

One of the old-timers said, "Yeah, come over here and help us lift."

I donned a pair of gloves and went into service mode, convincing myself that she was just a dummy (like those crash dummies they use for automobile testing), not a real person. I repeated, *She's not real* over and over in my mind, as I placed my arm behind her back and my other hand around her cold, stiff wrist. As we lifted her, a ghastly gurgling noise emanated from her body. I thought that I was going to throw up.

"I think she's trying to say something!"

This was when I discovered how warped some paramedics are. As I stood there, half-hunched, with one knee on the bed, the paramedic on the other side felt this would be a good time to tilt the woman's body backward to illicit another repulsive gurgle. *Where was O'Malley? These guys were tormenting me.* After the second attempted lift, I could hear the body crackling as we bent her into a seated position. With that, the paramedic said, "Let's take a break."

He released the body; now this poor dead lady was sitting in her bed with no back support. Rigor mortis had definitely set in. I couldn't believe my eyes—this was *not* my idea of fun. Then I peered around the room and realized that I was the butt of a cruel joke. They didn't need my help; there were four buff paramedics and firemen in the room! They seized an opportunity to torment the rookie with her first dead body call.

Then I felt a sense of relief. I looked at the old lady again and reached to find the humor in it. Meanwhile, they pushed her torso backward, which caused her legs to lift in the air like a teeter-totter. *What sickos.* O'Malley walked into the room, horrified. "C'mon guys," he said, "her daughter is in the next room."

I was more than happy to get out of there and followed O'Malley to the front door, where we held the screen open for the gurney.

Back in the squad car I asked, "Did you send me in there because you knew they were going to set me up?"

He said, "I had no idea they were going to do that. I sent you in because it's your job!" Knowing O'Malley's personality, I believed him. He took out his checklist and marked off, *Trainee handled a "code" today, grade "good."* I would learn later that many employees in the 'death industry' utilize this sort of gallows humor to relinquish any sort of personalization to the stressful emotions surrounding their abnormal exposure to death. I hated to think I may need to develop it as well.

Another time, O'Malley and I were dispatched to assist a man who wanted to have his wife involuntarily committed to a mental hospital. She was undergoing one of "her breakdowns" due to not taking her medication in a week, relayed the dispatcher. Sergeant Degnan, who was quickly becoming one of my mentors on the department and a backup officer, met us at the house. Aside from Degnan lending his support during my dispatching rumor crisis, he was an incredible role model, reminding me a lot of Sgt. Andrew from the Air Force. His uniform was always impeccable, and he truly exuded pride in his career. At the house, I discovered that situations like involuntary committals needed to be handled delicately. An ambulance team could not transport someone and have her committed to a mental hospital without the individual's permission. How to convince a person that she is mental and have her sign herself in was beyond me.

The husband allowed us in to remedy their situation. While his son was on the telephone attempting to contact her physician, his wife, Josie, was carving out a path pacing between the kitchen and the dining room. She ranted and chain smoked all the while. As Degnan and O'Malley attempted to retrieve information from the husband, I watched Josie and assessed her behavior. Then I flashed to the memory of my grandmother, who had passed away some years earlier.

My grandmother suffered from mental illness and lived with our family for many years. She took a variety of prescription drugs to control her state. Grandma, too, displayed some bizarre behavior when she had not taken the correct amount or proper combination of medication. It seemed Grandma's only pleasure was smoking. Even if she had a cigarette in her hand, she would request a cigarette from anyone who came near her. Grandma often sat fixated on something for long durations and would repeat some nonsensical line over and over. It was sad to witness the demise of a once loving, strong woman. Fortunately, I had this reference to draw upon for help.

I realized that Josie was completely uninterested in the goings on around her. The house could have been on fire for all she cared. As her husband explained to Degnan and O'Malley that Josie had violent tendencies and wouldn't hesitate to lunge at a stranger, I seated myself at the dining room table. Josie's route changed with the added dynamic of my presence. She began walking around the table, stopping intermittently to take a short drag from her cigarette and then tap her fingernails on the table's surface.

O'Malley approached Josie and tried to introduce himself. She ignored him. The other officer entered the room and said, "Hello ma'am. Can we ask you a few questions?"

Josie became irate and screamed, "Get out! Leave me alone!" She paced faster, oblivious to the trail of ashes descending from her cigarette.

I signaled to Degnan and O'Malley to permit me a few moments with Josie alone. I pretended to write notes on my scratch pad and purposely avoided eye contact with her. She stormed into the kitchen and poured herself a glass of water, gulping it frantically as it spilled down her chin and throat, drenching her shirt. Then she returned to the dining room and began tapping the table, standing closer to my chair. Without looking up, I asked her, "Could I have a glass of water?"

Like a Jekyll and Hyde metamorphosis, she responded, "Sure. I'm sorry I didn't offer." As she retrieved my water, her husband and my colleagues looked at me quizzically. I was just as taken aback as they were.

Then I thanked her and said, "I'm Lisa."

"I'm Josie," she replied, extending her hand.

I began asking her non-invasive questions about her family: how many children she had, where she was born, how many siblings, etc. She was an incredible conversationalist for a woman who was off her medication. Aside from a few nervous ticks, such as finger tapping and chain smoking, I managed to keep her distracted with conversation.

After ten minutes, her husband contacted her physician, who authorized her committal based on the knowledge she had not taken her medication in a week. The only way to get her regulated entailed a ten-day stint in the hospital. With that information we no longer needed her authorization for an involuntary committal; however, it was still necessary to have her transported by an ambulance, in case she lapsed into one of her violent episodes.

Degnan joined me and established rapport with Josie as well. When the ambulance arrived, I explained to her that her physician wanted to meet her at the hospital for a "check-up." Josie was surprisingly receptive. But as we escorted her out the front door, she spotted the ambulance and began screaming, "I'm not going in there! No! You're not taking me anywhere!" She flailed her arms and tried shoving her way past us.

Five of us attempted to restrain the now Herculean Josie. I soothingly said, "Josie, it's okay, it's okay…" as I held her hand. At one point I asked her if she wanted me to go with her to the hospital.

Miraculously, she stopped resisting, looked to me and asked, "You'll come with me?"

I looked at Degnan, who saw this as a great opportunity and nodded. With that, I led her to the waiting ambulance. She kept a death grip on my fingers as the paramedics strapped her into a gurney. I followed her into the ambulance and gradually retracted my hand from her grasp, saying, "I'm right here Josie, I just need to move out of the way for the workers." When she was calm, I slipped out the back door and allowed the medical team to do their job.

Josie's husband was effusive in his gratitude. Through tears he said, "Thank you officers. I can't thank you enough."

Back in the squad, O'Malley whipped out his trainee evaluation form and gave me exemplary marks on handling a "mental subject." Josie's husband followed up with a beautifully written letter to our department highlighting my role in Josie's committal. This was followed by my first Letter of Commendation for providing an outstanding public service.

After O'Malley I was transferred under the wing of Officer John Burke. He was an afternoon shift FTO sent to train me on midnights, so that I could be exposed to various shifts.

During the cold winter months beginning 1997, Burke brought his deep guttural cough and flu-like symptoms to "mids" with him. I was now forced to train under an FTO who was fiercely ill and had not worked a midnight shift in years. Burke's body was not prepared for this feat.

Halsted was one of the busiest streets in our district; it served as a main access road for commercial businesses. One of the first things Burke made clear was that we would not be "Halsted Rangers." This was his way of saying we would not be taking police action on this strip. Burke felt that Halsted was inundated with police from city, county and state municipalities who were hunting for offenders in hopes of one of them turning into "the big catch": a person with a warrant, a felon, or someone who just committed some heinous act. Instead, we would concentrate our crime enforcement efforts in the residential zones. *How boring. I wanted the real criminals too.* I buttoned my lips just like I did with O'Malley and adopted, "When in Rome..."

Burke made himself comfortable in the passenger seat and allowed me to drum up my own business. I stopped suspicious people walking alone in residential areas in the early morning and ascertained their identities, as well as their destinations. I wrote citations for parking violations and patrolled zones that required special attention.

After three a.m. on a frigid winter weeknight, the city became like a cemetery. Spotting a moving vehicle in a residential area was a highlight. Burke could barely keep his eyes open. He was running a pattern of blowing his nose and, as he would say, "coughing up a lung." It was *not* a pleasant experience. As the morning wore on, Burke perpetually fought the head nods. He directed me to cruise our beat to get acclimated with all of the streets. As I drove, he would engage me in non-police related conversation as a distraction, then without warning he'd demand, "What street are we on?"

After being stumped one too many times, I was on to him. He explained, "What if you're driving along and all of a sudden you hear a gunshot, how are you going to call for backup and advise dispatch of your location if you don't know where you are?"

Great point. Burke was adamant about officer safety issues. He would also say things like, "Arrive alive, Lockwood. What good are you if when you're responding to an emergency call you get into an accident on the way there?" *Another great point*; Burke was loaded with them.

One time, while enforcing the speed conditions on Canal St., I lifted the radar gun from its mount and pointed it out the window. Burke reacted sharply, "Hey watch where you point that" after witnessing me swipe it haphazardly in his direction.

"Why, what'll happen?"

"Didn't you hear that radar waves can cause sterility in men?"

I found this information amusing and mockingly pointed it toward his lap a second time. For some reason he didn't see the humor in my response and said, "Knock it off, I'm serious."

Later that morning, Burke unintentionally dozed off next me. After several minutes of this, he began to stir in his seat. Seizing another opportunity to play a prank on him, I powered off the radar gun and laid it on the computer console, angling it toward his crotch. When he awoke, he frantically picked it up and forcefully seated it in the dashboard mount.

"What the hell's wrong with you? How long was that there?"

"Whoops, I didn't realize I put it there."

After a giggle, I told him the truth. Burke was getting used to my humor and laughed with me.

Conducting traffic enforcement the following morning, Burke, still suffering from his grisly flu, drifted off. Parked in the entrance of a strip plaza, I hung the radar out the window and watched traffic. A short time later, an elderly couple pulled alongside our squad and gestured for me to roll down the window on Burke's side. As he lay fast asleep, snoring, the elderly woman requested road directions. Burke awoke from his slumber just as the couple drove off.

"What just happened?" he asked, horrified.

"Oh, they just needed directions."

"You left me sleeping in front of a citizen?" he asked in disbelief.

There was really nothing I could have done; it had happened so quickly. But I decided to add insult to injury and rile Burke a little more.

"Don't worry," I lied, "I told her you weren't feeling well, and even requested she whisper so as not to disturb you."

"What? Are you kidding me? You've got a lot to learn, Lockwood. Next time you see me doze off, nudge me or something!"

Every evening before we hit the street, I was required to inspect our squad. I would hear stories about how officers failed to find damage on their squad during an inspection and were later blamed for it; however, I had an advantage. In the Air Force, part of my duties was to perform a daily inspection of more than seventy-five trucks, buses, vans and cars. Aside from checking the operation functions of our lights and sirens, we were to ensure the interior of our squads was "clean;" i.e., absent any surprises secreted between the cushions of the back seat. Criminals were notorious for ditching drugs or weapons an officer might have missed on a pat down into the back seat. A good officer will inspect this area immediately after the criminal has exited the squad. Unfortunately, this is not always the case, and occasionally, a distracted officer will leave behind some contraband that will later be discovered during an inspection long after the criminal is gone.

One day, Burke lingered in the roll call room and sent me off to inspect our vehicle, and set up our squad with the shotgun and beat bag containing our street equipment. When I removed the back seat cushion, I felt a rush of excitement as I found a switchblade. I was jubilant. Search after search over the last few months had resulted in nil, but now I could impress Burke with my diligence. Ten minutes passed, and as the intensity of my elation in my find diminished, it occurred to me that Burke may have set me up. It was odd for him not to accompany me to the squad, and I knew he was big on officer safety.

When Burke finally did arrive, I decided not to mention the knife. He took the driver's seat and said, "How's our car?"

"Great," I replied.

As we pulled out of the lot he asked again, "Did you do a complete inspection?"

With that, I knew he'd planted the knife. "Yep."

"Rookie, rookie, rookie," he said shaking his head in disappointment.

"What?" I innocently responded as he pulled our squad into a parking lot.

He got out and said, "Follow me." Then he opened the back door and removed the seat. I stood over his shoulder, watching him, as he arrogantly rifled under the seat foam.

"What are you looking for?" I asked.

"Just a minute, you'll see."

I continued watching for another thirty seconds, until he became flustered. "I put a switchblade back here to see if you would find it."

I reached into my jacket pocket and held it out, "You mean this?"

Exasperated, he shouted, "Get in the car!"

In the car, I continued in a singsong voice, "Woo hoo, you tried setting me up, la, la, la, la. I got you instead."

He refused to look at me. "You think you're funny, don't you?" he said with a smirk, and turned up the radio, blasting the volume to drown me out. This sent me into a fit of laughter. I decided I was going to like working with the boys.

CHAPTER 8
THE BIG D

Shortly after my car accident and the announcement that I wanted a divorce, I began sleeping in the spare bedroom. I'd already shut Tony off from sexual intercourse a year earlier, and he finally came to terms with the fact that our relationship was unsalvageable. Meanwhile, I sought a divorce attorney and told him that we needed to start dividing our assets. He told me we could cohabitate until we decided what to do with the house.

One evening we civilly sat at the kitchen table with notepads and initiated the process. We would each keep our own vehicles, and Tony would buy me out of the house. But when it came time to separate the furniture and the Christmas decorations, he became emotional: "How can you be so cold about all of this?" he demanded. Suddenly, I was wearing the pants in the family.

"I'm trying to make it as easy as possible."

He pushed his chair from the table and stood up, rubbing his eyes and snapped, "I need a break."

I understood Tony's pain. I'd had over a year to mentally prepare for this day and was treating the matter like I was claiming my stake from the estate of some unknown deceased family member. Days later, we forged through the task, and I continued to sleep in our basement bedroom, maintaining a sibling-like relationship with him.

I soon found a townhouse under construction that fit my budget, continued working and spent time with my friends...gradually adopting the lifestyle of a single woman. Three months after filing for divorce, I noticed a series of hang-up phone calls and asked Tony if he was "seeing someone." He fearfully insisted he wasn't. *My how the table had turned; he was actually afraid of me.* I explained that I was okay with him moving on, and also grateful that he was letting me live in his house until the divorce was final and my new home was complete. Still, Tony denied all knowledge of the calls.

One day the telephone rang and—with Tony standing a few feet away from me—I answered it. As usual, I was met by silence, and replied without hesitation, "Hold on, Tony's right here." Then I handed him the phone.

Tony greeted the mystery caller and said, "I'll call you back in a few minutes."

"Aha!" I playfully accused.

He shrugged. "What?"

"Tony, like I said before, it's okay that you are dating someone else. I'm actually happy that you found someone. Please tell her that it's okay for her to call you. I'm a guest in your house and don't want to interfere with your future."

He said that he'd met a nurse at one of his construction sites and liked her. I truly was happy for him and elated that we were able to form this unconventional friendship before I vacated. We cohabitated for an additional three months after the divorce was final. Our families couldn't believe how maturely we handled the divorce. I was even invited to celebrate Christmas Eve at the in-laws' house. All the fears that I'd harbored of Tony killing himself or stalking me were a part of the distant past. I could never have imagined that things would have evolved this way.

In mid-December of 1996 my two best friends, Tracy and Kelly, thought it would be good to take me out for a night on the town. Spending time with the girls decreased to nil during the last year, with my dedication to my new career. They'd been raving about a band called Stormm, led by a singer who "was hotter than Steven Tyler" of Aerosmith. I knew I could use an evening of listening to the rock cover band and maybe even ogle the singer.

Needless to say, the girls were right. The singer was as hot as they described, and then some. He had brown, wavy, shoulder-length hair that framed his masculine face and cleft chin. With his blue eyes, combined with a set of the most voluptuous full lips I had ever seen, I was mesmerized. Once I moved past his appearance, I was free to permit his angelic vocals to permeate my ears, and when that was done all I could think was…Steve Perry, eat your heart out. He may have been as hot as Steven Tyler, but his vocals were as good as Steve Perry's. I remained transfixed on this rock god the entire evening as the girls gloated, "Told you so."

As he neared the end of his final set, he engaged the audience with his rendition of Journey's, *Lovin', Touchin', Squeezin'* by pulling up volunteers from the audience to sing the "na-na" part solo. After the second fan completed his bit, the rock god wove his way through the crowd, took my hand and yanked me center stage. I never so much as had the nerve to perform karaoke, let alone be center stage in the middle of a capacity crowd to attempt the high notes of Steve Perry. If it weren't for the three wine coolers I'd consumed, I would have surely fainted.

Mr. rock god continued holding my hand as he sung his part, prepping me to repeat his lyrics. I stood there hypnotized until he handed me the microphone. I took it, belted out the na-na's as best I could, and was immediately met by roaring applause and a look from the singer that translated to, "Not so bad." The girls anxiously waited for me to join them.

As the night ended we saw the singer emerge from a backstage door and get trampled by the bevy of female fans who wanted to at least touch him. We girls, still titillated by him, thought would we would appear more refined if we feigned disinterest by remaining on our barstools. I couldn't believe how attracted I was to this stranger. After spending eight years with Tony and completely losing my sexual desire, I was stirred. Feelings of sexual craving took hold of my entire body.

When the singer separated himself from the mayhem I rose from my chair, telling my friends, "I have to have him," and took off after him. *So much for refinement.* As I neared him, it dawned on me that I didn't know what I was going to say when the most cliché line spilled from my mouth: "Do you believe in love at first sight?"

The rock god grinned, looked me in the eyes with piercing intensity and said, "I do now." I stood speechless for an eternal second before getting blasted with a screeching, "Go home, we're closed!" over the P.A. system, which was followed by those dastardly floodlights. With that, Mr. rock god was whisked off by a band mate, and the girls collected their still mesmerized, soon to be divorcee.

They razzed their star-struck friend: "Boy you really got it for him." They were right.

"Girls, we have to see him perform again," I pleaded. "Find out when and where he plays next" was my frantic demand.

They laughed, "All right already, but you need to calm your ass down. We just got you back to ourselves; you've got plenty of time to meet men. Besides, every woman in that place was fantasizing about him. You've got a lot of competition."

The following weekend the three of us returned to see Stormm perform. We arrived early enough to be tortured by the caustically angry opening band, Twisted Savage. Trying to spare my eardrums from further damage, I sought refuge near the ladies room. That's when I saw *him*. Wearing a casual football jersey and Levi's, he sat at the end of the bar sipping a bottle of water. Suddenly I felt as if my feet were planted in two blocks of concrete. *What should I do? Approach him again? Would he remember me?*

Just then Kelly startled me. "He's over there," I said.

"Oh geez, now what are you going to do?" she asked.

"I'm goin' over," I said confidently.

"Well, you go then, sister!"

With that declaration I waltzed right up to him. Only this time, before I put my foot in my mouth, he grasped my hand and pulled me toward him, putting his arm around my shoulder, and introduced me to his buddy. "I'd like you to meet the future Mrs. Taylor."

Laughing off the compliment, I said, "Hi, I'm Lisa. By the way, you never told me your name."

"I'm Dean."

After some small talk, I said that I was a police officer. Appearing startled, he ran to the nearest wall, threw his hands up, spread his legs and stated, "Go ahead and search, officer." *His turn to be cliché.* Before he took the stage, he said, "Try and stick around after so we can talk." *Try?* That was an understatement. It would have taken a heat-seeking missile to get me out of that place.

His performance was even more powerful than the first time, especially with the knowledge that he wanted me to stick around. As the night ended, I grew as anxious as a child on Christmas Eve. Dean emerged from backstage and graciously thanked his entourage of fans before making his way to our table. Cutting right to the chase, he said, "Let's get away from this smoke and talk outside."

I told the girls, "I won't be long," as I was their driver.

Out in the biting cold of winter with nothing but a flimsy leather jacket, I asked Dean to join me in my car. As Queensryche's 'Silent Lucidity' played in the background, Dean reached over from the passenger seat and engulfed me with his lips. My head was spinning with euphoria until my poor friends pounced on my window, having been ejected from the closed bar. Before leaving, he handed me his business card and said, "Call me, I want to see you again."

"I'm in love," I lamented to the girls.

They laughed. "It's called lust, Lisa. Your well's been dry for too long, and you just need a good lay."

"Well, whatever you wanna call it, I'm taking it!" I exclaimed.

I couldn't wait to call Dean. Taking out his card the next day, I realized it only had his work number. I wondered why he didn't give me his home number. I surmised that he probably wanted to protect himself from female fans until he got to know them better. I phoned Dean Monday afternoon and left a message for him to call my cell so as not to alarm Tony. Even though Tony was in a new relationship, I wasn't sure how he would handle *my* moving on. Dean called back later and sounded happily surprised to hear from me.

"Why don't we get together for coffee tomorrow night?" he asked.

Coffee? This rocker wanted to take me for coffee? I didn't drink coffee, but liked the mature contrast from Tony's beer drinking and said yes.

At the coffee shop, the conversation was focused almost entirely on me. I told him that I was still living with my soon-to-be ex-husband, why the marriage didn't work and how exciting my new police career was. Finally, I asked, "So what about you? Married? Divorced? Kids?"

He hung his head and whispered, "Married." I nearly stopped breathing.

He continued about how unhappy he was and justified why he'd stayed on for ten years. Feeling betrayed, I cut our date short and said, "Dean I can't see you again. You really need to clean things up with your wife. Believe me, I know it's not easy but I pride myself on leaving my husband without the mess of an affair."

"I understand," he replied. He escorted me to my car, where I pecked him on the cheek and said, "Good luck." I drove off deflated with a tingling sensation running across the surface of my skin. *No wonder he didn't give me his home number.*

The girls were right. I could use some alone time. I'm having a town home built and starting a new career, and I'll finally be free.

CHAPTER 9
MIDNIGHT SHIFT FOLLIES

After some six months of field training I was banished, due to low seniority, to midnight shift. The shift was primarily made up of old-timers, folks who valued having their days available to work side jobs, mixed with an up-and-coming crew of young, spirited and driven rookies.

The liberty of driving my own squad and making independent decisions was a dream come true. Aside from handling dispatched calls for service, I was the master of my domain. I took an interest in enforcing drunken driving laws, amazed at how many intoxicated motorists endangered the streets between 11 p.m. and 3 a.m. I soon discovered the ease with which I was able to get intoxicated men to perform field sobriety tests, give true statements regarding their previous whereabouts and divulge exactly how much they had to drink. It seemed that their goal was to ask me for a date, and in their drunken state, they actually believed they would get the opportunity if they did as I told them. When it was time for me to testify against them in court, they would wave a hello and point me out to their attorney. Later their attorney would approach me and say something along the lines of, "It's no wonder my client was so cooperative."

Along with D.U.I. enforcement, midnight shift activity included domestic altercations, bar fights, gas station and mini-mart thefts and robberies, juvenile crimes and people who had warrants for their arrest. Between self-initiated police activity and dispatched calls, we remained hopping until 3 a.m.

I became consumed with my new job and had grandiose illusions of hunting down and capturing criminals nightly. The only way I thought I could achieve this was by making a lot of traffic stops and by asking the right questions on assigned calls. I did achieve the result I was after, first with minor arrests, and then managed to become skilled enough to graduate to felony arrests. The midnight shift old-timers did not greet my activity level kindly. I was told directly and indirectly to, "Slow down, you're making the rest of us look bad." Even some of the dispatchers were used to being complacent and despised the extra work I created for them. The climb to the top was not easy. If I wanted acceptance by dispatchers and senior colleagues I needed to be inactive; if I wanted acceptance from the rookies and my superiors I needed to be active. I chose to develop thick skin and tolerate the ridicule.

I found that working as a dispatcher had prepared me for some of the most bizarre and serious calls. One evening I was dispatched to a restaurant to save a raccoon with a paper cup stuck on its head. *Was this a real police matter?* I thought as I drove to the call. Exiting my squad, I spotted the pathetic overweight hairy blob wobbling in a circle. *How in the world was I supposed to get this thing off its head?* There's only so much one can train for in the academy. The man who'd called to report it stood at the restaurant door, looking to me to resolve this *important* police matter. I didn't want to get anywhere near the rabid rodent, but eventually improvised by using a broom to sweep the cup off.

On another evening, I was dispatched to a golf club where a wedding was being held. A groomsman called 911 to report that his drunken cousin had stripped down to his underwear and darted onto the golf course. The family put a search party together but was unable to find him. They feared that he might have passed out somewhere or made his way onto a highway and been struck by a car. As I listened to the cousin's story, his two intoxicated buddies were more interested in asking if I were single than confirming the safety of their naked cousin on this 45° night. *Hmmmm...track down naked drunk last seen running wildly toward the back nine? I think not; sounds more like a job for the K-9.*

The K-9 officer and I drove around on the course, shining our spotlights over the green. Then like a flash, I saw a blast of blinding white boxers leap from behind a tree and dart behind another. I sat stunned for a second, then broke into a fit of laughter; I tried to stifle it as I let the K-9 unit know I'd spotted our guy. We both got out on foot and walked toward the tree with our flashlights, ordering the streaker to reveal himself. As we closed in, he took off running barefoot at top speed. The officer opted to leave the K-9 in the car for fear that the dog would hurt the dimwit. We chased after him, over the hills, through the trees, into a sandpit, and back over the green. He finally stopped, turned and taunted, "C'mon coppers, come and get me!" With that my agitated, panting backup officer took a flying leap and landed on top of him. We wrestled his fat, sweaty body to the ground in an attempt to restrain him. I straddled his legs as my backup attempted to sit on him. He continued flailing, punching and kicking until the officer was forced to give him a dose of pepper spray. Within seconds, he surrendered and begged for help as he choked and screamed like a baby.

We escorted him back to the country club, where his friends and family members had gathered on the porch. They laughed and cheered for the sweating beast as they ran to meet us on the green. We found a garden hose and suggested his grateful family rinse his eyes and grass-covered body before bringing him back into the wedding reception. *Could you think of a better way to start a police shift?*

Yet another time, during roll call, the shift supervisor briefed us on the events of the last twenty-four hours. During the brief he relayed a call handled by an afternoon shift officer: "An ambulance was requested to respond to a residence for a woman whose head was on fire." (He paused to permit us to roar with incredulous laughter; gallows humor again). In summary, the husband explained that his wife's hair had caught fire from a cigarette she'd carelessly dropped as she slept. The police officer arrived before the ambulance and found the woman lying on the living room floor in a pool of liquid. The husband allowed the officer to look at his wife's burnt forehead and mass of scorched hair. He told the officer that he'd used a towel to beat out the flames and immediately poured a cup of urine on her head. The officer looked at the man in disbelief and asked him to explain what he'd done. The man proudly told the officer that he drank his urine every day, and used it as a disinfectant for wounds.

Abandoning his wife, he waltzed around the house showing the officer his fridge full of urine jars along with his extra stash in the cabinet under the sink.

As time passed and I became more comfortable with my colleagues, I realized, the more male-like I behaved, the more I was accepted. The men always seem to be pushing the envelope to create the illusion of bravado, whether it was behaving a bit more John Wayne-like when dealing with the public or breaking Nascar records when responding to a "hot call." As a woman, I didn't inherently have the need to portray myself that way. However, I found that if I could at the very least talk like the boys and become a part of their clowning around, I could earn points.

I soon found my niche. I actually began to amuse the guys by creating silly games and playing pranks to keep some balance between work and on-the-job socializing. I'd created a midnight shift game that required every officer working the street to incorporate a "word" into their radio traffic before the end of shift. Afterward we would vote to see who had the most daring or unique word usage, and I would ceremoniously hand them a prize. Would you believe, I bought toy trinkets from the dollar store as prize giveaways? The guys actually looked forward to receiving their cap guns, finger puppets, race cars and whoopee cushions.

The game went like this; I'd tell them they'd have to say "camel" over the air and somehow incorporate it into their call without being found out by a supervisor. One officer called in to say that he would be speaking with a group of juveniles in a park who appeared to be smoking Camels. Another time, the word was "hairball." The winning officer said to the dispatcher, "Could you please secure the sally port" (prisoner garage door), then he cleared his throat and continued: "Excuse me dispatch, I had hairball in my throat."

Another fun game I created to pass dead street time between the hours of 3:30 and 6 a.m. was the most obscure ticket contest. The officers would consult their ordinance violations and write warning tickets to the residents for infractions such as: failure to post house numbers or overgrown weeds. In hindsight, I'm sure the shift supervisor scratched his head on those days.

Tickets like those probably hadn't been given since the ordinances were created.

Once I started a game that entailed creating the most unusual officer initiated calls for service. One winning officer called into the dispatcher said, "I'll be out of my car momentarily to re-erect a 'For Sale' sign that fell over in a front yard." I called in one: "Dispatch, could you please log a dead black cat in the roadway at 35th and Armitage." The dispatchers always responded quizzically with slight hesitation: "Ten......four?" Not until we would go out drinking socially at a lounge, which opened specifically for the police at 7 a.m., would we clue in the perplexed dispatchers.

It seemed that one guy, Officer Flynn, would win most of the shift games. Knowing he was willing to go the extra mile on nearly everything, I took an opportunity to test his manhood. After roll call, I ceremoniously presented Flynn with a prize for the previous night's shenanigans. I came across one of those Mexican vehicle ceiling skirts made of velvet with religious emblems and little dingleberry balls hanging from the bottom. The guys roared with laughter as Flynn unwrapped this unusual gift. I then announced, "Now, this isn't just a prize, Flynn has to attach it to the interior ceiling of his squad and drive to every officer's beat to prove he affixed it properly. This was extremely daring when you considered that officers could not leave their beat without permission from the shift supervisor. If Flynn received a call for service he risked the citizens seeing the ceiling skirt. He also risked having the supervisor show up and see it. So Flynn's primary goal was to race from beat to beat and receive acknowledgement from at least ten different police units without getting caught.

Needless to say, Flynn succeeded. Days after, without another thought to the incident, a police lieutenant performed a surprise inspection. Flynn later showed me his evaluation...*Cleanliness: acceptable, but please remove religious items from the trunk.*

I also earned points with the boys by sharing tales of calls that went like this: I was dispatched to a home for a domestic disturbance. All I knew was that the husband—who'd called 911—was involved in an argument with his wife and wanted police intervention. As I pulled into the driveway of this elegant, million-dollar home and parked next to a red Mercedes, the husband stood at the front door, anxious to tell me what was happening. The marble floors and Scarlet O'Hara ascending staircase, richly encased by deep cherry wood railings took me aback. I'd only seen homes like this on TV.

He animatedly told me that his wife, from whom he was separated, was upstairs ransacking the house with her lesbian girlfriend. In response to this, I put on my game face and sympathetically asked more questions. Believe it or not, they actually did train for this in the academy. One instructor had us practice our "earnest look of concern face," to be used no matter what asinine story we were told. He even taught us the lowered head, sucked in lips, side-to-side head nod used for the compassionate, "I understand" response.

After uncovering the legal technicalities regarding the estranged wife's right to take her personal belongings, it was decided that I would stand by as the wife and lesbian lover packed a few bags of clothes. The husband escorted me up to his wife's dressing plaza. The space could have been in a magazine under the title "Every Woman's Dream Closet." The first room, used for dressing and makeup, was decorated with pink satin and cheetah's print. A heart-shaped, hot pink shag rug lay on top of a plush powder pink carpet. Pink satin love seat couches with cheetah print throw pillows sat against one wall. A twelve-by-twelve foot dressing mirror framed in pink boa-like feathers and round light bulbs sat opposite the couches. The second room held all of her clothing and shoes. It was organized like the dressing room of a high-end designer fashion show.

The estranged wife was stunningly beautiful. She had flowing blonde hair, deep brown eyes, pencil thin eyebrows, and full pouty lips. Her body was flawless. She hustled around the room bra-less in a white, spaghetti-strap tank top that barely contained her bouncing breasts. A black mini-skirt and high-heeled cheetah print boots completed her look. She smiled at me sweetly and said, "Officer, I don't mean to cause any trouble; I'll be finished in two minutes."

Her exotically beautiful Asian lesbian lover was whipping around the room, taking direction from the wife on what garments to pack. As this continued, the husband stood behind me, whispering, "That's what I get for marrying an exotic dancer."

I could have made a fortune handing this call off to just about any of my male colleagues. The way I earned points, however, was by describing the call in detail to the occasional cop who crossed my path over the next few weeks.

Whoever said that women were more likely to call the police in domestic situations should walk a mile in my shoes. Shortly afterward, I was dispatched to yet another call where the husband wanted the police to remove his wife from the house. When I arrived, the angry husband shouted, "I've told her a hundred times to lower the TV. I have to wake up early!"

I asked, "Sir, you called the police because your wife won't lower the TV?"

"Yes! And she has a friend over and they're talking too loud." Standing behind me, the sergeant raised an eyebrow, indicating that I should take the reins on this one. I went into the living room, where two middle-aged women sat on the sofa engaged in quiet chatter. The sergeant occupied the husband in the kitchen while I conversed with the women.

The wife sighed, "Just so you know, we are going through a divorce and neither of us is willing to leave the house. My husband's attorney advised him to start documenting, with police reports if necessary, how I treat him. I have been nothing but kind to him and it's killing him. I'm sorry you got called into this mess."

Fortunately the sergeant overheard the wife's explanation and had a few words of his own to share with the husband about making false claims to the police, before we left.

One day, out of the blue, I received a phone call from the rock god (Dean). Three weeks after "our coffee" he phoned to tell me that he'd filed for divorce. "Since you're nearly finished with the process, would it be possible to meet? I could use your input regarding some of the divorce laws." *Wow, he took my advice.* I was flattered. *Did I have that much of an impact on him? Would he have filed for divorce if he hadn't met me?* Still attracted to him, I was afraid of the answer. *What if I was the catalyst? Did he tell his wife he was interested in someone else?* I agreed to meet him for dinner.

With my legal papers in tow, I joined Dean at a restaurant. He seemed different. I didn't look at him like I had before. The rock-god was humble, respectful and appreciative of my support. He explained that his wife had left the house and would be retrieving her personal things when she found an apartment. Now the question remained: was that enough for me to start dating him? I consulted with the girls, who were blown away. "He really digs you. Of course he left her for you," was their collective response. I was in awe of the power I had over him. One day I was the chomping at the bit to get him to notice me, and a month later he is ending his marriage to be with me. I thought he was kidding when he introduced me as the future Mrs. Taylor. We started dating.

In March of 1997, I moved into the first place I could call my own since leaving the nest at eighteen. Being on my own was short-lived, however; after five months of dating Dean, he sold his home and became my new tenant.

Dean was completely different than Tony. He hated beer and ignored road rage; he was a musician and an accomplished singer on the Chicago-area lounge club circuit, and was impressed by my career as a police officer. He played keyboards, bass guitar, drums, and he recorded his own original music with hopes of selling his work later.

It was exciting for me to begin my next phase of life. I had a new career, a new home and a new relationship in less than six months. What a whirlwind of adventure!

CHAPTER 10
MY HUMBLE BEGINNING

Working as a policewoman on the midnight shift later created challenges in my relationship with Dean. We had been together for nearly two years and remained head over heels in love. He became accustomed to seeing me off to work every night in my blues, leather boots, ballistic vest, and Glock .40 handgun. *That must have been a sight!* Occasionally, instead of a kiss goodnight, he would jokingly salute me. I was out the door at ten p.m. six nights a week as he prepared to sleep alone. He admitted that he had nightmares about getting "the phone call," the one that informed him I'd been killed in the line of duty. I was in the habit of providing him with the play-by-play of calls and arrests, oblivious to his fear.

My fellow policemen often recounted how they protected their spouses from the ugliness they witnessed working the street. I never thought that Dean would also need to be protected. *He was a man; men can handle this stuff.* I thought wrong. I was filling a male role in our relationship in more ways than one. I dressed in a masculine uniform, carried a gun on duty (and occasionally off duty as well), and handled all of our home finances, travel and personal plans. I had become a take-charge woman and embraced my *male energy,* without really understanding what I was doing. I'd developed the belief through my eight-year relationship with Tony that if I didn't take care of things, they wouldn't get done. Dean didn't seem to mind. Honestly, I loved it; I wore Ms. Independent very well. In the process, Dean increasingly delved into his artistic and *female energy*. Because of this balance or polarity, the relationship flourished. We were content in our roles.

Still on midnight shift patrol, with a little more than two years under my belt, I was confident in my abilities as a police officer and had excelled in my department stats for citations and arrests. But driving alone and working the 11 p.m. to 7, a.m. shift was not something I thought I'd be doing for twenty-four months. Little did I know my efforts on the street were gaining the respect of members of the detective unit and that I would soon be asked to work my first undercover operation as a patrol officer.

Through trial and error, I learned how to quell many volatile police calls with the use of minimum force. For example, when handling drunk drivers, domestic altercations, warrant arrests or even bar fights, I built rapport with the offenders as well as the victims by treating everyone with respect, even after I determined who would be going to jail. I found that most of the offenders I dealt with were men, and being a petite blonde woman certainly gave me an advantage over my male counterparts. If I had a quarter for every time a male criminal or victim said, "Officer, aren't you going to pat me down?" I could have retired after two years.

I was the only officer on the midnight shift sufficiently conversant in Spanish to handle the Hispanic population in our district. Three years of high school Spanish took me farther than I could have hoped. Every time an officer got a call or an arrest dealing with a non-English-speaking Hispanic, I would be called to interpret. In doing so, I was able to build rapport with this group as well. They were flattered and began to revere the blonde police lady who made an effort to communicate in their language. My fellow officers said I'd developed a fan club amongst them. Sometimes the officers would call me into the lock-up to help get a confession from their prisoners.

In February of 1999, I was asked by the detective unit to work my first undercover assignment. They had an informant who had gotten into some trouble and decided to nark on his drug supplier to lessen his charge. They asked the informant if he could have his supplier come to town and sell acid (LSD) to an undercover officer. The informant said, "Yeah, but only if the person didn't look like a cop."

Burke, my former FTO, was now a detective and this was his case. He phoned me at home and said, "We need you for an undercover operation, you up for it?"

"Sure," I exclaimed, without even knowing the particulars.

"Swing by the department in two hours and dress like you would if you were going to a night club."

"You mean slutty?" I jested.

"I didn't say that. You want to get me rung up for sexual harassment?" he asked, "and furthermore, do you dress slutty when you go to a night club?"

I laughed and before I could respond he said, "Never mind, I don't wanna know. We need you to look like a Hooter's waitress. We just want to give the informant a look and then you can leave. If he approves, then we're going to use you for an acid buy."

I sprinted to my closet, ransacking through my skirts and dresses to prepare for my first undercover operation. Hastily, I tried on an array of outfits, with the cordless phone glued to my ear telling everyone from Dean to my mom what I was preparing to do. Dean was excited, but warned me to be careful. I explained that it was just a 'showing of the merchandise' today, not the drug deal. "Just remember, it's *my* merchandise!" he exclaimed.

Poor Mom, when will I learn? "Do you get to have your gun with you?" was her inquiry. It's funny to think that I didn't even care if I had my gun. My naiveté didn't even consider the potential dangers of the operation. All I cared about is that I was asked to work undercover. *This could lead to bigger things.*

I walked into the detective division and stopped my colleagues in their tracks; it was the first time most of them had seen me with my hair down and face made up, wearing a miniskirt and high heels. I overheard whispers and snickers from the crew. *This was the day that would change the way many of my colleagues looked at me.*

I was escorted to the interrogation room, where the informant was waiting. The detective asked him, "Will she do?" as he stepped aside to reveal me.

He froze for several seconds, his eyes fixated on my body. He finally said, as if I weren't there, "Is she really a cop?"

The detective grimly answered, "No, she's my wife, and do me a favor, put your tongue back in your mouth."

He finally assured the informant that I was a cop and would be posing as a Hooters waitress as a cover story. The informant made the phone call to his dealer, setting up the meeting for the following afternoon at 12:30 p.m. in the Hooters parking lot.

I arrived at the police department for my first official controlled-buy briefing at the infamous oval table in the conference room. I sat amongst the commander of the Investigations Unit, various detectives, and my mentor, Burke, who whispered to me, "Are you ready? Are you nervous? Are you sure you want to do this?"

My answer was a resounding, "Yes," every single time—although I didn't really understand the gravity of the undertaking until the briefing began. The room was scented with strong black coffee and dry erase markers. Briefing sheets, hot off the printer, were circulated, and Burke took center stage. He pointed to a white board with a diagram of the Hooters parking lot. He assigned officers to various undercover vehicles, mapping out who would be the blockers and who would be part of the hands-on, takedown team. There was a somber tone to the briefing as officers asked questions about bad-guy apprehension and a panic signal for Lisa. I remember previously thinking, some guy is going to jump in my car, hand me some "acid," I'll give him some cash, and he'll be on his way. When someone mentioned a panic signal, in case I got robbed at gunpoint, I sat taller. I tried to appear confident and seasoned as I listened and took notes. I would not be wearing a ballistic vest and my gun would be secreted in the small of my back. I was informed that if I had any indication of danger, I was to step on my brake so that rear surveillance could see my red taillights and close in.

Burke terminated the briefing with a callout list of last minute safety tips and equipment item reminders. The group exited at a pace far different than the arrival I'd witnessed some twenty minutes earlier. A new energy flowed through all of us. Burke and I were the last to leave the room.

"So, are you ready for this?" Burke asked.

I responded, "Yes!" for the umpteenth time.

"Do you have any questions at all about what you need to do if something goes wrong?"

I told him I didn't; finally, he gave me an endearing squeeze on the back of my neck and said, "Everything's going to go smooth." Then deepening his voice, he added, "I'll put a bullet in 'em if he tries to hurt you!"

I must admit the briefing had a sobering affect on me. The last thing I'd ever considered when I became a police officer was getting robbed on duty! I was actually putting myself in harm's way—proactively creating a potentially dangerous situation. This was far different than responding to a call in which a crime had already occurred, and I could remain in react mode. I was literally disguising myself as a sex bomb to throw off the scent of what I really was: a sworn police officer. *How long will Dean tolerate this?*

My adrenaline was pumping, and I needed to get my head in the game. My first order of business was to get more acquainted with the informant. He told the drug dealer that I was a chick who worked at Hooters and wanted to buy 200 hits of acid for some waitress friends. I began questioning him as to the quantity and price of the narcotic and came up with the cover story of our alleged history. I further obtained as much information as possible about the dealer, Eddie. I needed to know who might show up with him, if he was known to carry a weapon, would he pat down in search of weapons or wires, what type of vehicle he would be driving, and would he expect the buyer to sample the drug in his presence. I felt secure in his responses and left the room to suit up. I didn't have a Hooters uniform, so I wore something revealing to remain in character and provide a distraction. My blonde hair was now a striking platinum (a result of my liberation from Tony). It hung down, loose and wild. I went heavy on my makeup, wore my tightest jeans with a red form fitting v-neck shirt. As I exited the ladies locker room, I again caught sight of the stares and double takes from fellow coppers, and felt exposed and uncomfortable as I pretended not to notice. All of my efforts to appear professional were thrown out the window as word circulated about Lockwood's slutty appearance.

Most of the surveillance team and tactical officers went ahead to set up in the parking lot, before summoning the informant and me there. I backed into a parking space in the rear of the restaurant to ensure a quick visual on Eddie when he entered the lot. The informant and I engaged in small talk for a few minutes, then we noticed a pickup truck entering the lot and making its way toward us. The informant said, "I think this is them."

I asked, "What do you mean, *THEM*? I thought Eddie would be coming alone!"

He didn't respond. The pickup soon stopped directly in front of my car. *What was I supposed to do? We didn't plan for an extra bad guy. I didn't have time to phone the team. Surely they noticed there were two of them. Am I supposed to wait for their signal? Will they phone me? Did they expect me to abort the operation for my safety?* Too late; Eddie, the passenger, ran over to my car, both hands in his pockets. The driver remained in his seat and watched. Without any direction, I needed to improvise.

Eddie jumped in the back seat in a huff, commenting on the bitter cold day. The edgy informant introduced me to Eddie by saying, "This is Cindy. Hot, huh?"

As I turned to thank Eddie for meeting me, he smiled and said, "No problem. So you work at Hooters?"

"Yeah, I start my shift in fifteen minutes," I answered.

"Cool."

I improvised: "Why don't you guys come in after I punch in, so you can sit in my section?" (I was *well aware that they wouldn't be eating hot wings for at least three days*).

The informant said, "Yeah, let's get some lunch after."

Eddie seemed at ease and handed me two perforated sheets of acid in wax paper. I knew not to touch the LSD due to its ability to penetrate the skin and carefully opened the wax paper, smiling at Eddie with approval. I handed him $500 and thanked him again.

As he exited the truck I called out, "Don't go into Hooters yet, I want you guys to sit in my section after I start."

He smiled and arrogantly hand signaled me an okay. I tapped the brake pedal intermittently, signaling to the team that the "buy" was successful.

Within seconds, two undercover vehicles boxed in the pickup truck, and a team of cops poured out of a van, their guns drawn, shouting, "Police, don't move!" Eddie and the driver were extracted from the truck in one fell swoop, cuffed, and searched before they could even process what was happening. The informant and I were simultaneously extracted, cuffed, and searched. We acted like we didn't have a clue what was happening—*as if it were a coincidence that the police were in the lot watching our drug deal.* They searched Eddie's pocket and took back our $500, along with some cannabis.

The men were transported to the police department, where they were separated and interviewed. Eddie gave a written statement to the detectives, explaining that he received the drugs from the driver, Ben, who was his supplier. Eddie also stated that he wasn't going to be making any money from the deal, because he owed Ben from a former deal in which Ben had fronted Eddie the drugs.

Both men were charged with Unlawful Delivery of a Controlled Substance and pleaded guilty to their crimes.

At the end of the day, I knew it was my goal to continue to be aggressive in patrol to gain more street experience so that I might one day be promoted to detective. I also knew that the detective unit was grateful for their new asset and hoped they would use me again. *Who'd have thought that my physical appearance would grant me as much safety as a gun and ballistic vest?*

CHAPTER 11
MR. & MS. WEST COAST FALL FOR MISSY

How could I ever explain to Dean what that day meant to me? He was always supportive; yet I never really felt he understood me. I wasn't even sure *I* understood me. I kept a personal journal for days like these. I felt this was the only way I could truly express my thoughts. I was climbing the ladder in the department and wanted so much for someone to recognize what I'd achieved. This was big for the welfare kid who made something of herself—but who cared? Hearing Dean say, "Nice job babe" felt so cold and unattached. *Shouldn't I have just been proud for myself? Was my esteem just a charade? Who was I trying to prove myself to? I then wondered if Dean was just a convenient rebound guy.*

Detective Fester Rattan, our Internet Crime Investigator, was trained to look for people online who were sexually exploiting young children. To suss these individuals out, Rattan would frequent chat rooms created for the solicitation and exchange of child pornography—as well as pedophiles seeking young victims. Another door would be opening for me because of this dark phenomenon.

Rattan had the ability to perfectly emulate a fourteen-year-old girl with the written word. He was a family man and filled the role of a job most cops

93

hated. He employed the latest slang and instant message lingo, along with randomly intended spelling errors, to convince pedophiles that he was truly fourteen.

He found an adult couple, Tom and Patty from Oregon, who were interested in him—or rather in teenaged Missy, his undercover alter ego. They wrote to Missy after finding her in a chat room. Rattan embarked on a lengthy investigation to determine if the couple was authentic, using instant messaging and e-mail communication.

One day, Tom initiated an instant message conversation with Missy:

Tom: hi, do you like older couples?

Missy: ? maybe why?

It's rare to have a pedophile admit so freely in an early correspondence that they were looking for a young girl. Rattan was ecstatic.

Tom: great, can you send us a pic?

Missy: u first

Tom immediately sent two photographs of him and Patty. In return, Rattan forwarded them a photo of me when I was thirteen.

Tom: you are very cute and sexy

Missy: thanx

Tom: have you been with older men yet or other girls?

Tom: are you still a virgin?

Missy: yep, still a virgin

Tom: would you like to lose it with a couple, older man?

Missy: I think so will it huirt?

Tom: it won't hurt if we do it right, get you ready before hand. Have you put things in your pussy yet?

Missy: no I haven't, Im in Illinois is that far from you?

Tom: Yes baby, it's a long way, unfortunately. You need to start putting
      things into your pussy, to get it ready without it hurting.

Missy: oh ok but kinda scared to do that

Tom: good that little bit of fear will make more exciting and better

Missy: yep but we are far apart

Tom: yes we are but there are lots of ways to meet still,
      planes, biz trips, buses…whatever works.

Missy: way kewl ok

Tom: damn I would love to fuck you.

Missy: I never even seen a guy before

Tom: a young virgin, illegal, innocent, very erotic, kinky, never
      even seen a real cock before? OMG, I want you more now.

Missy: how old are you

Tom: I am 43 , my girlfriend is 27.

Missy: no way

Tom: Live with both your parents? Why don't you
      want a guy your own age or closer?

Missy: no Mom only, her and dad split, cuz they are jerks round here

Rattan knew pedophiles welcomed young girls who were from broken homes and searching for a father figure. His job was to make Missy vulnerable and

naive. But there was a fine line between soliciting the pedophile and portraying the vulnerable innocence of an average teenager.

> *Tom: are you alone, would you masturbate for me? Tell me what turns*
> *you on? Do you want to be with a woman too, touch her?*

> *Missy: im just a student sorry to bore you, Moms in the other room,*
> *I might try it, but scared because I never did anything*

> *Tom: is that a yes? What are you wearing now, can you touch your self?*

> Missy: jeans and a t shirt, you ever been with someone
> my age how you know it wont hurt me

> *Tom: I have not been with a young girl, just an*
> *18 year old, trust me it wont hurt.*

> Missy: ok

Rattan always avoided posing explicit questions to ward off the potential of turning his communication with Tom into "just another sex chat."

> Tom: I like to be called Thomas or Sir—do
> you get good grades in school?

> Missy: no, I haven't been doin good since dad left, hes a jerk

> *Tom: I am sorry, stay away from him then. Get your grades up,*
> *I will help you, ask q's by email I will help when I can,*
> *but mostly I want to fuck you, teach you to suck me.*

Tom's use of the father figure cannot help but give way to his real intentions towards Missy. The IM's continued a week later.

> Missy: any new pics of you?

> Tom: I am sorry baby…I got busy, and wasn't sure if you were real so I
> waited.

Missy: I am very real!!! are you

Tom: we are very real, I masturbated thinking about you the other night. Told my gf about you.

Missy: way kewl now what

Tom: now we continue to chat, explore, be open and honest with each other, then when you are ready, we talk on the phone, then if you want we can work it out, you come here or I come there to fuck you.

Tom: but I can go to jail just for meeting you or agreeing to meet you somewhere, so I have to be very careful and trust you and know a lot about you.

Missy: so why can you get in trouble I don't understand

Tom: because you are underage, arranging to meet an underaged girl, even just for friendship, is illegal.

Missy: I will not ytell anyone cause I want to meet u, Mom doesn't know how to use my puter, hehehehe

Tom: good girl. If your mother finds out, or friends of yours tells their parents, I could be in trouble.

Missy: gtg Mom is callin me to shop

Rattan now had confirmation that Tom was definitely interested but feared getting caught. He decided to wait and gauge the strength of Tom's motivation.

On July 11th Tom noticed Missy on line and wrote:

Tom: HI!! How is my sweet pussy Missy

Missy: good news, Mom told me she is going away for a week with her bf she will be gone July 31-Aug 6…ill b home with grnma

97

Rattan was opening a window in which Tom might feel he could safely visit without the fear of Mom being at home.

Tom: I may be able to come there

Tom: when we are there will you do anything
     I want you to do? Anything?

Missy: ill try but don't know much sorry

On July 17th, Rattan asked me to conduct an undercover telephone conversation with Tom, pretending to be Missy. Are you familiar with the old cereal commercial with the tagline, "Give it to Mikey, he eats everything?" A couple of brothers used Mikey, their youngest brother, as a guinea pig to test a new healthy cereal. After a few successful undercovers with the detective unit I realized that I was their "Mikey."

It was flattering to be thought of as the go-to-girl. At that point, I had the undercover experiences impersonating a stripper-cocaine-addict, acid-using-Hooters waitress and the occasional damsel-in-distress as a ruse for the SWAT team. I guessed I had given them enough references for pulling off a fourteen-year-old girl.

Rattan ordered me into his office for an audible test, I turned my back to him and said, "Hi I'm Missy," using my sweetest high-pitched voice.

"Ooooooh, that's good," he replied with a sinister grin. "Say some more."

We practiced together, using a series of getting-to-know-you questions, and Rattan was impressed. I had never imitated a young girl's voice before, so I just added pauses and displayed the lack of articulation of some of my younger nieces. I remembered how it was like pulling teeth to engage them in conversation due to their shyness. They giggled frequently and spoke in three or four-word sentences. This was good for me. The less I said to Tom, the better.

I prepared myself by reading all of the aforementioned IM and e-mail communication. Then Rattan and the FBI agent (Shannon) briefed me on how to use the recording equipment. Finally, we ensured the other telephones in the office were unplugged, and pagers were turned off. Rattan contacted the administrative section and temporarily prohibited them from using the intercom/paging system. The office was far from soundproof, however, so Rattan alerted the detective unit to stay clear of the office and keep communication to a whisper. It made me feel important to have such an integral role in the case.

Agent Shannon remained in the office with me while I awaited Tom's call. I tuned Rattan's boom box to a popular teenage music station as a backdrop—and to drown out any possible interruptions. Rattan was politely informed that I would need privacy. I was grateful for this. I'd assumed I would be conducting the phone call alone and was surprised that even Shannon would be there to observe.

But Shannon was sharp when it came to pedophile Internet cases. She encouraged me to relax and turned her back, pretending to sift through paperwork. I took a deep breath and began spinning in the office chair like a child, nervously awaiting the ring. Like clockwork, Tom phoned on the undercover line. I allowed the phone to ring twice, exhaled, and whispered, "Hello?"

"Is this Missy?" he asked.

"Yeah," I whispered shyly.

"How old are you Missy?"

"Fourteen, I told you that already."

He laughed and said, "I know, I just wanted to make sure you were you. What grade are you in?"

"Eighth."

"I could barely hear you baby…do you still want to meet me?"

"Yeah," I answered with a giggle.

"That's good my sweet baby, I want you to lay in your bed naked and touch your nipples with one hand and your pussy with the other," he said.

I could feel my body begin to burn from the boldness of his requests and had to remind myself, he actually believes he's speaking to a child.

"You know me and Patty are looking at airplane flights to Chicago. We plan on being their August 8th when your Mom is gone," he said with excitement.

"Cool, I can't wait to meet you and Patty," I said.

"We're going to have a lot of fun touching your body together, massaging your naked skin. You get to suck my dick while Patty plays with your nipples, won't that be fun?"

"Yeah." I said, all the while thinking, *not as fun as throwing your disgusting ass in jail.*

"Are you sure Missy, cuz we are taking a lot of risks flying to Chicago to be with you. We could go to jail if we get caught together. You have to want this as much as us and you have to keep it a secret. Will you keep it a secret?"

"Yeah, I want you guys to come and meet me, I like you both, I won't tell anyone," I said.

"Good girl. I want you to buy a calling card so you can call us from a pay phone so when you call us it won't show up on the phone bill."

I used this opportunity to remind Tom of my naiveté.

"I, uh, don't know how to do that."

"It's okay baby, I'll teach you. Have you been preparing yourself for our first fuck?"

"How do I do that?"

"You put small things in your pussy like a brush handle or your fingers to get it ready for me."

"No, I don't wanna put stuff in there," I whined.

Then Tom began masturbating and breathing heavy, saying, "I'm stroking my cock for you Missy, I'm imagining you licking me, keep talking to me baby 'til I cum."

I was speechless. This warped degenerate was actually stroking himself and getting off to the sound of my voice. In that moment, it dawned on me that I was actually getting paid to speak to a man on the telephone, pretending to be a fourteen-year-old girl while he moaned and masturbated in my ear. I made a frantic, hand-jerking gesture to Shannon to indicate what Tom was doing. She wrenched her face in disgust and drew her index finger across her neck, signaling me to stop the call.

"Tom, I have to go now I think I hear my gram's car in the driveway."

"No," he begged, "I'm almost there Missy, say you want to suck my dick, tell me you want to suck me."

I giggled and said, "I'm embarrassed, I have to go, bye Tom."

"Bye baby can't wait to talk to you again," he panted before hanging up.

Shannon snapped off the recorder and rewound the tape to prepare it for its entry into evidence. She put her hand on my shoulder and said, "You did a great job. Listen, I've worked a ton of these cases, and believe me, you convinced him. If he felt comfortable enough to jerk off to your voice, he doesn't think you're a cop. Also, when these creeps try get off, try to end the conversation sooner. A lot of these guys just want the free phone sex. You have to keep 'em wanting more."

Rattan stood outside the door and couldn't wait to be debriefed. He grinned when I told him the call was successful. But I went home feeling ambivalent about the whole incident. I was proud to assist Rattan and the FBI on the case, but grossly disturbed to know that this sort of thing was taking place. I also felt violated. I needed to find a way to separate myself from the emotions that were welling up inside me. Having this strange man speak to me with such explicit, graphic eroticism, moaning and reaching climax from the sound of my voice, felt vulgarly intrusive. It was as if I'd given this stranger a part of me.

I went home and recounted my undercover phone call to Dean, looking for some support to shake off the creep. I thought he would perceive Tom's explicit sexual banter as violating his woman. I felt that Tom crossed some invisible line and was certain Dean would be pissed off. This is where I discovered that I was confusing Dean with Tony.

Dean responded, "Cool, they're lookin' to do a three-way.

This marked the first time Dean would disclose his interest in a *ménage a trois*. Horrified, I asked, "You're interested in three-way sex?"

"I'll try anything once and twice if I like it," he replied.

It was a good thing my gun wasn't nearby.

"Are you telling me that you want to have sex with me and another woman simultaneously?"

"Why not?"

Looking at my dumbfounded expression, he laughed and added, "I think it would be erotic to experience that with you."

Ensuring I understood exactly what he meant I offered, "So this means you would share me with another man as well?"

"Sure."

As I wondered if this meant he had homosexual tendencies, he said, "I'm not saying we have to try it, but I think it would be an exciting experiment."

He then shared that he and his ex-wife attempted to experiment with a four-way with another married couple. They fell short of penetration when the other woman ran off crying at the thought of her husband cheating. I never entertained sharing Dean with a woman, ever! I loved him too much and the thought of being intimate with another man or woman, with or without Dean, repulsed me. *Was I a prude? Would Dean look at me in a different light? Worse, would he leave me and find another woman who would fulfill his fantasy? Was I not enough?* I was everything to Tony and now, the man I loved matter-of-factly divulges he wants to add people into our sex life. This realization forever marred my feelings toward him. *Why did I have to tell him about my undercover phone call?*

On July 21st Rattan arranged for me to speak to Tom on the telephone for the second time.

Holed up in Rattan's small office, I sat in his chair swaying side to side to shake off my nervous energy. *Heck, I should be nervous; I'm supposed to be a fourteen-year-old girl speaking to a man in his forties about the loss of my virginity.* At nine a.m. the undercover phone rang.

"Missy?" asked Tom, excited. "I have a surprise for you."

"What?" I asked, matching his enthusiasm.

"Patty is here, and she wants to speak to you before she leaves for work."

"Okay," I said. I wondered if Tom had asked Patty to ascertain if Missy was really Missy or a cop. I had to control the conversation so I asked naively, "Is this really Patty?"

She laughed and sweetly said, "Yes."

"Do you live with Tom?"

She boasted, "Yes I do, and I have been dating him for two years."

"Are you jealous that he is talking to me?"

She laughed. "Tom has told me everything about you and I saw your picture. You're really a beautiful girl."

"You are too," I responded, "I saw your picture too."

Patty never became graphic. She actually spoke to me in a protective, nurturing manner. I couldn't fathom this woman engaging in group sex with Tom and a child. I believe she was exhibiting caution and may have not been convinced she was speaking to a kid. She bid me a courteous farewell before giving the phone back to Tom. When he asked what I thought of Patty, I said, "She's really nice and sounds even prettier than her picture." *Whatever that means.*

Tom laughed. "She is...that's why I'm with her."

I ended the call, explaining to Tom that I wouldn't be able to reach him on the computer over the weekend due to a two-day getaway with Mom.

I made the decision not to share the substance of my undercover phone calls with Dean. I thought if I ignored his fantasy it would go away. The last thing I was going to do was incite more thoughts about what I consider a perversion.

On July 24th Tom e-mailed Missy to say he wouldn't be able to make the trip to Chicago because of commitments to his son and daughter. Missy blasted him in a response, accusing Tom of lying to her just like the "rest of the guys" on the Internet. He begged Missy to forgive him and pleaded speak with her again.

Later that evening, Patty sent Missy an e-mail:

Missy,

We both enjoyed talking to you this evening. We are trying to plan our schedules, so we can see you in August, We both want to very much. We hope we can work it out. But, regardless, we are planning on meeting you and teaching you things. Teaching you how to make love, and be our perfect pussy. To be our girlfriend. When can we chat on the phone again. We lost your pic can you please send another and when can we chat on the phone again?

Patty

For the next week, the intermittent exchange of e-mails and instant messaging continued in the same vein, as the couple tried to hammer out a date to meet in person. Rattan came to the conclusion that Tom and Patty were still leery about Missy not sounding like your typical fourteen-year-old.

Tom: Patty wants to ask you a question, What do you expect long term from us? What if it doesn't work out between us the way you want it to, will you be mad and what would you do then?

Again, Patty acted as the voice of reason, preparing for the possibility of coming into town for a one-time encounter with Missy, then leaving her high and dry. What they really wanted to know was would Missy become depressed and reveal their identities?

Missy: ????i don't know one thing at a time, maybe we could meet or I could come there

Of course, Rattan never intended to have me or anyone else pose as a teenager and show up on Tom and Patty's doorstep. The suggestion was a bluff, meant to convince Tom that he was truly speaking to Missy.

The following is a summary of my third telephone conversation with Tom:

"Hello, my sweet pussy," he said, upon my timid hello. "I love hearing your voice, hearing your breath and your laugh."

I giggled nervously.

"So here we are, it feels like forever since we spoke last," he said.

"Yeah, I feel a little bit of butterflies in my stomach," I responded. "Do you think you can visit before I turn fifteen?"

"We will definitely be having sex before your fifteenth birthday. Remember I'm planning to see you the weekend of September 9th."

"Sure, that's what you say now," I replied in a sarcastic, playful tone.

Tom laughed. "You know we're planning this the best we can. Are you sure you want to kiss an old man?"

"I think you're cute," I answered.

"Do you know I'm touching my cock right now as I listen to your sexy voice. How does that make you feel?"

"Funny," I said, giggling. I could feel myself perspiring and becoming flush and uncomfortable. I tried to remember what the seasoned FBI agent told me about ending the call when the offender began to "get off."

"Are you aroused," he asked.

'What do you mean?"

"Is your pussy getting wet?"

I knew I had to end the call. It was getting increasingly difficult to listen to him speak so explicitly without actually focusing on the body parts he called to my attention.

"Sorta," I said.

"I want you to touch your nipples for me. Are they hard?"

"Uh huh."

"Missy, I can't wait to be inside you, to lick you," he groaned.

"I have to go I hear a car, it sounds like Mom's," I said in a panic.

"Nooo, Missy not yet! I have to cum first…please wait a few more minutes…I, I, I'm almost there," he moaned.

"Bye I'll talk to you later," I rapidly replied before hanging up.

I think I let Agent Shannon down. I have no doubt the creep "got off." I didn't expect him to have his pecker in hand at the beginning of the conversation. As soon as the call ended, I pulled Rattan into the office and vented. "The jerk got off again!"

But Rattan grinned from ear to ear. "We got this fucker!" he exclaimed.

I thought we had too.

Little did we know that Rattan would continue communicating with Tom and Patty via the Internet for an additional seven painstaking months. The couple went so far as to send Missy $40 worth of prepaid phone cards, $50 in gift certificates for a teen shop at the local mall, and greeting cards for Christmas—all attempts to appeal to Missy's emotional weakness. Eventually, Rattan became exhausted with the pair and opted to turn over all of his evidence to the FBI for continued investigation.

Fortunately, the disappointing results in this case didn't sour Rattan's drive to find more offenders.

CHAPTER 12
SWAT COP

I remember one day as I was on my way to work as a 911 dispatcher, catching a glimpse of the SWAT team preparing to leave for training. (The SWAT team is a specialized unit that is called upon to handle highly irregular and dangerous encounters such as: barricaded gunmen, hostage situations, terrorist activity and executing search warrants.) As I watched the team of heavily clad uniformed men loading their SWAT van with rams, long guns, shields and duffle bags containing chemical warfare gear, I thought, *Wow! These guys are the real deal, the elite policemen of the department.*

Even though I was a dispatcher at the time, I was curious about the team and began to ask questions. *How does one become a SWAT officer? How do they train? How are they selected?* Commander Selleck, who was a street lieutenant at the time, was the SWAT leader. He would occasionally visit the dispatch center and proudly answer my inquiries. He was impressed with my military background and flattered by my interest in his elite team. Knowing that I was waiting to take the police exam, he asked if I was interested in helping the team with their training. Specifically, he was looking for a woman to emulate a damsel in distress. To be able to act and witness the SWAT team training was more than I could have asked for.

That time came several months later (I was still a dispatcher) when we participated in the annual South Suburban FTX (Field Training Exercise). This event, a conglomeration of SWAT teams across Chicago's south suburbs, was used to train as well as to measure the skill level of the various teams. It was sort of a quasi-competition of masculine energy, followed by an afternoon barbecue. While we prepped for the day, I could see how the men looked at me and whispered to their friends. A few officers from my department told me that the men were "checking me out" and asking a lot of questions about my status. It was nice receiving the male attention, considering my unhappy status with Tony. I also wondered if they took me seriously. *What would they think if they knew I was in the military and that I was taking the police exam? Would they be less attracted to me?*

My role that day entailed me donning protective gear: a helmet, goggles and one insanely heavy ballistic vest, as I took on the identity of a hostage. Each SWAT team had a turn to save the damsel from her heavily armed (with paint pellet guns) psychotic husband. Time after time, the muscle-bound teams of testosterone stormed our small wooden fortress, trampled my "husband" and delicately carried their petite flower off to safety (it's a rough life).

I must admit, the anticipation of observing how the teams strategized and executed different methods for the same outcome was exhilarating. Now I wanted to feel what it was like to actually be the bad guy and do some shooting. Lt. Selleck made that a reality. He explained how policemen often underestimate women in various criminal settings. So instead of permitting the SWAT teams to carry me off to safety while they contended with my husband, he added a new twist. During their escort, I would pull a hidden gun from my waistband and shoot as many members of the team as possible. How exciting! I'm not sure what it was that made playing cops and robbers so enticing to me. It could have been my desire to show them that I could be strong and powerful.

I gave it a go and deviously splattered the vests of at least five unsuspecting men, leaving them with bruised egos. I actually felt guilty after all was said and done. But later that guilt turned to power as Lt. Selleck debriefed the men. Pointing to me, he said, "Men, look at her. This exercise was done for the sole purpose of protecting you in the field. Women can kill just as easily as men...and do. Never assume all women are victims. They can easily turn on you."

With the last sentence, someone lightened the moment with the comment, "I know they can, I've seen it."

At the end of the day, Lt. Selleck empowered me and said, "What you did today will forever change the way these men think, and you may have even saved some of their lives." Wow! I was exuberant. That training day served as the spark toward my future aspirations.

Soon after my first undercover operation, I noticed a new posting for one position on the SWAT team. By that time I'd been used regularly over the last two years as a role player for the team, and I thought the guys were getting used to me. *Surely, they would be as excited as I if I were to apply.* I told Commander Selleck that I wanted to apply for the open position and he said, "I thought you might," before directing me to get acquainted with the City's General Order regarding the application process. To me, making the SWAT team equated to winning the lottery; especially if I achieved the honor as a woman, coupled with my low seniority.

Unfortunately, the events surrounding the SWAT selection were preceded by more drama than I was prepared for. One applicant, Officer LaRosa, was an expert marksman and was also a firearms instructor. LaRosa had many qualifications for the position. It just seemed that he was more focused on guns and shooting than actually hitting the street and arresting criminals.

LaRosa looked at the three other applicants, myself (a twenty-six-month veteran and a woman), Officer Sharkey and Officer Dudley (who did not officially qualify for the position because of his lack of tenure) and considered himself a shoe-in.

When rumors began to surface about my being the favorite due to my ability to be a team player, my aggressiveness in patrol, and overall dedication to the department, LaRosa got angry. So angry in fact, he began to spread rumors. A few of my colleagues shared this information with me and I felt my only recourse was a confrontation.

During patrol, I contacted LaRosa over our squad car computer and requested we meet for a chat. He agreed. I told him point blank, "I've been hearing rumors that I was the favorite for the SWAT position and numerous people on the department have approached me and told me you have been saying that I'm only being considered because of my breasts and blonde hair."

He looked at me smugly and replied, "Yeah, I said that."

Pissed off at his arrogance, I asked, "Do you really believe that's the reason why I am 'allegedly' being considered over you?"

He responded, "I don't know, maybe they want a woman on the team. I know Selleck has a 'thing' for you."

"Oh really? There's probably fifty cops that would say Selleck has a 'thing' for you," I shot back.

Commander Selleck had an affinity toward LaRosa because of their similar shooting interests. It was a well-known fact in the department.

LaRosa laughed at the comment, knowing it was true. I continued: "I don't know who they're going to choose for the position, but I want you to know if they do choose you, you won't hear me spreading ugly rumors about why you were selected."

"Sorry I said that shit but if they pick you, I want you to know I think they made the wrong decision."

"You're entitled to that," I replied before driving off.

The nerve of that guy. It was common knowledge that LaRosa was not a go-getter, had low arrest stats. Yet, he wouldn't allow himself to look at me as an equal, based on my gender and appearance.

Guys in the department made side bets about who would get the promotion. A few of my "friends" would secretly relay to me what was being said. Things like: Lockwood's a shoe-in, she's been licking Charlie's boots since she started." "LaRosa's got it all the way, he's Charlie's gun-bitch." "SWAT is never gonna put a woman on the team, some members have already said they're leaving the team if Lockwood gets on." "The guys are worried she's gonna file sexual harassment charges if they say 'fuck' in front of her."

I expected some slack from the men, but still felt hurt and betrayed. I'd been helping them train, socialized at lunch with them and even took off into the woods to relieve myself, trying to fit in. I was okay as their role player, but that was it. All they knew was an all-male team, and that's exactly how they wanted to keep it. I knew the team leaders were looking for a level headed team player who had proven him- or herself effective through proactive police activity and dedication to the department. It was the team members that wanted to keep it a boy's club. As much as I wanted to believe the guys would perceive me as an equal, the reality was that it wasn't going to happen. If I was selected, it would be like starting all over again. Yet another time for me to prove myself in a man's world.

Weeks later, on my day off, Selleck phoned me at home and said, "Feel like celebrating tonight?"

"Why?"

"I figured a new SWAT member would want to celebrate."

My heart raced. "Oh my God, thank you Commander!"

"Don't thank me, you earned it and the panel believed you deserved it."

So, after all was said and done, I proved to be the person they were looking for and became the first woman on the SWAT team. I proudly told Mom the news.

"Congratulations. Can you remind me again of why you want to do this?" She had been reluctantly adapting to her daughter's enigmatic ways. I explained that the SWAT team is more proficiently trained in the use of multiple firearms, gets to serve search warrants and handles some of the most dangerous police situations. *Like that was supposed to put her at ease.*

I told Tracy's father in person about my promotion, and he was appalled. A retired Chicago Police Captain, who had seen more than his share of homicides and shootings, barked, "Are you crazy? You don't need to be banging doors down to have some degenerate shoot you in the head over drugs!" *That was certainly a humbling twist.*

Dean knew that I was applying for the position and supported me. He, like Mom and everyone else who knew me, figured I was going to apply no matter what. In hindsight I think I would have preferred that Dean stood up to me and ordered me not to take the position. Not that I didn't want to the job; I did, and was truly excited at the prospect of the challenge. I just think I was hoping that he would have been more of a man like Tracy's Dad. If the situation were reversed, I don't think I could have easily accepted Dean intentionally escalating his chances of getting killed in the line of duty. There were times when I deeply desired to feel nurtured and protected. Even Tony wasn't ecstatic when I received orders for Desert Storm.

Shortly after, I was whisked off into a two-week basic SWAT training program. I was the sole female in a group of over forty men. The ratio of men who welcomed me was surprisingly in my favor. I had the fortune of knowing some of them through various police training classes. They either accepted me because they knew me and my reputation, or they tolerated me with the mindset that I was the token female. Or, perhaps they entertained the idea of "fresh meat."

Regardless, I was there to learn and do the same job as them. It was exciting to learn the various entry tactics for overtaking vehicles, private residences and commercial buildings. We were given all sorts of new "toys" with which to experiment; flash-bangs, battering rams, pry bars, scopes, shields and mirrors.

People were assigned to different positions based on the skills they brought to the team. As a general rule, the ram guy was short with a muscular upper body. This was so he could remain hidden in a squatting position behind the shield guy and hold the heavy ram for lengthy periods. Shockingly, as the days wore on, I noticed some of the so-called men who were assigned that position attempt to push the ram off on other people. After a break the instructor would grab the ram, hold it in the air and say, "Let's go, team," waiting for someone to relieve him of it. The ram guys could be seen meandering in the opposite direction, hoping someone else would take it. It was a disgraceful display. Not being able to tolerate the lack of initiative, I waltzed up and took it from the instructor. He smiled and asked, "You assigned to ram?"

I responded, "No, just thought I'd give it a try."

One entry team gathered behind me and we headed over to an abandoned house. The head training officer made his way to our group. Upon noticing the 'runt' holding the ram, he tugged at the eye socket of my neoprene facemask and asked, "Who's in there?" Everyone laughed, because he knew it was me. "Go for it, kid" was his order as he walked off grinning.

To the rhythm of a ticking clock we ascended the stairs, lined ourselves along a boarded up window and commenced our mission. The shield guy swung open the screen door and I rammed through the wooden door with all my might. The explosive guy tossed in the flash-bang and the bad guy slammed the door shut. It took a second for us to interpret what this meant.

As the flash-bang rolled back to our feet, everyone clamored to get out of harm's way. The explosion took a chunk out of my boot before I made my way down the stairs. That event served as one of the most electrifying eye openers of my life. During our debrief the instructor asked, "So what did you learn?"

They had been teaching us all along that no plan is perfectly executed in this business. There will always be a surprise, and we should expect the unexpected. We satisfactorily regurgitated this lesson. There was a whole new respect for the value of every position on the team, and we learned to support those who became weary without judgment. Just like in the military, we learned there is no "I" in team.

The final day of training brought us to a heavily wooded training ground. A number of the instructors became the "bad guys" for the scenario. Two of them maintained the positions of Command Post coordinator and scenario overseer. We were told that a notorious anti-government group, wanted for committing a string of armed bank robberies, were holed up with a hostage in their heavily booby-trapped, wooded fortress. Our training class was split in half. Each team would be given two hours to devise a strategy to find and infiltrate the fortress, save the hostage and arrest the bad guys. Guess who was selected to be the team leader? *This "expect the unexpected" thing was getting out of hand.* I did not see that one coming; however, I did know what had been working for me for the past ten years. *Act as if.* Acting as if I already had the skill or had done something before or knew the answer had become a way of life for me.

A few of the more experienced guys were pissed off. They were happy to have me as a team member but not a team leader. *Sound familiar?* This was their opportunity to shine. Surrounded by volcanoes of exploding testosterone, I sought out the alpha male and assigned him to assistant team leader. We corroborated a plan to allow the men to choose their various positions. Once the scouts, snipers, explosive experts, shield, rammer and entry team had been assigned, we headed out armed with paint guns. All the while I maintained radio contact with Command Post, giving and receiving intel. With all of my 911 and patrol experience on the radio, I sailed through the voice protocol.

Aside from briefly having a few scouts missing in action, we managed to locate and arrest some of the offenders after an exchange of fire in an angry shootout. Our final mission was to capture the barricaded gunman who was secreted in an L-shaped forty-bed dormitory with a hostage. As one of our rooftop snipers called out the movement of the "bad guy," I had our negotiator attempt verbal contact with the remaining offender. Because he chose to speak with us, he was forced to get closer to a window in order to give us his demands. I received authorization to order the sniper to shoot the offender at any opportunity, provided it didn't put the hostage at risk. When the sniper took his opening shot, the hostage managed to free himself from the building as the bad guy returned fire. During the shootout, the bad guy put a round into the leg of the hostage, sending him reeling to the ground.

Shortly after, the gunfire ceased and all that could be heard was the high-pitched scream of the wounded hostage. The negotiator was instructed to re-initiate verbal contact with the gunman as I devised a plan to extract the hostage from the danger zone. Unable to contact the gunman (it was a gamble to assume that he was shot or injured), I directed one of the explosive experts to launch a distraction device (flash-bang) toward the side of the building opposite the injured civilian. As soon as this took place, a smoke bomb was launched in front of the wounded man. As part of a four-person team, we darted from cover using the smoke screen to extract the man and carry him to safety.

With this successfully accomplished, we alerted the command post and told him of our plan to enter and search the dormitory for our assailant. Keeping the snipers in position, our entry team stealthily approached the rear door of the building. The shield man turned the door handle and discovered it unlocked. The rammer discarded his tool and the team rapidly entered the box-like corridor. Because of the L-shaped design of the building, we needed to be cautious in avoiding crossfire situations. I had half of our entry team cover the left hallway, while three additional tactical officers and I made a rapid entry into the first dorm. We swarmed the room, covering every square inch, searching under beds and behind curtains when I heard one of my guys shout, "Don't move!" The gunman was hiding behind a heavy gray curtain with both hands extended in an open palms up position. As one man held him at gunpoint, two of us instinctively pounced on the paint-riddled assailant, taking him into custody and handing him off to the cover team.

Even with the offender in custody, I needed to quell premature celebrations. We were trained to expect the unexpected. I reminded the team that we still had an entire dorm to search. With ten minutes to spare from our two-hour time limit, the remainder of our entry team systematically searched every nook and cranny of the last room.

After I radioed that the building was secure, our scenario overseer approached me and said, "Are you sure your building is secure and all of your offenders are in custody?"

My first instinct was to think, *Damn, I missed something.* Then I radioed Command Post and told him we were complete; second-guessing was not an option. "Yes I'm sure," I responded.

"Congratulations," he said, "You did it!" *I could breathe again.* Our team was jubilant. The room was filled with elation, smiles, high-fives and officers recounting the final moments.

Back at the command post we were told that the first team that entered this scenario fell apart after missing the hidden gunman and failed to search the remaining room. There was dissension among the troops and too much haste in extracting their wounded hostage. One of their tactical officers was wounded as a result. Just when I thought God had given me my share of proud moments, he gave me this gift. The upper echelon from SWAT school contacted my department's SWAT leaders and relayed my progress during the course. It was a monumental moment for me, in that now the team might truly appreciate the value of their newest "lightweight" member.

CHAPTER 13
THE STRIPPER &
THE CHICAGO MAFIA

A few months after wearing my little girl persona, I'd dolled myself up in short shorts, black stilettos and a slinky, purple tank top. My platinum blonde mane tussled wildly over my shoulders and stretched down to the small of my back. My lips were over-lined, a trick I'd picked up from the Miss Illinois pageant to give the illusion of a plumper mouth. Finally, my eyes—which could be my most valuable tool today—struggled to stay open as they lay heavily encrusted from the clumps of midnight-black mascara. Was all of this overkill? Not when this desperate rookie was at least smart enough to realize she'd be unwired, unvested and unarmed while escorting a snitch named Rocco into a Mafia–owned pawnshop with bags of "stolen" goods to sell.

My assignment was to infiltrate a Mafia-connected fencing operation on Chicago's south side, and Rocco was our informant. After having been arrested for shoplifting a felony amount of merchandise from a department store, Rocco had opted to flip on his source instead of going to jail for the crime. Rocco was in his mid-twenties, brunette, thin, and addicted to heroin.

My job, armed only with street smarts, was to become the cocaine-addicted stripper girlfriend of one of Rocco's drinking buddies. Sound confusing? I hoped so, because that's exactly what we were going for. The sketchier my relationship was with the informant, the better it was for Rocco. We needed to do what we could to protect his decision to "nark." If pressed by the Mafia, Rocco was coached to say, "Her boyfriend told me she was an expert thief and needed help unloading stuff." Rocco was prepared to casually brag, "Yeah I told her I'd get her in, but she's gonna have to give me a cut for the connect."

We were convinced that we'd created an airtight story to get me inside the quasi-pawnshop to meet the players. Then again, what did I know? I was just an undercover rookie willing to do anything to impress the guys.

The "pawnshop's" lobby was dark and barren, furnished with nothing more than two metal folding chairs. Filthy orange linoleum, circa 1970s no doubt, lay scuffed and faded beneath our feet. A solid wood-paneled wall stood directly before us, encasing a small, clouded bulletproof glass window with a money exchange slit at the bottom. To the left of that window was a seamless door with no knob and a doorbell. *The elusive entrance.*

My mind raced momentarily as I considered my mission. Aside from convincing the Mafiosi that I was a cocaine-snorting thief who made her living as a stripper, I had additional tasks. This is where my cake-lashed eyes would be called into action. The team made my assignment clear: ascertain the identity of the players, discover whether or not "hot" merchandise was secreted in the warehouse, pinpoint the guy who was actually conducting the day-to-day business operations, locate where the cash was stashed, identify the locations of all entrances, exits, doors, windows and stairwells *and* conclude if anyone was carrying concealed weapon. Additionally, I had to remember anything that would present an officer safety concern in order to prepare for the eventual execution of a search warrant on the business, provided that probable cause was established. All of this was expected from an inexperienced patrol officer who was chosen for the undercover because, like Greg Brady's Johnny Bravo from *The Brady Bunch*, "I fit the suit." I'd made it easy for them. I was attractive and sexy and, most important, I was willing.

Rocco walked up to the bulletproof glass and said, "Hey buddy, open up!"

The young dark-haired, olive-skinned man monitoring the door deliberately shifted his eyes toward me with disdain. He furrowed his eyebrows and squinted while nodding his chin upward at Rocco, as if to say, "Who's that?"

Rocco crept closer to the window. I stood to the side trying to remain aloof and gazing around the lobby as if I didn't give a rats ass if he let in that back room or not. I listened as Rocco pleaded with the guy (Tony), whom he referred to as Tone.

"C'mon Tone, open up. She's okay; it's my buddy's girl..."

After several seconds of peering down his nose and scowling at a groveling Rocco, Tony relented and buzzed the door open. *Showtime.* Following Rocco past a small, grungy office, I noticed Tony icily locked onto me. Immediately beyond the office was the warehouse, where a short pudgy, fifty-five-year-old Italian man made his debut. He wore an untucked, wrinkled dress shirt and tired black dress pants. The musty warehouse reeked of sewer odor. It was poorly lit and...Bingo! Loaded with hot merchandise. Shelves were packed to the ceiling with TVs, DVD players, laptops, stereo equipment, and an organized assortment of toolboxes and power tools, all in their original packaging. To the left were clothing racks overflowing with men's suits and sports jerseys. Two rows of bicycles lined the back wall, most with the store tags still hanging from them.

Rocco walked straight up to the pudgy guy, extended his hand and said, "Hey Danno. This is Lisa." (I was told by the veteran detectives to use my real first name undercover so as not to trip up some of their 'rocket scientist' snitches.)

Mr. Pudgy acknowledged me by correcting Rocco: "Danny."

Again, Rocco spewed his rehearsed line, "She's my buddy's girl," and added..."for now" (not rehearsed). Rocco's nervousness manifested itself with a case of diarrhea of the mouth. "She's a stripper," he said, as if I weren't there, "ain't she hot?"

As Danny blatantly eyed my now-perspiring body up and down, I corrected Rocco and sarcastically said, "That's *dancer.*"

Now that the formalities were over, I followed Rocco's lead by dumping our bags of 'stolen' razor blades and jars of Tylenol on a card table, and then neatly laid out the men's suits. Danny's eyes lit up; he began sorting the items. "How much?"

119

Rocco said, "Three hundred for the suits."

Pleased with the load, Danny shrugged, puckered his lips, and nodded his approval as he caressed the fabric. Before I had a chance to name my price he said, "I'll give you a hundred."

In no position to negotiate with Danny head on, I looked at Rocco and asked, "Whattaya think?"

Rocco snapped, "Take it."

Before I had a chance to agree, Danny picked up one of the suits and walked away as if the deal had already been settled. Suddenly, he searched the suit and barked, "Where's the store tag on this? I told you before, this shit has to have the tag on it for me to get a good buck for it!" Then he noticed the size and expressed further disappointment. "Next time you get a forty-four short."

Rocco, not intimidated, said, "Okay, man."

It was evident Danny wanted the forty-four short for himself. He pulled out a large roll of cash, gave me a hundred-dollar bill, and began counting out Rocco's share. "You still owe me fifty bucks," he grunted, handing him $250 instead of $300. Rocco didn't flinch. *How often does a bad guy get to use police money to pay off a debt to the Mafia?* After the transaction, Danny escorted us out.

As we passed the office, Tony and another young man were comfortably reclined in their leather office chairs watching a movie on a brand new large-screen TV. When they looked up, I seized the moment by smiling flirtatiously and purring, *Goodbye,* as I scanned the room for a safe and any sign of a weapon. Rocco said, "See ya man," to which Tony just nodded. *I wondered if Tony was a mute or preserving his vocal cords for a Sinatra karaoke night.* They each returned my smile as we left.

We crossed the street to a parking lot where the surveillance van loaded with back-up detectives awaited us. Rocco and I entered our undercover car, all too aware that the guys in the store could still see us as we drove off. A tail and lead car escorted us to a predetermined rendezvous point for our debriefing.

We arrived at a park only minutes away from the business, and Rocco was swiftly transferred to an undercover vehicle with heavily tinted windows.

I felt like I was under a microscope, surrounded by high-ranking members of the Southwest Major Case Unit along with various superiors from my department. They were anxious to hear the play-by-play, and I reveled in all the attention as I handed over $350 to the case detective. "We did it!" I exclaimed.

I overheard one of the Commanders whisper to a detective, "Hell, I *know* she's a cop, and I'd still buy stolen shit from her."

Consumed by adrenaline, I'd forgotten what I must have looked like dressed as a stripper in a crowd of policemen. I considered that I would no longer just be the petite, no make-up wearing, French-braided blonde rookie they barely saw for the last four years on midnights. Now these men had an actual visual to fantasize about "Lisa the stripper." Everyone was beaming about our success, including me. Only now I glowed for an additional reason: would these guys still respect me or did I just unseal Pandora's Box? Regardless, it was done. We had successfully infiltrated a Mafia-tied fencing ring and I was now a crucial operative. I remained on a high for the next two days, recounting our successful sting in my mind. I shared what I had accomplished with my boyfriend Dean, my two closest friends and a few family members—short of the case-sensitive information, of course.

Days later, with an inflated ego, I was back inside the seamy pawnshop with Rocco, attempting to sell more suits and power tools. This time, Tony was quick to buzz us in, and Danny was already waiting for us in the warehouse as we placed our items down on the card table. Rocco and I replayed a rehearsed story about how we were nearly caught by store security as we fled with the power tools. To tighten our case against Danny and the fencing operation, we needed to ensure that he knew the merchandise we were bringing him was stolen. As Danny examined our wares, I made an intentionally loud aside to Rocco: "You're only gettin' $25 from me on the suit split because I took more risk." It worked…however, a bit too well. Hearing me sound so assertive this time piqued Danny's suspicion. With furrowed brows, he looked into my eyes and started his interrogation.

"Where you from?"

I'd learned, when trying to convince someone of a false identity, to keep the story as simple as possible. Besides, I'd always enjoyed role-playing pranks with friends and strangers to see how convincing I could be, and had learned from an early age to intertwine real events with fictitious stories to make my accounts more believable. This was definitely a moment when I was thankful for indulging in such a silly pastime.

"Bridgeport," I replied.

"Where'd you go to high school?"

"Kelly High." This wasn't true, but my sisters had been students there and I thought at the very least I'd be able to recall some things about it if necessary. I'd attended an all-girls Catholic high school, but I wasn't sure Danny would buy that a Catholic schoolgirl would graduate to a coke-addicted stripper.

He paused for a second, then asked, "You got any ID?" That was the question that dried my palate. It was evident that today's Daisy Dukes and a skin-tight cleavage-revealing shirt were not going to be enough to distract Danny this time. Since I hadn't done much undercover work, the detective division hadn't bothered to create the usual wallet of fake credentials for me. They had, however, at the last minute, thrown together a traffic citation for speeding, which bore my undercover name. There was only one problem: I'd forgotten it in the undercover car parked across the street.

I answered Danny with a hint of sarcasm: "Yeah, it's in the car, in my purse."

To my horror he said, "Go get it."

A quick decision had to be made. I dared not get into an argument with him and risk leaving without a sale. The other option was to retrieve the ticket, but this meant leaving Rocco alone. (It would have seemed suspicious to ask him to accompany me to the car.) But this option was an officer-safety "no-no," posing a number of possible risks: without a wire I had no way of alerting the guys in the back-up van that I would be leaving the pawnshop without the informant.

Meanwhile, I ran the risk that Rocco would betray the police and voluntarily reveal my cover; it was not uncommon for an informant to play both sides. Or, Danny could either shake Rocco down or entice him with a reward to reveal my identity.

I needed to show that I was unmoved by his request, so I exited the shop and hastily crossed the street, pretending to act like it was more of an

Me at four.

1988 Miss Illinois USA Pageant.

U.S. Air Force Saudi Arabia 1992.

Saudi Arabia driving a dump truck.

Chicago Police Academy with "the now late" Officer Tero.

Still a Pre-SWAT volunteer.

2002 - My last photo as a SWAT member.

Detective Leary (Boz) and I
awarded Co-Officer of the Year 2002.

Rock, my new man, treating me to Rodeo Drive.

Driving Nascar in L.A. after my Law Enforcement resignation.

inconvenience than anything else. As I approached the undercover car and grabbed my purse, I could feel the tension and confusion filtering out of the hot, beat-up panel van less than two feet from where I stood. But I couldn't communicate with SWAT for fear that someone inside the business was watching. The decision was ultimately mine. I could abort the sting by not returning to the shop, or return and hope that my cover had not been compromised. I made the rookie decision; risking my safety, I opted for the latter and hurried back across the street.

Tony buzzed me in without question, and Danny greedily snatched the ticket from my hand. "You got somethin' with a picture on it?" he asked me, agitated.

"Yeah, my license has a picture on it but the cop took it when he gave me the ticket!" I tried to sound equally agitated. I couldn't understand why he was so pissed off this time around.

He headed toward the front desk to consult with Tony, whom I would later discover was his brother and in charge of running the business. As I tried to eavesdrop on their conversation, I began thinking of an escape route. I stared at Rocco for any indication that Danny had extracted information from him. But Rocco appeared carefree as he rode a kids' bike he had found in the warehouse between the tables and boxes of merchandise.

This was no time to relax. A minute later, Danny pounded toward me with Tony on his heels. I scanned them both, looking for a gun bulge, trying to appear calm and also keep Rocco in my sight. There were three of them and one of me and the SWAT guys were clueless. All the police academy training in the world couldn't prepare me to take on three men without a weapon, and I felt naked without my vest. Danny flicked his wrist toward me, indicating that I should take it my ticket back as if it were contaminated, and posed *the fateful question*. The one everyone has heard asked on TV dramas and in movies: "You a cop?" *Damn!* I felt nauseous. Did Rocco nark me out? Were Danny and Tony preparing for my final 'sleep with the fishes' in the Canal Street river? I dared not look down to see if I was standing in the middle of a disposable area rug. How could this be happening to me? I thought the other day went brilliantly. This wasn't fun anymore. Could all of Mom's worries have been right? Surely I didn't push myself all these years to achieve goal after goal, just to die so foolishly.

There was no time to think. I quickly responded with a sly, flattered smile and breathy laugh, "Are you serious?"

Rocco morphed from his deer-in-the-headlights expression and chuckled. This made me believe that he wasn't shaken down. I felt relieved. There was no need to say anything else.

In an instant, Danny abruptly lightened up and smiled. I'm not sure if it was one of embarrassment for the false accusation or a grin to show his Napoleonic power of intimidation. Regardless, they must have seen that I was unmoved because Tony passed him a piece of paper to have me sign, indicating that the items I was selling him today were not stolen property. *Piece of cake.* Giggling, I rolled my eyes and said, "Gimme a pen." I signed the 'contract,' which was about as valuable as a three-dollar bill, considering all I had to prove in court was that he was verbally aware the stuff I sold him was 'stolen.' Tony, who still hadn't uttered a peep, handed me a mere $75 for the suits, then forked over $80 to Rocco for the power tools.

After all of our transactions changed hands, the men couldn't repress their rising testosterone level. *Thank goodness. I was starting to question my sex appeal.* This time, instead of the rush to the exit, Danny said, "How long you been dancin'?"

"Two years," I told him.

"Do you do private parties?" he coyly asked. *Does a bear shit in the woods?* Now that I had them hook, line and sinker, there was nothing I didn't do.

"For the right price," I boasted.

Then, Tony piped in with his first words: "You go to da boat?" he asked in a deep Rocky Balboa voice.

"Sometimes, but mostly I'm a slot girl." I winked. *C'mon, did I really just say that?* As we all caught the accidental sexual innuendo, grins erupted. It was evident that the 'cop issue' was now the farthest thing from their minds. I took advantage of my sluthood and flirted with them as Rocco stood by and listened. I meandered into their front office as if I owned the place and noticed a safe under a desk in the far corner. Tony and Danny gave me their personal cell phone numbers in case I ever needed to get rid of anything.

This meant I didn't need Rocco to bring me back here. I thought it bold of them to cut Rocco out right in front of him, but I went along with it. Rocco was small-time and I'm sure Danny, with his Napoleon complex, was used to letting little people know where they stood.

When I thought things couldn't get better, Tony asked me, "Wanna go on the riverboat?"

"Sure," I replied, sounding flattered.

Tony, acting like the stud of the pair, beat Danny to the punch and said, "Give me a call Friday night if you're not doin' nothin', I'll take ya out dere."

Smiling, I said, "I'm in." They were clueless, and I knew that this would be our last deal at the pawnshop; our team would be arresting them during a search warrant later that afternoon.

I breathed easily, convinced that neither of them was the wiser regarding my true identity. Rocco and I left the pawnshop as Tony and Danny, appearing smitten, watched us from the front window. I crossed the street, playfully placing Rocco in a headlock and feinting punches at his head, landing a few light ones for good measure. He struggled all the way to the undercover car. We were again escorted to a new rendezvous point. This time, however, I would have to reveal my screw-up with the ID to the team. Rocco was immediately hustled into the undercover car, and I had to explain why I'd put us in such a precarious situation. I glossed over the purse-in-the-car bit as quickly as possible, trying to downplay the event, and highlighted all of the good things that had transpired upon my return. Everyone was satisfied with the outcome, but admittedly shaken by my mistake.

After receiving a few handshakes and pats on the back, Detective Burke discreetly took me aside and read me the riot act. He—the king of officer safety and my former field-training officer—was pissed off and scolded me accordingly. "Nothing is worth you gettin' hurt, Lockwood! There's no glory in dyin' over a property crime!" He glared at me in admonishment.

"Got it," I said, swallowing hard, knowing he was right. Burke was like an older brother to me; the last thing I wanted to do was disappoint him. I knew I deserved this and stoically took my lumps as I nearly choked on my short-lived pride. I darted off to the safety of a blacked out suburban just in time to hide the eye-blurring wells of tears pooling up, hoping they thought I was just in a hurry to change out of the slut ensemble. I was shocked by Burke's authentic show of concern. How could this man care about me so much? I mean, Dean, my lover of two years, would occasionally throw in a "be safe tonight." My ex-husband, Tony, flippantly asked me to go AWOL when I received orders for Desert Storm and my own father was emotionless when I told him I was chosen for the SWAT team. Burke's gesture was overwhelming. Was he just being protective, or is this how men are supposed to treat women? I knew two things in that moment: it made me feel weak and uncomfortable, and at the same time made me feel loved and special.

With the two successful pawnshop deals under our belts, we were ready to put together a search and arrest team. The SWAT team, along with other task force members gathered at a local police department, where the preparation was initiated. The team leader circulated all of the intelligence on the suspects to the eager police officers. In a pair of jeans, a black tee-shirt with white POLICE lettering emblazoned across the front and back, a low hanging pony-tail and a monochromatic finish to my face, I was back in my element as one of the boys.

A buzz of euphoria flooded the air in the prep room as I diagrammed the floor plan of the business, labeling all of the exits and entrances on the large dry erase board in front of the eager squad. After the SWAT team leaders formulated their entry plan, nearly everyone made their way over to offer a compliment for my undercover work and efficiency in recalling, in detail, the layout of the pawnshop. I was excluded from participating on this search warrant; it was imperative to keep my real identity a secret as long as possible to protect Rocco.

Later that afternoon, members of the SWAT team, along with officers from the Southwest Major Case Unit, assembled near the pawnshop to execute the search warrant. It was decided that one of the detectives would stage a ruse to get the reinforced door buzzed open. Jake, the chosen detective, dressed as a construction worker and walked inside hoping to hock a power tool.

Meanwhile, we had a team stationed at the back door of the warehouse, and another team lined up against the building directly next door to the pawnshop. This time Danny stood behind the bulletproof glass when Jake entered.

Jake asked, "How much will ya give me for this?"

Danny's guard was up and, not recognizing Jake as a regular, he said, "We don't buy stuff like that." After some desperate pleading on Jake's part, it became evident that Danny wasn't going to open the door, so Jake gave the green light for the teams to enter and then calmly identified himself as a police officer. He handed the search warrant through the slit in the glass and demanded that Danny open the door.

Danny tried to pretend that nothing was wrong as he told the officers to go right ahead and search, acting the part of a perfect gentleman. (There was no one else present, so Tony would have to be reckoned with later.) Danny was cuffed, and a bankroll of more than ten thousand dollars was retrieved from his front pocket.

After he was taken into custody and transported to the police department, I was allowed to return to the pawnshop, where I had the painstaking job of assisting with the seizure of stolen inventory worth well over one hundred thousand dollars.

While Commander Wheeler, a highly respected team coordinator, and I searched the office two young men in their late teens entered. Ignorant of the fact that we were police, even with my black and white police shirt, they asked, "You wanna buy two brand new lawn mowers?"

Not missing a beat, Wheeler said, "Bring 'em in so I can see what they look like."

As the boys left to retrieve the mowers, we were dumbfounded and clued the other detectives in. When they returned, brand new mowers in tow, Wheeler and I met them in the lobby. Wheeler asked, "Where'd you guys get these?"

The boys proudly exclaimed, "We stole them from Sears in Burbank mall!" Ironically, this was in Wheeler's jurisdiction.

"Well guess what, boys? We're the police and you're both going to jail." Wheeler took out his badge. We cuffed the stunned boys and brought them into the warehouse. As we waited for a marked squad car to take them away,

I felt compelled to ask them what they'd planned to do with the money they would have received from the mowers.

The older boy said, "I got a bad drug problem and use it for acid."

The other boy sat silently in the chair, his head sunk low between his legs, fighting tears. They further revealed that they'd been doing business with Danny and Tony for the last three months. Both started crying, expressing the devastation their parents would feel upon notification of their crime. In response to what hard-nosed cops looked at as a cowardly emotional display, one of the detectives said, "When you play with the big boys, you go down like the big boys." I fought the feminine urge to counsel and console the lost boys. I had an image to uphold around my comrades. The boys were both charged with a felony crime.

Shortly after, Commander Selleck made a special point of addressing me in the alley behind the shop. "You did good today. What do think about this type of work?"

His approval meant the world to me. He had been one of my mentors early on. He'd encouraged me in my rookie years to embrace the highest of standards. He had attracted ridicule for having the confidence to send me—a rookie—to Firearms Instructor School. He'd supported my decision to apply for the SWAT team, aware that this would make him unpopular in the eyes of his colleagues, as well as certain members of the team. It wasn't long before my envious colleagues started to call me Sgt. Lockwood, due to the rapid pace my law enforcement career was advancing. Now, I was being pulled out of patrol to perform undercover operations with joint agencies. With the exhilaration of our success fresh in my mind, I forgot about the near death experience I'd endured just hours before. I was too naïve to wonder if I was doing this for their approval or for my own self-esteem. I gave Commander Selleck an adamant, "Yes!" in response to his question. *I loved the thrill of working undercover!*

We all celebrated our successful day with pizza back at the station after unloading the contents of our vans and trucks into an evidence warehouse. We heard that Danny was giving the lock-up keepers a hard time, behaving boisterously and demanding to make phone calls. Later he would complain of chest pain, a symptom the police often refer to as "Felony Flu." (In many cases, when an individual is made aware of the gravity of their crime, he trumps up some type of ailment that can get him out of his cell and transported to the hospital. Whether we believe him or not, protocol insists that we assume it's a valid ailment.) Danny was transported to the hospital, where he remained for two days before he went in front of a judge for bond hearing.

Tony eventually turned himself in, with his attorney attached at the hip, and was free on bond within forty-eight hours. Several months later, still awaiting trial, he was discovered dead in his hotel room in Las Vegas. The cause of death was an alleged overdose. Danny ended up cooperating with the police and was given probation for his participation in the fencing operation. The entire recovered inventory was sold at a police auction.

Later that year, I received the Grand Cordon award. This would only be the beginning.

CHAPTER 14
THE ANGEL IS PAIRED WITH BOSLEY

In October of 2000 Selleck called me into the department for an "official meeting." Usually these were related to some type of investigation regarding a potential misconduct involving an officer. In my last official meeting I was called in to give my version of a call involving a criminal who claimed to be injured by an officer (I backed on the call) during his arrest. Being on the other side of an interrogation, even when innocent, is not a pleasant experience. I racked my brain trying to think what could have happened in the last week that could possibly be conceived as an infraction. Even though I came up empty, I was not looking forward to the meeting.

I arrived for the meeting nervous and perplexed and was completely unprepared for what I was about to be told. Noticing my tension Selleck said, "Relax, this is good news. You've had a very impressive career as a patrol officer…and you've probably already heard rumors that the existing drug team was not getting the results the department anticipated."

"Yes."

"Well…the current Drug Unit has been given their notice and will return to patrol next month."

I knew what was coming and could feel the butterflies well up in my stomach. "We are putting together a new male and female drug team and I want to know if you're interested in the position."

There was no hiding my feelings. I knew I looked like a deer in headlights. "Yes," was all I could muster as beads of sweat formed on my forehead. I grinned.

"Great. I'll get the paperwork started and will be announcing your promotion to Narcotics Detective as soon as we decide on your partner."

The following week, they still hadn't decided on my partner and I was sent off to a weeklong class on narcotics investigations. Rumors were surfacing that I was a "golden child" with the brass. I had already received several specialties (certifications above and beyond patrol officer) over the duration of my brief career, and jealousy was par for the course. Secretly, I was being referred to as "Charlie's Angel." I wasn't complaining; there were far worse names I could've been called! I was truly honored—and even more so when I heard that after a mere four-and-a-half years, I was in a class of my own. It was uncommon for a patrol officer to be promoted to detective with less than seven years' experience.

There were two strong candidates vying to become the other half of the drug unit. One of them, Officer Leary, had been a cop a year longer than I. In fact, I'd been a dispatcher when he was hired and had formed an immediate opinion of the rookie. He projected the image of a bookworm and was overly polite, never offering more than a concise yes or no when questioned in person. To our dismay, he was notorious for excitedly yelling his transmissions over the radio; yet when it was necessary to give or retrieve information from the dispatchers in person, he would enter the radio room, meekly stand in the back, and then approach using the least number of words possible to communicate. In the beginning, I honestly didn't think he had what it took to be a police officer and figured he would be eaten alive on the street. I couldn't have been happier to be proven wrong.

As Leary became more familiar with the job, he began to develop a reputation of "the shit magnet," because every call he was involved with seemed to turn into some kind of fiasco. Even so, he always worked them through, going above and beyond the call of duty. Leary was like a bloodhound on the street—he had an uncanny ability to seek, find, and arrest criminals. Not just your everyday run of the mill criminals—don't get me wrong, he got those too. Leary was unparalleled in finding the worst felons, no matter what beat he was assigned, and this was an impressive feat.

Leary and I worked different shifts, so we never formed any kind of working relationship. But I would hear about him through roll call and saw his arrest stats every few months on the postings. One could say I admired him from afar. Then we were both selected to become juvenile officers, in addition to street officers, and were sent to a forty-hour training class. Every day we would drive together, sit next to each other in class, and have lunch. During that time I established that he was married, received his opinion about the department union, and discovered he'd been in construction prior to becoming a police officer. Talking to Leary was like pulling teeth. I felt fortunate to get that much out of him. In the end, the bookworm received a hundred percent on his certification. His mind was like a sponge. He could recite criminal procedure and case law from memory. I was looking forward to getting away from Mr. Excitement and getting back on the street.

When I discovered that Leary was in the running to be my partner, I told Selleck that I respected him and thought he would be make a great detective—after all, he was "the shit magnet." I figured I could work through the personality issue. Leary was ultimately chosen and we were brought in together to receive official notice of our promotion. The Chief asked if we thought we were compatible. We were both so excited to be offered the position, we embellished our relationship, highlighting the *great* time we had at juvenile officer training. Then we found our way to our new closet—it was actually a tiny windowless office—and began to set up shop.

With no one available to show us the ropes, we winged it. We had a file cabinet with a few drawers of information on past informants, and one filled with not so hot tips about possible dealers from anonymous sources. We spent the day sifting through the files and obtaining a few equipment necessities. As I tried to organize our personal things, I came across a congratulations card belonging to Leary. Our fellow patrolmen personalized the card with individual blurbs. One comment, in particular, caught my interest: "Make sure you don't get bushwhacked." When Leary returned I asked what it meant. He blushed as he snatched the card from my hand.

"It doesn't mean anything."

"C'mon *partner*, don't hold out on me."

"It's stupid, the guy's a goof."

"If you don't tell me what it means, I'll just think the worst."

"Geez, you won't give up…okay, just remember it was just a joke. It means don't get pussy whipped," he said, frowning.

"Haaaaaaaaaaa! Really? The guys think I'm gonna pussy whip you?"

"No, it was just a stupid joke, that's what guys say. Can we drop it now?"

"No way! I'm the bushwhacker. You better watch out, I'm the bushwhack Queen."

"Great. Here we go," he said dismally.

Leary was getting a taste of his new partner's humor and wasn't sure how to take it. I think he was trying to hang on to professionalism as long as possible; or at least until he could assess if I was for real (truly not offended by the comment).

Graduating to plainclothes, the buckle badge and holster was a monumental moment. We couldn't believe the freedom afforded to us! We made our own hours, dined on our schedule, and had free reign of the city and adjoining towns. When we drove past someone in our unmarked car, they had no idea we were the police. It was like a dream come true. *Didn't you ever wish that when someone made some idiotic move in traffic, a cop was around?* It was even better when someone made an idiotic move like cutting *us* off, and we were able to throw up the gumball, hit the siren, and pull them over. Even better than that, was when they gave us "the finger" with "the cut off." We knew we were going to love this job.

About eight weeks into our new unit, Leary and I received information about a teenage dealer who was selling weed out of his parents' home. The father had a reputation for being a troublemaker and a wife beater. After conducting surveillances in the bitterness of winter, Leary and I determined there to be significant drug activity. Cars would pull up and honk their horn;

then our suspect, Jim Scarfo, would run out half-dressed, reach into the car and run back inside. It didn't take a rocket scientist to figure this one out. Now that Leary and I had a fair amount of evidence, our goal was to get into the house. *Ask and you shall receive.* A week into the investigation, one of the street coppers picked up a kid for underage drinking. The kid told the cop he had drug information and asked to speak to a Nark. He didn't want his parents to find out he'd been arrested and asked if he could work a deal with us. To our delight, he bought weed regularly from Scarfo and agreed to become an informant. If he did everything according to plan, we'd offer him assistance with the State's Attorney regarding his underage alcohol case.

The first day our new informant, whom we nicknamed "Rainman" for his slow nature and short attention span, phoned to cancel our meeting, using car trouble as an excuse. But Leary and I were so pumped to be working with our first informant; we weren't going to let that hold us up. We told him to meet us on the corner by his house. We picked him up and briefed him. We needed to repeat our simple directions to him, like we were spoon-feeding a baby. "Take the money into the house, buy the drugs, leave the house, and meet us behind the strip mall."

"So should I ask him where he keeps his stash?" Rainman offered helpfully.

"No!" Leary shot back, "Listen to me! Take the money into the house, buy the drugs, leave the house and meet us behind the strip mall. Repeat after me, take the money…"

Rainman laughed and said, "Okay, I get it."

I set up surveillance in a minivan across the street, several homes down from Scarfo's residence. Leary tailed Rainman in and set up farther down the road, opposite my location. We radioed to each other, calling out Rainman's movement. Rainman went inside for less than five minutes and headed back toward the strip mall as ordered, with Leary on his tail.

Rainman handed over the bag of weed and smiled with elation at accomplishing the task—*like it was the first time he ever bought a bag of weed.* We stroked his ego and told him we never had an informant conduct a buy so smoothly. *He didn't need to know he was our first informant and that was our first official buy.* Rainman was so proud of himself; he was more than ready to do it a second time. Leary and I dropped him off and had our own high-fiving mini-celebration. Then we packaged our evidence, wrote our report, and started looking up case law on the various types of search warrants.

The next day, Rainman arrived on time, eager to do his next buy. Leary briefed him: "Just like last time, in, out, and meet. Got it?"

Rainman smiled. "I got it. Don't worry."

This time, as I sat down the street watching Scarfo's house, I noticed a car roll up loaded with teenagers. They honked, and Scarfo ran out to do a drug sale right under my nose. I alerted Leary to have Rainman standby, so that I could ensure Scarfo was back in his house. It would have been a throwaway deal if Scarfo delivered the drugs outside his residence; we needed Rainman inside to get probable cause for the residential search warrant. I noted the teenagers' license plate for the future as they rolled past me obliviously. Then I relayed to Leary that the coast was clear, so Rainman could proceed. But this must have been a hot sell time for Scarfo, because he noticed Rainman in the driveway and met him at the car to do the deal—exactly what we *didn't* want to have happen. Had Rainman been sharp, he could have told Scarfo, "Hey man, I don't wanna do this outside, let's go in the house," or, "I gotta use the can." But then, there was a reason we named him Rainman.

He met us at the rendezvous point and apologized. "There was nothing I could do." We told him we understood, and suggest maybe next time he could offer an excuse to get into the house.

Next time came two days later. For some reason Rainman wasn't as excited about doing the deal as he had been in the past. Someone had gotten to him. He started getting squirrelly, asking questions about testifying in court and wondering if Scarfo would know he'd narked him out. Leary and I believed he opened his mouth to someone. If that were the case, it was almost certain that Rainman had blown his own cover. This wasn't good. So we took Rainman through the steps again regarding how we couldn't protect his identity if he told people he was working with the police. Obviously lying, he said, "I swear I didn't tell anyone." Leary and I knew from criminal deception training that as soon as someone prefaces a statement with *I swear...* they're lying 90 percent of the time. There was nothing we could do at this point but believe him if he was still willing to go ahead with the next drug buy. After that conversation he said, "Okay let's just get it over with."

This one went like clockwork. Now Leary and I were ready to start the procedure for obtaining a warrant. The detective unit was impressed. We'd infiltrated a known drug house with less than two months experience, and within a week of receiving information about the sore spot. Leary handled our first search warrant. You would have thought he was writing the Declaration of Independence given the amount of time, care and attention to detail he put into it. I felt a bit left out.

"You done yet?" I asked in passing.

"Should I get a sleeping bag?" I offered an hour later.

What finally got a rise out of my new partner was my inquiry, "Should you be typing that in all caps?"

He glared at me, abruptly pushed himself away from the keyboard, and snapped, "You wanna do this?"

Wow, my partner has a pulse. I put my tail between my legs and slithered back to our closet.

"That's what I thought!" I heard him say.

Twenty minutes later he came in holding his Holy Grail as if it were going to disintegrate from human touch and apologized. I told him sincerely that *I* should be apologizing, that he was right. "I just felt a bit left out."

He extended one of his hands. I stood up to pat him on the back, and he nearly cracked his head on the door, trying to get away from such an intimate act! I laughed and said, "Geez, I was just gonna pat you on the back." We laughed and forgave each other.

Leary and I conducted our first search warrant briefing. The Chief even sat in to oversee our plan. The SWAT members, K-9, and his handler were all in attendance, anxious for some excitement. We drew the diagram of the rooms and marked off the two locations where we believed the weed was hidden. Scarfo had a stepbrother that lived with him who also dealt but had his own customers, so we were hoping to find additional contraband in his room. The ruse was simple: "Use Lisa to knock on the door." *I was growing accustomed to being used as the pawn.* The team would then align themselves next to the attached garage, and I would knock. When the door opened I'd signal to Burke, who was the first guy on the stick (line of officers ready to make entry), and they would storm past me to secure the occupants.

En route to Scarfo's, squashed between eight guys randomly seated on the benches and inner wheel wells of our undercover panel van, I started singing, "I can see clearly now the rain is gone, I can see all the obstacles in our way..." and before I knew it two guys jumped in for the next verse and several others thereafter mouthing the words: "it's gonna be a bright, bright, bright sun shining day." It was a surreal moment accompanying all these hardnosed combat-ready men loaded to the hilt with weapons and shields, singing along with little miss sunshine on cold snowy day minutes away from storming a house.

While the perimeter guys held their assigned positions, the team hustled into place. It was a blustery evening and time was of the essence. A car of buyers could pull up any minute and alert Scarfo to our existence. I scurried to the front door and knocked. A young man answered and I sweetly asked, "Is Jim here? Jim overheard me and began to rise from the couch. At that moment Burke swung open the storm door, pushed me aside, and trotted past with the team. I jumped into the last position of the stick. The highly trained tactical team ended up looking like the Keystone cops; heavily armed and fully geared coppers skidded with their snow entrenched boots across the slippery ceramic tiled foyer. We were grabbing for air, trying to break the domino-like falls.

Through this unfortunate circumstance, however, we could see a houseful of occupants, including mom and dad. As we scrambled to regain our balance, orders were barked out from all directions. "Police Search Warrant! Get down on the ground...get down on the ground, show me your hands!" Within twenty seconds, all nine of them were cuffed.

Dad started in with his usual mouthing off: "Let me see da paperwork, dis is bullshit! You don't need to cuff everyone. I wanna call my attorney. This is police brutality! Who's da boss here?"

Commander Selleck made his way in and diplomatically dealt with Scarfo Sr.

Leary and I scanned the residence to look for things that might injure the K-9, before we allowed him to conduct his first official search with the new

Nark Unit. The handler, Leary and I started our search in Scarfo's bedroom. Scarfo had decorated it with psychedelic black light posters, candles, and a coffee table loaded with overflowing cigarette butts and ashes. Beer bottles were strewn amid the laundry that lay scattered about the floor. Photographs of Scarfo and his friends showed him next to his cannabis garden, smoking from a bong and holding a pound of "dank" with one hand and a wad of cash in the other. A six-foot cabinet served as host to an assortment of multi-colored glass bongs in all shapes and sizes. *Scarfo certainly went to extreme measures to conceal his criminal activity from his parents…NOT!*

The K-9 made his way around the room, excitedly sniffing. I think he was experiencing sensory overload, indicating positively on nearly everything he came in contact with. As I followed the dog around the room I identified a few loose joints, seeds and cannabis leaves.

All of a sudden, the K-9 started an insane scratching on the second drawer of a bureau. When his handler pulled him away, Leary reached in and retrieved a key (kilo) of cannabis. We were elated. As the evidence technicians began securing and packaging the contents in Scarfo's room, Scarfo Sr. fell mute. There was no question that the parents had knowledge of their son's actions, and now Scarfo Sr. became compliant.

The search continued. We made our way into the stepbrother's room. The K-9 entered and stood in the center of the room on his hind legs, sniffing and barking toward the ceiling. A black fabric skull and crossbones banner was tacked up there. The K-9 handler swatted the fabric with the back of his hand repeatedly, until a large bag of cannabis plummeted to the floor. "Good dog!" we repeated excitedly as he vigorously wagged his tail and rubbed himself against our legs. The K-9 continued hitting mark after mark, revealing a sizeable quantity of joints and cannabis pipes.

The evidence collection team had their work cut out for them. We, however, were wrapping up. As an afterthought, someone asked if we had searched the daughter's room. She was thirteen, and mom and dad Scarfo were extremely protective of her. They made quite the scene when she was temporarily handcuffed, stating, "She's just a baby, leave her out of this!" The search warrant included all rooms in the house, and since we had the dog there, we decided to have him do a quick sweep.

To our shock, the K-9 did his freak-out on top of the girl's dainty white vanity table, knocking all the contents that lined the shelf onto the floor. Assuming it was the dog's first false indication by his handler's display of irritation, I began scrambling to pick up the items before mom and dad went berserk. But as I gathered the tiny pieces of scattered jewelry that lay spilled from her Tinker Bell jewelry box, I couldn't believe my eyes—a joint! The Scarfo Princess had a joint stashed in her Tinker Bell jewelry box! One of the evidence techs immediately came in to seize a photo-op before running down to show ma and pa Scarfo what little Miss Innocent had in her bedroom. Without even questioning their daughter, dad cried, "You assholes planted that in there!" All we could do was shake our heads and laugh; some people just don't understand the concept of accountability.

After arresting nearly the entire family, a celebration was in order. Leary and I treated our colleagues to a pizza party back at the Department. The K-9 and his handler definitely proved their worth and were recognized as our MVPs. Leary and I had a private moment in our closet. We gave each other knowing looks, and the dreaded handshake made its way toward me. But this time I went in for a hug, which he stiffly tolerated.

"Well, you did it, Charlie's Angel," Leary said with a hint of sarcasm.

"You know what they're callin' you behind your back?" I asked in retaliation.

Leary exhibited paranoia regarding what people said about him.

"Bosley," I said.

He laughed. "What! Who's sayin' that?"

No one actually said it. I'd made it up a few days earlier when a fellow cop referred to me as Charlie's Angel. Trying to take the heat off I asked him, "Know what *they* call Leary?" When I said, "Bosley," the cop laughed so hard I figured it was a keeper, and I wouldn't be pegged as the originator. I told a white lie: "I heard it in roll call the other day." Technically, I did hear it... after *I* said it, that is. Leary was still laughing so I surmised he was receptive. From that day on it stuck. Boz and Angel were on their way.

* * * * *

The Boz and Angel dance card became full over the next year. We were working so many cases at the same time, we could barely keep track of our informants. Our pagers and cells buzzed all hours of the day and weekends. Our colleagues were calling us on our days off to interview their criminals who always had "great drug information." We could never say no. This caused some strain on Boz' relationship with his wife, Pam. He'd often have to leave family events to do surveillance or interview a criminal. Pam struggled between trying to be supportive and making Boz choose between their relationship and the job. Even though I, too, had a man at home, Dean was different; he just kind of went with the flow.

I'd often return home after a shift and recap my exciting day. When I asked Dean about his day, *which was usually a complete replication of the one before for my truck-driver-by-day, rock-star-by-night boyfriend,* he would try to compete by sharing the stress of dealing with his inept dispatcher. A dinner conversation would go something like this. Me: "Wow sweetie, so they made you drive clear across town for a delivery when another driver could have handled the run. That must be so frustrating for you. By the way, yesterday, when I executed that search warrant, I found a Mac-10 assault rifle hidden under a false plate under this gangster's bureau. Tonight I'll be on surveillance with Bosley for that armed robber we think may be one of the kingpins for the West Side Chapter of the Hell's Angels. Oh yeah by the way, remember that Ecstasy case I was workin' on for the last six weeks? Boz and I are two days away from setting up the top soldier with a controlled buy."

After one too many days of sharing my stories, Dean started to feel intimidated. He would share less and less. Because of this, I'd tone down my day to keep it as equally placid and mundane as his. For example, I'd say; "I went with some informant and bought a couple of pills of ecstasy from this scraggily dude, pretty uneventful." In reality, it was a boatload of Super X and the guy was ready to flip on the main supplier from Texas. I was trying to become less significant in order to show Dean that my job could be just as ordinary as his. All to salvage his precious ego. But, just like Tony, he was also frightened by my education. While I was going for my Master's Degree, Dean questioned his self worth. He would often say, "What are you doing with a guy like me? You should be with a doctor or lawyer."

This form of rejection made me want to prove to him that he was worthy and I was the same spontaneous sexy woman he'd first met. I was still physically attracted to him and even more so after I saw him perform on stage.

For a large part of 1999 and 2000, I made every effort to get the weekend evenings off to support him at his performances. While there, I had to deal with intoxicated fans and groupies coming on to him, girls flashing their tits and sneaking their phone numbers to him and offering him blow jobs left and right. I wore my bravest face during all of this and even resorted to dressing more and more provocatively to keep my guy interested. He enjoyed the attention from the women and often egged on their behavior. When I questioned this, he explained, "It's all part of the performance. You know I love you."

On the flip side, Dean was tantalized by having other men ogle me...it was a huge turn-on for him to see men approach me at his shows. We even played these games where we pretended not to know each other at some of his performances. When some unwitting guy would hit on me, Dean would walk up and plant a sultry kiss on me and walk away while I pretended not to know him and vice versa. I wasn't sure if this was his way of acclimating me for a potential ménage, or if he just enjoyed the cheap thrill. Of course I was hoping for the latter. If this is what he needed to keep our relationship stimulating, then I was happy to oblige.

CHAPTER 15
ANOTHER FAREWELL

Dean and I had sustained our four-and-a-half- year ride together by remaining perfectly content in our easygoing relationship. I suppressed his three-way sex-capade offers. We had no routine during the week because of our conflicting work schedules but enjoyed weekends at his performances. We remained physically attracted to each other, due largely to the fact that our time together was so limited. We shared the household chores and expenses and rarely argued. It was a simple existence. Dean liked things simple. Simple worked for me too, as I devoted more time to my career and education.

But in July of 2001, I reached a turning point. While vacationing in Europe with my two best friends, Tracy and Kelly, I asked, "Do you think it's possible to have a relationship with a man like *we* have together?" This question provoked some deep soul searching. One of the minor differences Dean and I had was our feeling about travel. My friends and I loved to travel and ventured overseas annually. Dean had no interest in it. He believed that was something "old retired people do."

We visited places like Buckingham Palace, drove across the Highlands of Scotland, walked through castle ruins, and experienced the splendor of Ireland, and all I could think was, *I need a man in my life that can appreciate and share this magnificence with me, now! Not when I'm retired.*

I needed a man in my life that wanted something more. As I achieved goal after goal within the department, maintained straight A's in grad school, and began volunteering at a homeless shelter, I became dissatisfied with the lack of *variety* Dean brought to the table. In 1999, Dean missed an opportunity to audition as the replacement for singer Steve Perry in the rock band Journey. His lack of drive and ambition to move beyond driving a truck wasn't enough for me anymore. I had my life mapped out. Every year I would set goal after goal and do whatever it took to achieve them. He would watch and cheer me on. I wanted to cheer him on, but he would tell me time after time, "I'm not like you. I don't care about what's going to happen three months from now, let alone next year."

I couldn't swallow what he was telling me. He truly had no interest in any of my extra-curricular activities. I felt as if I were the only one who initiated conversations, and I desperately needed more mental stimulation.

During that European vacation, I also noticed that I didn't miss him and phoned less frequently than I had on trips past. In my mind I decided that Dean and I were finished, and three weeks later, after one of his performances, I clued him in.

It took another one of those strange catalysts to push me. While watching Dean perform, a female fan realized I was his girlfriend and hurled verbal insults at me. Her drunkenness got the best of her, as indicated by her desire to "kick my ass" for no reason more than that the man she longed for was in a relationship with me. As usual, I ignored the comment. She approached me with a mini-entourage and *accidentally* spit in my face as she slurred more profanities. With that, I grasped her hair and swiftly brought her to her knees. The bouncer, whom I knew, arrived in a flash and escorted her and two of her friends out. This moment of truth shot through me, as it had with Tony, and I knew it was time to say goodbye. Such an ugly incident over a man I knew I would be leaving. It was as if I needed this event to solidify my desire to end "us."

I was speechless on the drive home. Dean was confused about what had occurred, because he was in the middle of a performance; but he knew I was not proud of it.

The following morning after a silent breakfast I said, "We need to talk."

"I know…things have felt different since your return from Europe."

"I don't think either of us is getting all of our needs met together and I want to dissolve our relationship."

His eyes became transfixed on a wall. After an uncomfortable silence, he said in a robotic tone, "When do you want me out?"

"As soon as possible."

He abruptly stood and proclaimed, "Geez you don't waste any time giving me the boot!"

This reminded me of Tony's sentiment during the dispensation of our household goods, and I couldn't help but feel a bit cold about how I handled it. Recovering, I said apologetically, "Well, of course, I don't expect you to leave tomorrow...do what you need to do to find a place."

Tony had allowed me to continue living in his home for nearly three months after the divorce was final.

Several days later I headed downtown for a three-day Anthony Robbins seminar. I was grateful to be getting out of the house, away from Dean, and even more grateful to be attending a seminar that I believed would get me on track for what I was truly looking to accomplish in my life. The seminar proved to be more than I expected. I found new ways to understand my driving forces and broke through some barriers I'd held regarding self-worth in relationships. Because I believed that kind of psychology was something I could swallow, I signed up for the whole program and would be leaving for Hawaii in a few weeks for the next event. I called Dean to give him the green light to remove his belongings from the house while I was away to avoid any emotional drama for either of us.

Somehow I returned from Hawaii rejuvenated, considering 9/11 occurred during the event. Valuing life even more after the terror attack on the U.S., I made the decision to take all areas of my life to another level. One of the most rewarding exercises of the seminar provided clarity by showing me how I could actually design the kind of man I wanted in my life. I even decided to run my first marathon in New York City that fall. I was growing and ready to challenge my former way of thinking and embrace yet another new beginning.

CHAPTER 16
WOLF SINGS

For me, transitioning into single life meant devoting even more time to the J.O.B. Boz and I were on a roll with no end in sight. Our days bled into one another as we continued to chalk up arrest after arrest; developed a large database of viable informants, worked long grueling hours on surveillance, wrote lengthy airtight police reports, developed probable cause for search warrants (keeping the SWAT team busy) and should have set up cots for the amount of time we spent in court testifying. I wondered how a person could actually juggle a personal life in the midst of all of this.

I adapted to the solitude at home and rather enjoyed living alone. Emotionally I was through with Dean. But sadly, as time passed, out of pure carnal desire I would occasionally seek out a more than willing Dean. I was controlling our encounters and felt empowered. I really knew what it felt like to think and behave like a man.

On November 6, 2001 Detective Burke was asked to follow-up on a string of similar retail thefts occurring at a local department store. Several suspects, two men and one woman, were developed from information provided by the store clerk to the initial reporting officer. When Burke realized several businesses in surrounding cities were experiencing similar thefts, he activated the Southwest Major Case Unit (SMCU) to assist.

Next day, Burke and the SMCU conducted surveillance on the three suspects, who were observed entering an electronics store. Members of the team posed as shoppers while they watched the suspects work their way through the store. The two male suspects began looking at cordless telephones. Shortly after, one suspect distracted an employee with questions while the other managed to smuggle a telephone into his jacket and leave the store. Several minutes later the remaining male and female left the building and met the other inside their vehicle.

The idea was to tail them to see where they would try to get rid of their stolen items. The surveillance tail led to a pawnshop, where one of the suspects attempted to sell the phone. All three were apprehended and brought into the station for investigation. Of the three, Bone confessed to being the mastermind and admitted to more than a hundred thefts, spanning seven towns within the last four months. Burke certainly had a gift for making people feel comfortable about revealing their innermost thoughts! Bone also said that he was a recovering heroin addict and was using the money to support his lady's heroin habit. He had a personal incentive for providing information about his main source for unloading the stolen items: by assisting us with the apprehension of a main fencer, Bone might receive a lesser charge in court.

Later that afternoon, the dicks (detectives) contacted me for an undercover. I looked forward to another chance to sell stolen goods. Last time was with the Mafia, and I'd learned a lot since then. I was introduced to Bone and told that I would be posing as his girlfriend, in order to meet Wolf—Bone's source. Bone was about 5'9" and thin with sandy brown hair, a quick talker, articulate and street smart. He had zero trepidation over my escorting him to sell Wolf stolen goods.

"Yeah, you could come with me, but I'll do the first sell. That way he can get used to you," Bone said.

At 9:30 p.m., with three cordless phones to sell, I drove Bone to a seedy bar called the Dark-n-Low Pub on Chicago's south side. "On the way there Bone said, "I always wanted to be a cop." *They all wanna be cops.* Boz and I noticed a pattern with these criminals. Once they've gotten a taste of working as informants, they mistakenly believe that buying drugs or selling stolen goods is all that cops do. They're clueless about what it takes to put a case together, process crime scenes, collect evidence, formulate a solid police report and credibly testify against some of the most dangerous criminals on the streets who are represented by the best attorneys that their drug money can buy. I'd gotten used to humoring these guys.

"So why don't you go for it?"

"Yeah, I should. That's what my mom tells me I should do. Once I'm done helpin' you guys out, I'm gonna start lookin' into it. If I had a felony arrest in the past do I still qualify to become a cop?"

How utterly ridiculous.

Still feigning support, I sighed. "Well that's a tough one. There are ways to get your felony record eradicated provided you stay outta trouble for a specific amount of time."

"Yeah, that's what I thought."

I'm sure he did.

The Pub was in the middle of a residential block in a rundown area of town. Bone told me that Wolf lived next door to a vacant lot that separated his residence from the Pub, but spent most of his time at Dark-n-Low. We pulled up, and Bone hopped out of my car to see if Wolf was inside. Seconds later, he returned; Wolf had instructed Bone to meet him in front of his house while he got cash. We watched as Wolf exited the back door of the Pub, crossed the lot and entered the back door of his residence. He stood about 6'3" and 260 pounds, resembling a woodsman with his flannel shirt and black, scruffy beard.

After several minutes, Wolf emerged and walked up to the broken chain link fence in the middle of the lot. I stayed in the car for the first transaction, so as not to spook him. I opened the window and shouted a "Hey" to Wolf when Bone pointed in my direction. Bone introduced me as "his babe" and said, "She helped me pick up today's load."

Wolf gave me a disinterested nod. He was preoccupied, looking up and down the street and over his shoulder for cops. Bone handed our three cordless phones to Wolf through a two-foot hole in the fence. Wolf accepted them, but explained that he'd only brought enough cash for two phones. He handed Bone $70, promised to be right back with the balance, and returned to the Dark-n-Low.

Bone gave me the money and assured me that Wolf wasn't suspicious of my presence. I told him, "Yeah, especially now that he knows no cops are in sight."

Bone laughed. "Now that the intro is behind us, next time you can get out of the car and do the deal with me."

Wolf returned with $25, ten bucks less than usual, because the third phone didn't have an answering machine. *Finicky thieves.*

Bone then told Wolf that I worked at an electronics store and could steal anything. Wolf's eyes lit up, and he smiled. "Oh yeah? Have her get me CD burners, 35 mm cameras, small portable TVs, headphones and telephones with answering machines." *Geez, this guy really knew what he wanted.*

I shouted out, "I could do a pick-up tomorrow."

Wolf nodded, and Bone gave me a thumbs-up—they both beamed at me. Then Wolf walked back to the Pub and called out, "Give me a jingle tomorrow."

The SMCU was satisfied with the success of the operation, and Bone was returned to his jail cell until tomorrow's deal. *Piece of cake.* I truly found my calling.

On November 8th, at around five p.m., Bone and I arrived at the Dark-n-Low with three small televisions and a cordless telephone. Bone ran inside the pub and returned, claiming, "No one's seen Wolf all day, so I hit the bartender chick up for his home phone number."

It turned out Wolf was indulging in a siesta, but he agreed to see us in ten minutes. A short time later he met us both at the hole in the chain link fence, and we handed him our wares. Wolf started to play hardball with the prices.

"I can only give ya $30 for the TVs. I only get fifty for 'em. It's gotta be worth my while."

Bone whined, "C'mon man, my girl steals this stuff and we gotta split."

I interjected, "Those TVs sell for one-twenty-nine. Can't you give us forty?"

This agitated him. He snapped, "I know how much they go for, I got all kinds of this shit in the house!" Still trying to show us who the boss was, he added, "You're only getting twenty for the phones because they don't got answering machines!"

Not wanting to push him as I did with the Mafia pudge pot, I changed the subject. "Can you unload laptops? I got a buddy working the dock at the store."

Now composed, he collected his wares and said, "Yeah, no problem, I'll be right back."

Bone and I waited at the fence snickering over how cheap Wolf was. He returned with $110 and said, "Catch ya later," before sauntering back to his house.

Once again, the SMCU was pleased with our success and immediately got the ball rolling for the execution of a search warrant. Our original intention was to search Wolf's residence, but since he'd gone into the Dark-n-Low to retrieve cash for one of the sales, we now had enough probable cause to search the pub as well. *A double whammy!*

Within minutes of our sale, I deposited Bone with a uniformed officer and climbed into the back of a waiting van, where I geared up with my vest and Glock. A case unit sergeant, three detectives, and I coordinated to simultaneously storm the Dark-n-Low, while Selleck, Burke, and his posse of detectives did the same at Wolf's residence. Like two rows of falling dominoes, our teams hit our marks as planned. Wolf was immediately taken into custody. I guess looking over one's shoulder is overrated. It's the "babe" in the car that'll get you every time.

Burke again worked his magic and had Wolf howling about everything he knew. After being read his Miranda Rights, he promptly told Burke he'd hidden stolen property in a crawlspace in the basement and might have a few items in the apartment above the Dark-n-Low. All of the property Bone and I had sold him was still in the house, as well as boxes filled with additional stolen merchandise. A plate of cannabis was also found on top of Wolf's refrigerator. *Drugs and thievery go hand-in-hand.*

Meanwhile at Dark-n-Low, Sgt. Degnan asked Jill, the bartender, for identification. She asked if she could retrieve her license from her purse. Degnan asked if she had any drugs or weapons in the purse, and she replied, "Yes," before handing over a small folded piece of paper that contained a white powdery substance. *Talk about honest criminals.* As I took Jill into custody for possession of cocaine, another detective conversed with a man who was making his way down the stairs from an apartment behind the Dark-n-Low. The detective explained that a search warrant was being conducted for stolen property; the man said that he did not have any stolen property in his apartment but did have some "blow" in his bedroom. *Yet another criminal with good moral ethics.*

There was something about the contagious integrity of these criminals on this particular day that threw us all for a loop.

The man further signed a consent-to-search form and did everything short of opening the door for the detective. The cocaine was recovered from the suspect's room, and no other stolen property was found. That suspect, too, was taken into custody and brought back to headquarters, along with Jill.

At the police station, Burke interviewed Jill and informed Boz and me that she was willing to "cooperate" with the police by supplying information about her drug source. After two weeks with no contact from Jill, we assumed she'd changed her mind, as many criminals do when weighing the pros and cons of "narking" on their source. Bone took his lumps, cooperated with the state and pled guilty, thus receiving a minimum sentence.

CHAPTER 17
BLACKIE'S DOUBLE-CROSS

Here's an example of how cases can bleed into one another. A few weeks after Jill's arrest at the Dark-N-Low Pub she called Burke, having decided to work off her crime by providing information about her drug source. But when Burke asked what information Jill could provide, she became nervous, confessing she feared for her life if she named her source, let alone set him up. What Jill had in mind was to have "a friend" work off her crime. She'd been socializing with one of the bar patrons and had told him about her dilemma. The patron, a sixty-eight-year-old man named Blackie, was enamored with Jill and willing to tap into his pool of drug resources to assist her. Burke requested that Jill have Blackie telephone him.

Blackie called Burke the following day. He spoke with a gravelly Southern accent, asking Burke matter-of-factly, "Whatta y'all want me to do to get this kid outta trouble?"

Burke asked, "What can you give us?"

He became angry. "I asked you, whatta y'all need to get this kid outta trouble? I ain't playin' games!"

Burke, the king of rapport, told Blackie he wasn't into games either and wanted to know if he was able to put us in contact with a major cocaine supplier. After Blackie responded, "It's my dime, that's why I called," Burke told Blackie to contact the drug unit and turned the case over to Boz and me.

Blackie came into the police station to be interviewed. He looked more like eighty. He wore a black nylon heating-and-cooling supply jacket and a pair of faded blue work pants. His hair was gray with sparse strands flapped across the top; his face was wrinkled and weathered, like that of a farmer. His body was skeletal and he stood maybe 5'6" tall. After receiving his requested black coffee, he sat in the interview room he'd already contaminated with residual cigarette smoke and muttered, "I ain't got all day, git a pen, this is what I got!"

I read Boz' anguished face and saw that Blackie's crusty attitude was getting to him. I, on the other hand, got a kick out of the old crank and got my pen ready. Blackie provided us with two sources. One of them was promptly investigated, but we determined the bad guy didn't trust Blackie enough to go along with our plan, so we nixed it. Instead we opted for Blackie's second source. He told us about a woman who was a crack whore and a heroin addict. She was well connected to major drug dealers on the south side of Chicago, and he felt she would be an easy target.

A drug deal was set up at Hooters Restaurant in June of 2002 between Kiki the prostitute and me. Blackie had supposedly told Kiki that I was a stripper looking to buy cocaine. Two hours before the scheduled purchase, Boz and I got a phone call from Blackie, who said that he would be bringing Kiki to Hooters to meet me. We didn't like surprises and suspected that Blackie was trying to take advantage of what he thought were two rookie detectives. *Why would Blackie want to be so close to the operation if he didn't have to be?* We knew that he was out to impress Jill. Perhaps he was getting anxious to get this over with, so he could collect his "reward" from her. Finally we decided there wasn't much harm in having Blackie bring Kiki to Hooters; after all, it was his decision to get burned. Knowing Blackie, we didn't take him for a man who was concerned about some "crack whore" seeking retaliation against him.

Selleck and one of the female detectives sat at a bar table in Hooters, wearing plain clothes, pretending to be patrons. Bosley and Burke sat at the table to my rear. I sat at the bar alone, keeping an eye on the front door. I sipped a glass of wine, as if I were a high-end stripper, and looked over the menu. Fifteen minutes later, Blackie—who'd cleaned up a bit by slicking his hair over to one side—walked through the front door with a blonde. Her scraggly hair was uncombed, and she wore tight jeans and a low-cut blouse that exposed her bony chest. Dark rings framed her eyes, and her cheeks were gaunt and sunken. She wore at least six tarnished silver necklaces, twisted and tangled, with an array of tacky charms. Her fingernails were cracked, and dirty, and she reeked of cigarette smoke.

Blackie walked toward me, kissed my cheek, and said, "Hi sweetie."

I instantly felt skuzzy and knew my comrades were going to be razzing me later for Blackie's surprise move. But I smiled and said, "Hey buddy."

Kiki nervously waited for direction. Blackie said, "Well y'all go ahead and take care of yer business, I'll wait for ya outside."

I rose from my bar stool and told Kiki, "Let's go into the bathroom."

She followed like a lost puppy. Once inside, I opened my purse and reapplied my lipstick as I waited for a woman to finish washing her hands. Kiki said, "You got pretty hair." Deliverance *flashed through my mind.*

With the hand-washer barely out the door, Kiki suddenly handed me a small cardboard ring box. I opened it and saw two 1.5 gram baggies of cocaine. I asked her, How much did you want for this, again?"

"I don't know, how much did Blackie tell you?"

I replied, dumbfounded, "Did you get this from one of your regulars?"

"No, Blackie had it in his car before he picked me up and told me I was gonna meet some stripper and give it to her. He said he'd give me thirty bucks to do it."

Son of a bitch! He'd set *us* up. I had to laugh inside—Blackie thought he could outsmart us. I decided to continue with the sale and handed Kiki the $250 that Blackie had originally quoted, then allowed her to walk out the front door, where detectives waited to scoop her up.

I immediately phoned Bosley and told him, "Take Blackie down too!" He'd been seen pulling out of the parking lot earlier. Two exterior surveillance cops tracked him down less than a mile away and pulled him down. When Boz and I arrived at the site, Blackie was already in cuffs. Bosley jumped out of the car and got nose to nose with him.

"Because you want to play games and waste our time, you're both goin' to jail! You're lookin' at six years for delivering cocaine to an undercover cop."

Blackie exclaimed, "Why? What'd she tell you? She's a lyin' bitch!"

We brought both of them to lock-up, where they sat less than three feet from each other, cuffed to the bench. Kiki ordered Blackie, "You better tell them the truth."

Blackie barked back, "I don't know what you're talking about, shut your mouth!"

We brought Kiki upstairs to our interview room and allowed her to give her version of what happened. Through tears, she again claimed that Blackie had asked her to take a ride with him and hand some cocaine to a stripper at Hooters for $30. We believed her. She further revealed that she was a heroin addict and never messed with cocaine. She worked as a call girl to support her habit. To our surprise, she revealed that she meets her "Johns" at a motel in our jurisdiction. She said that she would be willing to set up one of her main heroin suppliers to get herself out of trouble. Boz and I truly felt that Kiki was a victim of circumstance and put her back in lock-up until we decided what to do with her.

Bosley decided he wasn't finished reading Blackie the riot act and reminded him how much time he would be spending in the penitentiary. "You won't be free again until your 84th birthday!"

For the first time Blackie looked scared and said, "Get me outta deez cuffs and let me talk to y'all."

Bosley told him he was finished talking, and we returned to our office to assess a new game plan. As we thought about exploring Kiki's heroin supplier, we learned that Blackie was having a heart attack in his cell and had been transported to the local hospital. Selleck made the decision to release Blackie without charges; it seemed the horny old man had enough problems with his medical condition.

CHAPTER 18
THE CALL GIRLS
GET THEIR FIX

The case gained momentum. Kiki was forthcoming with information regarding her main heroin supplier. She revealed that literally hours before she'd arrived at Hooters to sell me cocaine, she picked up heroin from Caruso. He had been supplying Kiki regularly for four years.

Her usual order was six "bags" (heroin wrapped in a tiny square of folded tinfoil), which cost $20 each. She described Caruso as late thirties, short with a medium build and a hot temper. Kiki had been to his apartment on many occasions, knew that he was unemployed, and she'd seen where he kept his "stash."

Boz and I decided to set up a controlled heroin buy with Caruso later that evening. Kiki was nervous and asked if she could smoke a cigarette before making the call. We escorted her outdoors to a secluded area, where she could make calls and smoke. We rehearsed a simple explanation for why Kiki was buying twice in one day. As she nervously finished her cigarette, I spoke to her calmly, assuring her that she was going to do fine.

Kiki placed the call on our undercover phone: "Hey it's me again. I was wondering if you can do another run today."

"For you?"

"Yeah, this girl at the service needs a few."

161

"What girl at the service?"

"Tawny, she's okay, I've known her for two months."

"You getting 'em for her?"

"She's meeting me at the motel on Damen in an hour."

"You know I don't work like that, Kiki."

"I know…just meet me this one time, she's got cash, and I'll get a few more for your trouble."

"How many you want?"

"Fifteen…five more for me and ten for her."

"I'm down to four; I'll have to take a ride to Western first. It's gonna be three hundred plus another fifty for traveling."

Kiki repeated Caruso's statement out loud and asked me if that was okay. *Not part of the plan. Now Caruso was aware that she's relaying the information to someone.*

I got into call-girl character and responded abrasively, loud enough for Caruso to hear, "Yeah, but tell him to hurry, I've got a *date* in a couple of hours."

Kiki began to repeat my words to Caruso, but he cut her off.

"I heard her, you idiot! "Don't be callin' me in front of people."

"Sorry. She's cool, she won't say nothin'."

"I'm headed out and should be there in about an hour. I'll call when I get close…and Kiki, don't fuck me on this!"

Now I needed to transform quickly from a high-end stripper to a heroin-addicted call girl. Bosley loved this, advising me to "dirty up" in order to resemble Kiki. I started scrounging around the department and borrowed things from the female staff. They found it amusing when I requested the use of mismatched hair accessories and aid with ratting my hair. I traded classy jewelry, black satin flare pants, and a lace camisole for a pair of tight jeans, a faded black t-shirt and gym shoes. I put a few mismatching barrettes in my newly ratted hair. I removed most of my makeup but piled on the mascara, trying to create unappealing clumps and smears on my eyelids. I topped everything off with Bosley's oversized Notre Dame jacket. Then I tucked my gun into the small of my back and was ready to go.

At 7:30 p.m. we had Kiki phone Caruso for an ETA. He said, "I'm tied up in fuckin' traffic. Meet me near the restrooms of the restaurant next to the motel," and abruptly hung up.

Not good. There were two restaurants next to the motel, and it was imperative that we had the right one. We were forced to have Kiki call her supplier back, well aware he was already agitated. This time Caruso didn't pick up the phone; instead it was his driver, Barberio. He told Kiki that Caruso had stepped out of the car to take a leak. Kiki had told us earlier that Barberio might be driving Caruso and usually showed up in a black Jeep Wrangler. I instructed Kiki to ask him if he was going to be in his Jeep. Barberio confirmed that he'd be in the Jeep.

Barberio did not know which restaurant Caruso wanted to meet at, however, and asked us to call back in ten minutes. I surmised that Caruso was not in a men's room, but was actually picking up drugs.

Ten minutes later, Kiki called back. Caruso answered. "You didn't tell me which restaurant," she said.

"I don't care, go to the chicken place, I'm almost there."

We needed to scramble. Kiki and I went inside; I ordered a chicken sandwich for her and fries for myself. There were only two other patrons in the restaurant. I led Kiki to a table next to a window where I could see the traffic on Damen, as well as the entrance to the parking lot. We needed bodies and arranged for Selleck and Rattan to order food and sit six tables away from us, with a visual of the front window as well. We had two officers in the adjacent parking lots and one parked at a restaurant across the street.

A few minutes later, I watched a black Jeep pull into the same parking lot across the street. Seconds later, a man climbed out and crossed the busy four-lane street.

"It's him, it's him!" Kiki exclaimed.

My heart began to thud. I told Kiki to face me and stop watching Caruso. He came in the side door, looked our way, and ordered a drink before casually walking over to our table. He sat next to Kiki, avoiding eye contact with me.

Kiki started in, "This is my friend—"

Caruso interrupted. "I don't like this, I don't know her and you know I don't work like this."

I interjected, "Listen…don't get pissed at her, it's my money and I wasn't gonna let her walk with it."

He looked at me as if I were his worst enemy, *intuitive criminal,* and sat silent a moment. I broke the silence: "If you feel more comfortable we could go in the motel and make the exchange."

My instincts told me Caruso was anxious to get the deal over, and with the rise of cop programs on television showing police busting down motel room doors after drug buys, I felt confident he didn't want a change of venue. Thank God he didn't, because we didn't have a motel room, and my surveillance team would have freaked if they'd seen me leave with them.

Caruso looked me in the eye again and asked, "You a cop?"

I sarcastically responded, "Yeah, a cop that moonlights as a whore for extra cash."

I then extended my hand under the table and attempted to pass him his $350.

"No disrespect but I'm late for a date."

He looked around the restaurant and snapped at Kiki, "Get the money, I'm not takin' it from her."

Caruso, like many ignorant criminals, thought that if he didn't physically take the money from me, then he had not committed a crime. When he saw the cash in Kiki's hand, he snatched it from her. Then he reached into his back pocket, pulled out a black nylon wallet, and handed it to Kiki, who gave it to me. I ripped open the Velcro to ensure the heroin was inside. There were fifteen tinfoil packets wrapped in cellophane; satisfied, I told Kiki to meet me in the bathroom to claim her share.

Before we could stand up, Caruso headed for the door. I lifted my hair three times, grasping it into a ponytail to signal to the indoor detective team that the deal was successful. They scurried from their table and followed Caruso, signaling the exterior surveillance to get him in custody before Barberio had a chance to see what was happening. Meanwhile the detective watching Barberio waited for the signal that the buy was successful. Caruso tried to make a run for it when he heard, "Stop, Police!" Unfortunately,

Barberio heard the screeching tires of cop cars closing in on Caruso and saw him being tackled to the ground. Barberio peeled out of the parking lot as police officers approached and demanded that he exit his vehicle. He was eventually boxed in by two marked squads four blocks away.

Back at the station, I gave Kiki a cover story. In the event Caruso or Barberio contacted her, she would pretend she had no knowledge that I was a cop. She would tell them that I must have infiltrated the service to put them out of business—that she was just as shocked as they were to discover Tawny was an undercover cop. I then released a grateful Kiki and made myself scarce, allowing Bosley to interview Caruso.

"You ain't got shit. I was goin' to the motel to get a fifteen dollar blowjob and she didn't show, no crime there." Caruso refused to make any further statements without a lawyer and was put back into his cell. Barberio, on the other hand, cried and sent Caruso down the river without a paddle, as most accomplices do. He divulged in a written statement that he has driven for Caruso at least twelve other times for drug deals. Today, Caruso gave him $10 up front for gas and promised him an additional $20 after the deal.

After the interviews, I visited the boys in their cells individually. *It was time for damage control.* We had placed them on opposite sides of the jail so that were not able to communicate. I thanked Barberio for being forthright with his statement. He was a big boy, also in his late thirties. I told him, "While I was infiltrating a prostitution ring, I met Kiki. When I found out she was addicted to heroin, I took advantage of her and asked her if she could score some heroin for me."

Barberio barely looked up at me as he said, "Am I gonna do time?"

I gave my cliché response, "That's up to the judge, but Detective Leary and I will be sure to tell him how cooperative you've been in our custody."

I then walked over to Caruso's cell. He lay on his back with his hands behind his head. I said, "Hello Jim, I'm Detective Lockwood."

He glared at me and said, "I knew it, that bitch set me up."

"Yeah she was the easiest one at the service. I worked there for two months, locked up a couple of "Johns" and pretended to be her friend. Next thing I knew she trusted me enough to set me up with her heroin supplier, and here you are. She still doesn't know I'm a cop but I'm sure when you get released you'll be making it public so I guess I'm finished at the service, but that's okay there are more fish…"

Caruso appeared to have believed my story and for the first time looked concerned and said, "So what's gonna happen to me now?"

"That's up to the judge."

Both men made their bond two days later and I received an alarming phone call from Kiki soon after. She told me that two men entered her apartment and ripped her and her sleeping boyfriend out of their bed and pummeled them. They were thrown across the room and beaten for several minutes. They said, "You know who this is from."

Kiki told me they were friends of Caruso's and she believed the landlord was paid off to let them into her apartment. Her apartment was out of our jurisdiction so we were not able to take an official police report. As much as we wanted to follow up with the battery and go after Caruso for tampering with a witness, it didn't matter, neither of them wanted to sign complaints against the men or report it. We told Kiki it would be difficult for us to protect her if she didn't cooperate, but she decided to endure it alone.

After checking in with Kiki over the next few weeks, we learned that there were no new threats, and Blackie even showed up to apologize for setting her up with us the first time. Fortunately, we learned that Caruso had not retaliated against her again. Ironically, she thanked us for not arresting her and wasn't too concerned about Caruso any longer.

For Baberio's decision to make $30 assisting Caruso, Boz and I (and the department, of course) became the proud new owners of his black Jeep Wrangler. Caruso served thirty days in jail and was given two years intensive probation. Ironic how our criminal justice system works at times; the getaway guy pays more for his crime than the actual dealer.

Days later, Blackie called and apologized for setting us up. He had undergone triple by-pass surgery and was grateful to be alive. Seizing the opportunity to play a prank on Bosley, I pulled out a Polaroid photo we had taken of Blackie and wrote in red ink along the border, "Bosley's 1st Kill."

When he arrived in the office and saw it taped to his cabinet, he grinned and said, "Take that down."

I told him, "No, its official, the first man you killed in the line of duty."

He wasn't amused. "He's not dead. He had a heart attack, asshole."

"Yeah well, you're the reason he was taken to the hospital, telling him he won't see the light of day till his 84th birthday, thus bringing on the heart attack that caused his death. I just got notice from the hospital."

"Are you serious?"

I started singing an impromptu tease song to a tune from the *Wizard of Oz:* "Ding dong Blackie's dead, Blackie's dead, ding dong my partner killed the old man."

He looked at me with daggers. "Fuckhead, are you serious, did he die?"

I looked at him earnestly and said, "Yes, I better let the Commander know; I'm sure there's going to be a lawsuit. Don't worry; it wasn't really your fault."

As I started for the door, he still appeared skeptical.

I returned to the office and sat down with my back to Boz, allowing him to stew for a few more minutes. Finally he ripped down the Polaroid and said, "Are you nuts putting this up on my cabinet, advertising that I killed someone?" Now I had *him* admitting to killing someone. "What if the Chief walked by and saw it?"

"I would tell him that it was just a joke. That the guy is not really dead."

"He's not dead?" Bosley asked.

"No, he called me today to thank us for releasing him and was sorry for what he did."

"You're demented, Lockwood. I'm serious, there's something really wrong with you!"

All work and no play makes Jane a dull girl. Yes, it was time to hit up Dean again for another interlude. I justified it by telling myself I was too busy to meet people socially. Besides, it was easy to show up on his doorstep and indulge in unadulterated, no-strings-attached sex. It was a revelation for me. Maybe Boz is right, I am a man trapped in a woman's body. It was easy for me to carry on this way and go home to an empty house and live for my career.

On December 6th, nearly four months since we broke up and what would have been our five-year anniversary, I paid Dean another visit. He escorted me to my car and said, "You know I'll always love you, Lisa."

I was speechless. The last thing I wanted to do was lead him on and end up hurting him. I asked, "Do you harbor any thoughts of us ever getting back together?"

"Does *will you marry me* answer your question?"

Gulp. That came out of left field. My throat dried and my eyes welled up.

"I'm so sorry, Dean. I didn't mean to lead you on. I really enjoyed our time together and thought it was win/win. I don't want to do this anymore. The last thing I wanted to do is hurt you."

He never said another word to me and walked back to his house. I broke down in tears as I drove off. *Marry him? He asked me to marry him.* That was the last thing I would have ever expected. I swore off Dean and decided I would only date men who wanted a win/win situation. Bosley may be right about me after all.

CHAPTER 19
CANDY WOWS THE CARNIES

I was truly starting to feel like a man and wondered how long I could live like that. I loved the power of the gun and badge and the challenge of the job, yet still yearned for something more. After 9/11 it seemed that nearly every American turned into a patriot and I, too, felt an inherent urge to protect our country. As soon as the news broke about a need for Federal Air Marshals, I applied. Surely with my background, and the fact that I don't look like a cop, I thought I'd be a shoe-in. As it turned out, me and about fifty thousand other Americans had the same urge and I was put on a waiting list. I kept my application a secret and went back to doing what I did best.

In late May of 2002, Boz had the night off and I hung around the office doing paperwork when I learned about a "hot" call at Hooters restaurant. A waitress thought a drug deal was in progress there. She was serving a group of six rowdy men and noticed a black man take a silver, cylindrical item with a small screen from his pocket. She believed the item to be some type of drug equipment. The manager did not believe the men were locals and feared having a drug transaction take place in his restaurant.

As I finished reading the notes I received a page over the P.A. system. The supervisor requested that the Drug Unit "handle it." With Boz out, I coordinated with the K-9 officer to stay available in the vicinity while I went in to investigate the matter.

I had frequented Hooters over the past seven years for both personal and work related matters, and was familiar with the managers and waitresses. I put my gun and badge in my purse, rapidly freshened up my appearance, put on a pink blouse and added lipstick. Then I walked into Hooters as "Candy."

The manager immediately made eye contact with me and smiled as I entered the establishment. I nodded, signaling for him to meet me in a corner near the restrooms. He pointed in the direction of the men and summoned their waitress to give me an update. She again attempted to describe the metallic item she'd observed in the hand of the black man. I could only assume it was a crack pipe, until I saw it for myself. She added that the group was in town for the next four days as ride-hands, aka carnies, for the carnival that was due to start the following day.

I told the waitress and the manager that I was going to take on the identity of a Hooters employee that had just completed a shift. I noticed a vacant bar table alongside the window next to the carnies and made my way over.

I walked past the group, extending a hello and my brightest smile, making flirtatious eye contact with three of them. I sat alone at my table, facing them, and pretended to make a call on my cell phone. Laughing, I created a welcoming space for my observers as I continued my animated, one-sided conversation.

They had already started whispering and talking about me. The men with their backs to me would occasionally steal a glance in my direction.

They were definitely not locals. I could hear a distinct Southern accent; one of them wore a Confederate flag shirt, and three wore ball caps, one advertising Lenny's Towing Company, another with a bright yellow John Deere, and the third a tattered Radio Shack cap. Two of the men wore greasy slicked-back ponytails, one short, one long. The only African-American in the group—the man I was most interested in—appeared to be in his mid-forties. He wore a short Afro that seemed to magnetically attract small white fragments of fuzz. His teeth were mostly brown with one capped in gold. He wore a pair of maroon dress pants with both pockets bulging out. He wore a tired, gray "Members Only" jacket with one front pocket struggling to hold on by three threads. The lot of them had grease-filled fingernails and reeked of beer and body odor. I knew I was in for a treat.

After my simulated phone call, "Flagshirt" mustered up the nerve to smile and wave at me again. I returned both as the waitress approached. Music blared as she asked if I wanted anything. I reminded her that she did not have to wait on me because of my cover as an off duty waitress. She laughed and said, "Oh yeah." It occurred to me that I should seize the opportunity and retrieved my own glass of water from the waitress station located directly on the other side of the carnies. I followed her past the men and helped myself, then returned to my table, again smiling at them.

Flagshirt finally made his grand approach, which entailed turning 180° and taking all of one step forward to reach at my table. He introduced himself and asked my name.

"Candy," I said sweetly.

He smiled from ear-to-ear, flashing his cracked and nicotine-stained teeth. "I'm from South Carolina. I've been traveling with the carnival for eighteen months."

Meanwhile his entourage was laughing and nudging one another, expressing their astonishment that Flagshirt was speaking to me. Moments later, John Deere and Long Ponytail decided to join him. They started tag-teaming me with questions, competing for my attention. I told them I was a Hooters waitress, had just gotten off work, and was waiting for my sister. John Deere was so impressed by this news that he turned to share it. "Hey, she's a Hooters waitress!" Within ten minutes from the time I first sat down, I had the entire carnie team swarming around me. The waitress came over, smiled at my progress, and served them another pitcher of beer.

I expressed an interest in their work and asked who ran which rides, assuring them how much I loved carnivals. They invited me to visit over the weekend and enjoy their respective rides for free. Unfortunately, Gold Tooth, the target of my investigation, remained reserved throughout our socializing. I knew I needed to start working him.

After all of them had revealed that they were from various Southern states and would only be in town for the long weekend, I singled out Gold Tooth and asked where he was from.

"I'm from the west side. I don't travel with the carnival. I'm an independent contractor. I run the water pistol game."

After several more flirtatious minutes, I asked Flagshirt if he smoked, gesturing with my pursed thumb and index finger, as if I were holding a joint. His eyes widened with approval, and he nodded. I asked, "You got anything on ya?"

"Naw, not wit' me, but I could get some tonight."

Once I felt Flagshirt was comfortable with this line of questioning, I asked him if any of his buddies had anything on them. They all said they didn't, but were also quick to say they, too, could score some later.

Long Ponytail opened the floodgates I'd been waiting for when he asked, "You need anything else?"

Twenty minutes in the door, and I had five out of the six willing to supply me with drugs.

"What can ya get?" I asked.

Meanwhile, Gold Tooth appeared interested in the topic of conversation and began inching closer to my left side. When I inquired about Ecstasy, none of them had a contact; "X" was too designer and too expensive for this group. I knew it, but didn't want to let on that I had any idea they were more likely to have crack or heroin. Also, Hooters waitresses do not fit the profile of crack or heroin addicts.

When I least expected it, Gold Tooth said, "I used to sell heroin, but got out of the business because it killed my brother."

"Have you ever sold crack?" I inquired.

"I don't mess with that poison anymore."

Then he laughed, lightening the moment, and said, "I stick to beer and blunts."

Now, it was no surprise that this group had smoked cannabis, nor was it a surprise that they could get their hands on other drugs. They were carnies who, after all, had a reputation of working ten or twelve hours in the hot sun, then settling into their trailers at closing to smoke pot, drink beer, and if they were lucky, solicit a few young groupie girls to join them. My job tonight was not to take down Carnie-Land. I'd gone to Hooters with the specific assignment to investigate what management thought was a crime in progress. It was evident to me that the men were not carrying any dope and were simply out to drink beer and be stimulated by pretty girls at Hooters. It didn't matter if it meant letting their guard down and disclosing all of their drug resources to an undercover Nark.

They all bought Hooters t-shirts and asked me if I would autograph them. As I sat there signing "Candy" and personalizing each shirt, Gold Tooth reached into his pocket and pulled out a small shiny metal cylinder with a screen, then began poking it with a toothpick. Still encircled by the men and their shirts, appearing mildly interested, I asked Gold Tooth what he was working on. He handed me the cylinder and told me to press the button on the back with the toothpick. I followed his instructions and was surprised by a blue flashing neon light. It was the new fad that could be seen in the hundreds at music concerts. The kids wore them on their clothing, in their hair, and even managed to stick them on their tongues—an upgrade from glow wands and necklaces. I made a spectacle out of Gold Tooth's toy, pretending to have never seen one before. I even called the waitress over to the table to show her the cool item. She took it and glanced at me with a hint of embarrassment, indicating that she was sorry for my trouble.

The carnies requested that she and I pose for a picture with them as they donned their autographed t-shirts.

So, there I was, Candy the off-duty Hooters waitress, posing for a photo with the real Hooters waitress, Gold Tooth, Flagshirt, Lenny's Towing, John Deere and Long and Short Ponytail.

As I drove back to the police department, I reflected on the event, feeling proud of my "unsung" accomplishment. Not one person on the department would really know how I'd handled the call, or recognize how the value of being a woman in that situation gave the establishment such an immediate remedy. I knew that any male colleagues would have had far more difficulty infiltrating the carnies—if they'd been able to at all—which truly made me appreciate my femininity.

CHAPTER 20
MISSY LEARNS ABOUT VD

In the midst of work, I dated men casually. During this time, I ended a month-long relationship with a commercial airline pilot. Luke was a stunner; had that sort of clean-shaven babyface look, sparkling blue eyes, a perfect set of choppers and a square jaw. The only flaw was that he was getting too serious. I couldn't let another Dean incident happen. I explained to him that I wasn't looking to start a serious relationship. It was my priority to stay focused on my career." "I understand," was his wimpy reply. Maybe it was me, intentionally attracting these weak men; like I had undergone a complete role reversal since the demise of Tony. Needless to say, I ended it with Luke and started a new relationship with a mega-fit personal trainer I'd met at a conference. Jack, from Michigan, was geographically desirable as far as I was concerned. He was Greek with a thick accent, and acted the part of a macho man. We'd see each other every other week or so for several months.

Work was still on the fast track when Rattan again borrowed my voice for the benefit of another adult male looking to make a love connection with fourteen-year-old Missy.

Even after taking all of the usual precautionary measures to prevent telltale background noise in Rattan's office, there still existed a measure of uncertainty—namely the risk of having the paging system bleed into my conversation with the alleged pedophile. So on August 2, 2002 I settled into an idling, air-conditioned squad with an undercover telephone.

Rattan had timed his last instant message with Ken to allow me ample time to cool off the squad, tune the radio station to something appropriate for a teenager, and await Ken's phone call. When Rattan logged off, he raced out to tell me, "He should be callin' any minute!"

I rolled the windows shut, took a few deep breaths, and sang along with the radio to calm my nerves. This was my second time playing Missy and I hoped, finally, that Rattan's efforts would result in an arrest.

Rattan milled around, growing anxious as minutes passed with no incoming call. He would shrug his shoulders with a palms-up motion, inquiring—pointlessly—if the phone had rung yet. He was funny to watch. Rattan desperately wanted to sit beside me and listen to the conversation, but he knew not to ask. I could understand his curiosity—after all, it was his case. He was responsible for building the existing relationship with the pervert, and all I had to do was review the previous e-mail correspondences and conduct a five-minute conversation. But Rattan knew that last time, when Agent Shannon sat in the room with me while I impersonated "Missy," I'd found it highly distracting. It was difficult to remain in character and speak so explicitly about sex in the presence of a colleague. So Rattan had faith that I could pull off the conversation and respected my request.

The phone rang. I lifted it to my ear and Rattan gave me a thumbs-up. When the caller asked, "Hello, is this Missy?" I returned the gesture.

"Yeah," I said, sounding meek.

Ken sighed with relief. "So, I finally get to hear your voice."

"Uh-huh..."

"Where are you?" he asked.

"In my room."

"What grade are you in, seventh or eighth?" He sounded more comfortable now.

"I'm gonna be in ninth grade this year."

"I can't wait to have sex with you!" Ken blurted out.

I gave him a surprised, nervous laugh.

"I already checked the map and it looks like it will take me about eight hours to get there by car. It's too expensive to fly."

Excited, I replied, "When are you gonna be here?"

"I'll be on vacation on August 14th, so how about then?"

Damn. I knew that Rattan was going to be on vacation during that time as well, so I needed to postpone the meeting.

"I'm gonna be at my Gramma's cottage that week," I whined with disappointment.

"Aw, really? I'll still make the drive as a dry run, so I know exactly how to get there and get familiar with the area. I'm gonna get a rental car."

"Have you met any other girls on the computer?" I asked.

"Yeah, one time I was talking to two sixteen-year-old girls and drove all the way to a mall in Omaha to meet them and they never showed up."

"Really? How come they didn't show?"

"I don't know, but I want to make sure I can get in touch with you when I get there. Do you have a cell phone?"

"No, but maybe my friend will let me borrow hers on that day."

"If you can't get one that's okay, because they have businesses that allow people to pay to go online, and I could send you an e-mail when I get there."

Someone did his homework.

"That's a good idea," I said, stroking his brilliant ego.

"Do you want to have sex with me?"

"I think yes...but I'm a little afraid."

"Don't worry; I'll use a condom so you won't get pregnant, because I'm not ready to have kids."

"Me either. I have to hang up, my Mom is gonna be home soon."

I heard Shannon's voice in my head: *Leave them wanting more.* I'd learned my lesson from the last pedophile, who'd manipulated me into explicit phone sex conversations.

Rattan jumped into the car and demanded like an anxious child, "What'd he say? What'd he say?"

I was convinced Ken thought he was talking to a fourteen-year-old girl. I had zero indication that he'd been spooked in any way. Rattan was sold when I told him about Ken's intentions of taking an eight-hour "dry run" to navigate the route.

On August 10th, after a few more e-mails and instant messages, Ken arranged another call.

"Missy?" he asked.

"Yeah," I whispered.

"Hi, it's Ken."

As if I weren't expecting his call.

"Hi!"

"So, what do you like to do for fun?"

"I go to the movies and I roller blade and...swim," I replied.

Now that the obligatory small talk was over, he cut right to the chase.

"I've been checkin' out stuff to do where you live and found a really nice motel in your neighborhood."

"Really?"

"Yeah, it's called Essence Suites, have you heard of it?"

I had an internal chuckle as I recalled assisting an ambulance at the Essence Suites with an unconscious woman. When I arrived, the boyfriend was in his underwear, a graphic porno was playing on the ceiling-mounted TV, and the woman lay passed out naked on the heart-shaped bed—from acute intoxication. As the paramedics worked on her, the remaining emergency crew leered at one another, trading mischievous smirks waiting for someone to turn off the porno, or not.

"Yeah, my Mom drives past it all the time when we go to the mall," I lied.

"Could you meet me there?"

"Yeah, it's not that far from my house."

"It'll take me seven hours to get there from Omaha; I plan on leaving right after work on the 30th and probably be there on the 31st before ten in the morning. When I get there I'll check and see if the hotel has an Internet service so I can get in touch with you."

"Okay and I could ask my friend to borrow her pager so you can page me," I said, allowing Ken an additional piece of certainty. I still needed to cover for Rattan's impending absence, so I added, "I'm gonna be leaving for my gram's cottage tomorrow and will be there till the 24th, so I won't be able to send you e-mails."

"That's okay, I'm gonna miss you."

"Me too… I hear a car in the driveway."

I quickly ended the call so I could share the great news with Rattan.

Rattan resumed his e-mail conversations with Ken immediately upon his return—or rather upon Missy's return from Gramma's cottage.

On August 28th, two days before our much anticipated meeting, Ken phoned Missy. "Hi," he said, with sadness in his voice. "I'm not going to be able to meet you on the 30th."

"How come?"

"I just feel that we haven't really talked to each other enough and the last time I tried to meet girls on line, I got burned."

I figured Ken had gone ten days without communicating with Missy and had either met someone else, or was getting cold feet. I was not, however, prepared for what he was about to reveal.

"I was really excited about seeing you, don't you like me anymore?"

"Yes I like you…but there is other stuff going on," he said cryptically.

"Like what?"

He hesitated.

"I went to the doctor's a few days ago and I have some type of genital ailment—the doctor said it's not HIV or an STD."

Whew, what a relief, it's not HIV or and STD. Suddenly remembering how young I was supposed to be, I asked, "What's an STD?"

"Like a sex disease, but it's not that, I'm just really swollen right now."

Grateful for the visual Ken candidly supplied, I decided to sound concerned.

"Does it hurt?"

"It burns when I pee."

Lovely.

"I'm so sorry this happened…I really, really want to see you, but it hurts too much right now. If everything is better, I will see you at the end of October and we will be able to have sex then."

I couldn't believe I actually wanted this pig's genitals healed so we could meet and arrest him sooner.

"I hope everything goes okay at the doctor."

Actually, I hope the "thing" rots and falls off.

"Ok. I have to hang up now; I keep hearing my gram in the hallway."

I had about enough of the drama and visualization surrounding his ailing genitals.

Rattan was livid about the change of events. He had already notified FBI agents of that date and bragged to the Commander that this was a go. Rattan barked, "Is his fuckin' dick fallin' off, or what?"

I laughed, but really felt sorry for him, knowing the hours invested in this case.

Rattan maintained his daily e-mails with Ken, but kept him at bay regarding the phone conversations because it was logistically difficult to coordinate phone calls with my work schedule, Rattan's work schedule, and Ken's availability—but also because Rattan wanted to punish him for canceling the first visit.

As it turned out, Mr. Personal Trainer, too, wanted more. He hinted that it was time for him to leave Michigan and venture into a new city to start over. He even went so far as to say he had an offer from another woman-friend to move to San Diego. I was growing tired of our relationship, feeling as if he was spending one too many weekends at my place and infringing on my freedom. Even with all of his brawn I realized, as I have with many of the men I'd been attracting, they become too soft and accommodating. *Where were all of the strong, masculine men?* I was looking for a man who could ravish me and leave my head spinning. I wanted a man who was an intellectual, yet powerful. I wanted someone who had the nerve to put me in my place when I acted tough. I was tired of my dominating men.

So, as far as I was concerned this was my perfect out. I politely encouraged him to move to San Diego and said, "You're a great guy I wish you the best in San Diego." After his move, we maintained phone contact, until it gradually dropped off.

Rattan still had Ken on the wire, so on September 29th I placed another call to him. Things once again looked promising.

"Missy? I've got great news, I made a reservation for a hotel called the Comfort Inn for October 5th!" he exclaimed.

"Really?" I gasped.

"Yep. I should be there by noon and I'll be stayin' 'til the 8th."

"Wow, three whole days, I can't believe it!" I was beaming and giving Rattan the thumbs-up from inside the car.

"I'm gonna book a rental car next week."

"Are you gonna rent something cool?"

"No, I can't afford a sports car—whatever is the cheapest."

"My Mom is gonna be out of town that weekend so I could tell my gram I'm stayin' at my girlfriend's house and we could spend every night together. I could even have my friend call the school and say I'm sick on Thursday so I can see you as soon as you get here."

"Wow, that's perfect, only one thing—I still am a little bit swollen and am taking medication but my dick feels better when I have a hard-on."

What? Did he really just say that? By all means, let's revisit the ailing dick once again. The sacrifices men will make for women.

Call me a glutton for punishment.

"Are you sure *it's* okay?"

"Yeah, I'll be fine. How 'bout I pick up some raspberry wine coolers and have them in the hotel for you?"

"Okay, I'll try 'em."

"I thought I could take you to a movie and the Olive Garden for dinner one of the days."

"Are you my boyfriend now?"

"Yes, but it's gonna be hard to see you a lot because I live so far away."

"I can't wait to see you."

"Oh yeah, the hotel has a pool, so make sure you bring a bathing suit… we're gonna have a great time."

"Oh, one more thing, I was thinking, when we go out to dinner and the movies, we should probably go somewhere not close to my house so no one I know sees me with an older man and tells my Mom."

"I already thought of that, don't worry, no one will see us together and we won't hold hands. People will think you're my little sister or something."

"Good idea…I have to go now."

When I briefed Rattan and Selleck, they were ecstatic. The FBI was notified and a record search was conducted at the hotel to see if Ken had really made a reservation. Everything checked out and the planning began.

October 5th—D-Day—had arrived. Two FBI agents set up surveillance vehicles in the parking lot of the Comfort Inn during the early morning hours. At headquarters, it was decided that after Ken contacted me by phone, I would walk to the hotel from a half block away and meet him in his room. Due to my age and the obvious difficulty of *physically* impersonating a fourteen-year-old girl, I would wear a baseball cap with my long, blonde ponytail hanging through the back, and keep my face turned away from the door at all times. All that was left to do was wait for Ken's phone call.

Meanwhile, the FBI had located a rental vehicle in the hotel lot with Nebraska plates on it. Ken was already at the hotel and his phone call was two hours late. We were relieved that the car had been sighted, but anxious that Ken hadn't phoned.

Soon after, the FBI identified a white man, approximately twenty-seven years of age, leaving the hotel and entering the rental vehicle. A tail was initiated. Ken drove to the local Wal-Mart, spent a short time inside, returned to his car with a small bag, and drove back to the hotel.

Fifteen minutes later, I received the call.

"Hi Missy, is your Mom gone?"

"Yes, what took you so long to call?"

"I wanted to make sure your Mom was gone."

"Can I come over now?"

"Yeah, I'm in room 312, how long will it take you to get here?"

"Maybe twenty or thirty minutes."

"See you soon, bye," he replied, without a concern in the world.

Back at the station, everyone was beaming, giving me high-fives and patting me on the back. We were ready to go. We left two FBI agents in the parking lot for surveillance; one remained in the lobby reading the newspaper. I was dropped off around the corner from the hotel, while Selleck, Rattan, Detective Blazer and another FBI agent made their way down the corridor on the third floor. I arrived shortly afterward, spotted my backup down the hall, and headed to room 312.

Two months of e-mails and telephone correspondence had come down to this moment.

As I approached room 312, the takedown team moved closer and aligned themselves against the wall in the corridor. I turned to them a final time, gave a nod indicating the ready signal, and knocked three times. I kept my face angled away from the peephole.

"Who is it?" the familiar voice called out.

"Missy," I replied, and he opened the door.

I never saw his face. The takedown team shouted, "Police!" and stormed the room. Ken was pinned to the bed before I could even turn around.

I entered the room once he was cuffed.

"I didn't do anything, I didn't do anything!" he screamed.

The room was neat. He had unpacked, and my raspberry wine coolers sat on a table alongside a Wal-Mart bag containing a receipt for condoms and breath mints.

For Ken's decision to cross state lines with intent to sexually assault a fourteen-year-old girl, he was charged in a Federal court, found guilty, and sentenced to six years in the Federal Penitentiary. Rattan and I proved to be a great team and were finally able to celebrate the fruits of our efforts.

CHAPTER 21
SNIPER NIGHT

Chained to a SWAT pager 24/7 was my life. But because of the infrequency of call-outs, wearing the little black box became as common as wearing deodorant. When I was promoted to detective it changed and I grew accustomed to the round-the-clock beeps from informants, without ever thinking it could be a SWAT assignment. When it was the real deal, rest assured: some fun personal outing would be disturbed.

One time I was attending the wedding of a fellow SWAT member. Dressed to the nines, and escorted by my friend Kelly (it was too dangerous to invite one of my casual boyfriends to such a romantic affair), I heard the high-pitched beep screaming from my purse. Unaffected, I retrieved the pager that I'd nicknamed "the Anti-Christ" for interruptions such as these, fully expecting to placate some informant and enjoy the evening's festivities. As I zeroed in on the code displayed, I saw that it was the witching hour, an official SWAT callout. *You gotta be kidding me!* As I began to follow the precinct's response procedure, I was approached by another wedding guest, who said, "We gotta go, I just checked in and we have a barricaded gunman." Fortunately, the groom and his SWAT member best man were given amnesty. Unfortunately, seven of us had to vacate immediately, leaving behind our dates or spouses. I went from an evening gown to SWAT gear and arrived on site in less than sixty minutes. The only remaining evidence of my femininity was my mascara-dressed lashes, which peeped through my masked eye sockets.

The ideal SWAT call-out, if it could ever be regarded as ideal, is when we're called while on duty. It's so much more convenient to receive the information first hand, hustle to the SWAT room, gear up and be the first reaction team on the scene. One evening I had the fortune of just that. In my office, I caught a glimpse of the police assignment screen and noted that officers were responding to a domestic call at the notorious Pacella household.

It was 10:30 p.m. and Mrs. Pacella (the woman who told me she'd shot her husband while I was a dispatcher) was requesting an ambulance for difficulty breathing after an alleged physical altercation with Mr. Pacella. Moments later her husband commandeered the phone and told the dispatchers his wife was upset about the result of her son's death. He kept refusing to put Mrs. Pacella back on the phone. When Mrs. Pacella managed to re-seize the phone she told dispatchers that her husband pulled her hair.

With that, Mr. Pacella stripped her of the phone and told the dispatcher, "She's too upset to talk" before slamming it down.

Within thirty seconds of the hang-up, officers were at the Pacella residence. One officer observed the wife through the front window as he attempted to raise someone at the door. Mr. Pacella refused to open the door and could be seen running around inside. Another officer, with his ear pressed against the front door, overheard Mr. Pacella ranting about the officers' safety if they attempt to come inside. The call officer was still able to see the wife and notified the dispatcher that she appeared safe. As the dispatchers continually attempted to raise the Pacellas via telephone, the officers remained at the door and in surrounding perimeter positions calling out the movement they observed inside. Mr. Pacella resembled a caged animal, pacing to and fro before becoming irate and pulling the window shades down to cut off the officer's view.

After several minutes of receiving a busy signal, the dispatcher finally got through. Mr. Pacella answered and said that his wife was distraught over the death of their son, refused to open the door for the officers and again slammed down the phone. With that, the officers who had maintained their positions on the porch pounded on the front door. Mr. Pacella shouted, "If you try to come in you're dead!"

As I sat at my desk in the station, Selleck came in and said, "Get ready, SWAT may have a call-out at the Pacellas' very soon."

I raised the volume of my portable radio to monitor the officer/dispatcher transmissions.

Nearly twenty minutes had passed since Mrs. Pacella made her original plea for help and officers had yet to make contact with her. Due to the strict guidelines regarding unlawful searches and seizures, the officers' hands were tied regarding entering the residence without an invitation. The dispatcher was again able to get Mr. Pacella to answer the line. This time he simply told the dispatcher he was in his bedroom and hung up.

Moments later, Mrs. Pacella opened the front door and was rapidly whisked out of harm's way by the officers. She told them that Mr. Pacella had locked himself in his bedroom and had a machine gun. With that, I flew from chair, raced down into the SWAT room, grabbed my equipment and began dressing. A SWAT team of five was sent to the scene. The first responding street sergeant and backup officers, some of which were also SWAT members, entered the residence and set up on the stairwell leading to Pacellas' bedroom. They concealed themselves behind a ballistic bunker and attempted to talk Pacella out. As he continued to threaten the officers, they could hear him skidding furniture across the floor, barricading himself inside.

Mrs. Pacella, who was inebriated, told the officers that her husband definitely had guns in his bedroom. An ambulance was called to treat Mrs. Pacella, who continued to complain of difficulty breathing. SWAT's first order of business was to clear the residences surrounding the house. If Mr. Pacella decided to sling his gun out a window and take shots at officers, we needed to ensure a stray bullet didn't make its way out.

Officers knocked on doors requesting that residents vacate their homes for their safety. The department compensated rooms at a local hotel for some; others opted to stay with relatives.

By 11:45 p.m. the SWAT Command Post was set up on the far end of the street. Because Mrs. Pacella was considered to be out of any physical danger, it was decided to keep her on-scene and use her as a continued source of information until Mr. Pacella surrendered. As SWAT members maintained perimeter positions, I and members of the initial react team remained situated on the inner perimeter, standing guard until our leaders decided on our next recourse.

After gaining perspective of the location of Pacella's bedroom window, we realized that attempting to have an officer enter the alcove between the home and a neighbor's home proved too dangerous. Mr. Pacella had a blinding spotlight illuminating from his back porch, which poured direct light into the alcove and his bedroom window.

We wanted to ascertain if Pacella actually had a weapon or was just bluffing. If we were able to ascend a ladder outside his bedroom window (under the cover of darkness) and peer into it, we could give the officers, who cautiously stood outside his bedroom, the green light to storm the door and take Pacella into custody.

One of our beanbag-certified riflemen was given the order to shoot out the porch light that illuminated the passageway under the window. Even with the less lethal beanbag round, precautionary measures had to be taken. The officers on the outer rear perimeter needed to relocate temporarily in the event the marksman was "off." After everyone was in a position, the rifleman took his shot—and missed. I watched the rifleman lower his head in temporary defeat. He knew everyone was watching.

Like a professional, he instantly reloaded and fired off another round, this time striking his intended target. The blazing light responded like a Fourth of July evening, hissing, buzzing and spitting sparks before slowly fading to black. Mr. Pacella grew alarmed and screamed out more threats. As we hustled into the alcove directly below the bedroom window, our next order of business was to get a peek inside his room. The riflemen and I carried our ladder over and raised it just under his bedroom window. I remained at the bottom to support the ladder as the rifleman crept up. Once in position, he raised his extended SWAT mirror to get a visual of Mr. Pacella.

Unfortunately, the window blinds obstructed his view and it appeared all of our efforts were fruitless. When the rifleman conveyed that he could not get a visual inside the room, he descended the ladder and we reconvened in front of the residence to brainstorm. I noticed Selleck and another SWAT officer huddling at the adjacent neighbor's house and sought them out. Selleck asked me about the blinds on Pacella's window. I explained that they were not completely shut. He asked if I thought we could see a silhouette if we had a rooftop angle from the neighbor's home. "Worth a shot," I said. Without further deliberation, Selleck and the officer permitted me to sink my combat boots into their shoulders as I scaled the first tier of the neighbor's raised ranch-style home.

I was flattered to be considered for the plum position and wanted to be able to provide the officers inside with intelligence as quickly as possible. I gripped the rooftop and nearly exhausted all of my upper body strength pulling my small frame with the added equipment weight of thirty-five plus pounds, including my MP-5 slung across my back. By the time I was finished with the first tier, I bent the gutter while sliding my torso and swinging one leg onto the roof. The guys below laughed as I quickly jumped to my feet, rearranging my twisted knee pads and gun sling.

Halfway there, I thought as I glanced at the second tier. It looked easy enough, until I realized I wouldn't have the assistance of the guys below for a boost. Feeling the heat of the eyes gathered below, I experienced what the rifleman felt moments earlier. *I have to make like a monkey and conquer this roof as if my life depended on it.* Initially, I thought I could simply reach above my head and hoist myself up. As I dangled there a mere foot from the roof of the first tier, I realized that I did not have the strength to pull myself up. Knowing everyone was watching this sad display I jumped down, took a running start and used my feet to scale up as my arms pulled me forward. I did it!

Now, all I needed to do was crawl on my belly up the incline of the roof and take a peek into Pacella's window. As I popped my head over the rooftop, I could see that he slid a bureau and a sofa chair in front of the door. I radioed my compadres about the obstructed door and continued looking for him. Lying on my tummy, holding my MP-5 aimed at his window, I thought, *I could stay perched here all night and watch this imbecile.*

"Expect the unexpected" haunted me in the next moment. I finally had Pacella in view as he darted past the window. While maintaining my position, I reached for my radio transmission button on my shoulder, heard a loud "pop" and was instantly exposed under a raging spotlight. "Shit!" I whispered as I ducked my head, extracted my weapon and shimmied down the side of the roof. Mr. Rifleman's light from hell decided it was not time to die. All the men in the passageway under Pacella's window scurried for cover as we waited to see how he would respond. With my heart pounding, I could hear the rifleman being directed to take out the light...*again.*

This time he did it on the first shot and everyone, including me, got back into position. Pacella heard the commotion outside his window and decided to close his blinds. Still, I managed to pick-up his silhouette through the tilted slats that were just shy of being completely sealed. The rifleman tiptoed back up the ladder and extended his mirror pole to have another look. I could see Pacella sitting on his bed but could not make out if he had a weapon nearby.

Nearly an hour and forty-five minutes had elapsed since the original 911 call and the brass was growing weary of Pacella's drunken threats. It was decided that the rifleman would use his mirror and tap on the window to get Pacella across the room opposite the bedroom door. I remained in a sniper position to protect the rifleman if Pacella greeted him with a weapon; meanwhile, the entry guys just outside the bedroom door would pummel it down and storm the room.

The rifleman tapped the glass three times. Instead of walking to the window, Pacella launched a pillow at the blinds, bending the slats and allowing a better visual inside. I radioed to the guys outside the door that Pacella didn't bite, so we tapped again. Annoyed, Pacella moved toward the window. I radioed the team and they blasted through the door. Pacella turned to them and stood frozen as the men climbed over the furniture, tore across the room and shoved him onto his bed.

At 1:15 a.m., Pacella was in custody. As if we didn't have enough going on, twenty minutes later he complained of neck pain (felony flu?) and was transported to the hospital. One hour later he was returned to his cell where he awaited his bond hearing.

Pacella was charged with: Domestic Battery, Possession of Fireworks/ Explosives, Interfering with Domestic Report, two counts of Aggravated Assault against a Police Officer, one count of Assault and one count of Resisting Arrest. For all of our trouble, he was merely found guilty of the first two. His sentence: ten days community service, a fine of $250 and one year Conditional Discharge (probation).

Shortly after all of that excitement, I managed to get away and enjoy a ten-day trip with Tracy to Vienna and Prague. The trip served as a way to connect with my best friend and come up for a bit of air. My goals were sightseeing, running, and getting pampered at the hotel spa. On the second day I scheduled a massage with a home-grown Austrian therapist named Dieter.

Dieter was attractive in a Lance Armstrong sort of way, thin but toned; a thirty-year-old Austrian who spoke like Arnold Schwarzenegger. When I asked him if he could recommend any attractive running routes in the area for me he said, "I compete in Iron Man competitions, I could tell you where to go or show you myself."

Well, well. Dieter wanted to show me himself. I couldn't refuse an offer like that.

The run took us through a forest, up and down mountains and to little ponds where we drank from fresh springs. At the end of the run he offered to show Tracy and me around that evening and took us to dinner with a group of his friends.

The whole experience was utterly charming. As the evening wore on, I caught Dieter staring at me. Meanwhile, Tracy seemed to be getting along brilliantly with Dieter's young friend Max. After several glasses of Austrian wine, Max took Tracy by the hand to show her a bit of the history in the quaint cobblestoned town. Soon after, the others parted and Dieter escorted me to a nearby harbor. Under the stars, as the waves thudded against the rocky coast, Dieter, noticing my chill, blanketed me with his sweater and pulled my shivering body to his. He looked into my eyes, tilted my chin upward and kissed me softly. At that moment, off in the distance, I heard Tracy call out, "Hey, there you are!"

The remaining days in Austria and Prague consisted of daily runs with Dieter, more massages, dinners and touring. The night before my departure, Dieter insisted I join him for a home-cooked meal. After such beautifully romantic connections with Dieter, I knew exactly what could happen and welcomed it. The evening went exquisitely and the following morning he prepared tea and offered Viennese breads, croissants and an array of jams and honey out on his flowered terrace.

Upon bidding Dieter farewell, he mentioned that he'd never been to the U.S. and wondered if he could visit Chicago. Like most people who create friends or have liaisons on vacations, it was customary to offer an opportunity for a future visit. In the moment, the intention feels authentic, yet in my experience, the visits never seem to materialize. So it was easy to say, "Sure."

CHAPTER 22
THROW MOMMA FROM THE TRAIN

It turned out that Dieter truly wanted to maintain contact and phoned twice a month and e-mailed regularly. Coming back into my reality, I looked at our encounter as a fond memory that would soon dissipate. My male energy had returned.

A few months later, mid-September of 2002, I was flown to New York City by a surgeon, Dr. Ferro, whom I'd met in Hawaii at the conference last year. While attending that conference, he asked me if I'd consider running the New York City Marathon the following year. Never having run more than six miles at a time in my entire life, I said no. He asked, "Why so quick to say no?" and added, "It's for a worthy cause." Dr. Ferro explained that it was for a charity. After spending twenty minutes with the good doctor, he found his leverage and asked, "Are you telling me that you don't think you could do it?"

I thought, What if I couldn't do it? Twenty-six miles is a long haul. If I tell people I'm running a marathon they're going to expect me to finish. Lisa always finishes what she starts (except with men, that is). I'd developed this new mantra of "If I can't, I must." So I'd told Dr. Ferro and everyone who knew me that I would be running the New York City Marathon in 2002.

Two months before the race, Dr. Ferro generously offered to fly me to there to get a taste of running through Central Park. He explained that he invites a group of thirty runners to his place intermittently throughout the year to train, hang out and see the city. Boz warned me not to go.

"Are you attracted to him?"

"No," I answered.

"Well then don't go! I'm tellin' ya right now, this guy wants to bone ya."

"C'mon Boz, he's a perfect gentleman. He's never come on to me. I could tell these things…men are so obvious."

After my second day in the Big Apple, it turned out Boz was right: the good doctor had a little more than training on his mind. He dressed in a tux and provided a limo for our secret night out to the Opera. He even arranged for a romantic seven-course dinner. When we arrived back at his posh skyrise, I practically ran to my room to put on my unappealing baggy flannel pajamas. When I resurfaced in the living room, he had mongo-sized chocolate covered strawberries and champagne set up by candlelight on the coffee table. I hate you Boz. I feigned an exaggerated yawn, explained that I never drink champagne, grabbed a strawberry and nuzzled into the end of the sofa farthest from him. I kept him at bay, explaining that my boyfriend (one of my casual relationships) and I were becoming serious. Realizing that I was uncomfortable, Dr. Ferro switched on the TV. I remained in the living room for what I thought was a respectable amount of time, pecked him a thank-you goodnight on the cheek and retired. I felt so uncomfortable the following day. He behaved a bit coldly during our morning run, but recovered later as we took in my first Yankees game at the Stadium. I phoned my flavor of the month back home whenever I was sure Dr. Ferro was in earshot, compelled not to hurt his feelings by making him believe there was really someone special back home.

Back at the precinct I meekly put my tail between my legs and admitted to Boz that he was right. "You've got a lot to learn about men, Lockwood," he said. Yes I did.

At work later that month, Bosley and I set up a controlled cocaine buy. The bad guy, Dinky Thomas, whose father was put in jail for delivering multiple kilos of cocaine ten years earlier, had assumed his father's business years later on a smaller scale. Dinky lived in an old beat-up, red, two-story farmhouse on a semi-wooded lot. The backyard was decorated with an array of junk cars, auto parts, and a dilapidated white barn. Fortunately for us, the informant, trying to save his own hide on a petty theft charge, thought it would be better to nark on Dinky rather than take his own lumps.

It was nine p.m. when the informant and one of the patrolmen we had borrowed to work undercover were waiting for Dinky's arrival in the McDonald's parking lot less than a quarter mile from the farmhouse. Par for the course, the bad guy was late. After thirty minutes and three phone calls to Dinky, he finally showed up. Boz and I had the eyeball from our trusty white van, which we'd parked behind a strip mall across the street.

Everything had gone smoothly. Dinky handed our undercover officer a baggie holding about twenty grams of cocaine, received money from our undercover officer, and left. The felony transaction of delivering a controlled substance to an undercover officer took less than sixty seconds.

About two weeks later, after receiving all of the necessary intel to execute a search warrant, we had a new concern. The informant relayed that the occupants of Dinky's house consisted of at least three toddlers, Dinky's mother, an uncle, a cousin, and a teenaged girl. Due to the number of people living there and the age of the children, a plan had to be devised to ensure that no innocent parties were put in harm's way upon the execution of a Narcotic Search Warrant. Our goal was to get Dinky out of the home to arrest him without disrupting the family, then return to the house for the search.

The plan was for me to drive as close to the farmhouse as possible, feign auto trouble, knock on the door, and hope Dinky offered to assist a damsel in distress. SWAT would then exit the van and rapidly take him into custody while the remainder of the team performed the search of the house.

I pulled up in my beat-up van about forty feet past the farmhouse, on a slightly tilted gravel lane. I hesitated momentarily as the SWAT guys in the rear gave me last-minute fatherly morsels like, "Don't go into the house; safety first, Lockwood," and finally, "good luck."

I exited the van, wearing painted on jeans and a creamy white, breast-accentuating shirt with my hair down and flowing freely. Approaching the front, I was met by an eight-foot wood fence with a locked gate. *Strike one.* I phoned my compadres and advised them of the dilemma—if I use the rear door of the farmhouse, I would be out of the team's sight, and therefore at risk, being unarmed and unvested.

A senior member of the team assessed the situation and gave me the green light to knock at the rear door. What I didn't understand, however, was his reason for changing the ruse before the original damsel-in-distress plan was attempted. He noticed a Suburban truck on the side of the lawn adjacent to the house with a "For Sale" sign in the window, had an epiphany and said, "Instead of feigning auto trouble, pretend you want to know the price of the truck." I thought the damsel story carried more credibility, and my attire was more suited to that role. Now I was supposed to feign interest in a rusted-out truck with a snowplow attached to the front. There were probably five SWAT guys that would have been more convincing than I for that kind of ruse, but I had to do what the senior guy suggested.

Venturing alongside the house in my quest to raise someone at the back door, I was met by the likes of Satan in dog's clothing. *Cujo* was unleashed, salivating and barking ferociously like a rabid wolf. I froze, my heart lodged in my throat, fixated on my imminent death. Cujo stood twenty-feet from me in pre-attack stance, waiting for me to so much as blink. At that moment, a farmhouse window abruptly flew open and this "thing" resembling the character from *Throw Momma from the Train* screeched, "Henry, no!" Momma was attempting to disguise Cujo as Henry but I wasn't buying. Suddenly, I wasn't sure who I feared more. Fortunately, Momma's order to Cujo worked, and someone summoned Henry to the rear of the house. With *Cujo* out of sight, Momma wanted to know who I was and what I wanted.

When my heart decided to find its way back to where God put it, I sized her up as she hung half her body out of a window approximately five feet above me. She wore a dingy gray smock-style nightgown with a pattern of tiny flowers, my only indication that she was a woman. Her hair was multi-shades of gray parted down the middle, greasy at the roots and frizzed wildly. Her eyes drooped and her loose skin appeared to be melting from her whisker-laden face. If she had ten teeth in her mouth she was fortunate; I only saw six.

Flanking her were two curious, filthy-faced little girls. I coolly responded to her inquiry by asking, "Can you tell me the price of that truck out front?"

To my horror, she said, "I don't know. It belongs to my son's friend, and he'd asked to park it on the lawn for exposure. Why don't you call the phone number on the For Sale sign?" *Strike two.*

I was ready to hang the cop responsible for changing the plan. Still, without skipping a beat and determined to get the bad guy out of that godforsaken house, I said, "Oh great, thank you. By the way, as I was pulling over to take a look at the truck, my van died and my cell phone battery is nearly gone."

To my second horror, she said, "C'mon 'round to the back, I'll let you in to use the phone."

Replaying the "Don't go into the house" directive, I had to once again trump up an excuse. I replied in an embarrassed tone, "Well ma'am, to be honest, I really don't have anyone available who I could call to come out and help me."

She looked at me sympathetically and I seized the moment: "By chance do you have any men at home that could come out and take a look? It might just need a jump."

"My nephew is here but he's sleeping."

I was now forced to reach the groveling point of no return: "Do you think you might be able to wake him up?"

She hesitated, apparently shocked by the boldness of this stranger at her window, then directed one of the kids to wake the guy up. Meanwhile, Momma tried to engage me in small talk as I drifted away from the window, pretending to search for a better signal on my cell. I hung around the side of the house, awaiting the mystery man, hoping it would be the bad guy, all the while whispering on the phone to the SWAT guys that a man might be coming out to save the damsel and, "Oh, by the way the truck-interest ruse was a disaster, thank you."

Momma disappeared and I was left to wait. Nearly ten minutes passed, and I was sure I'd been forgotten. The SWAT guys called me back, demanding the reason for the delay. I sympathized with them; I knew it wasn't the most comfortable thing to be crouched down in SWAT gear in a confined space for any length of time. While debating whether to throw a pebble at Momma's window, a disheveled looking man exited the back door and walked toward me. From a distance, I thought it was Dinky; he had the same build, weight, and hair color. I smiled and introduced myself.

He returned the smile and told me his name was John, *not Dinky*. He was now just several feet from me, and I was certain it was not Dinky. *Strike three.*

He began walking toward van to save the day when I realized, first, the van was in perfect working order and, second, it was fully loaded with a team of crouching SWAT guys. There was no way I could permit this guy to get anywhere near that van, and I had seconds to relay to the SWAT team that John was not the bad guy before they prematurely pounced and exposed the entire operation. I slowed down and promptly got on the phone with the SWAT guys, pretending to have a conversation with my husband. I said, "Oh great sweetie, you're only five minutes away, because this nice man named John was gonna take a look at it for me. Okay, I'll tell him, no, no I'm okay, see you in a few minutes."

I hung up the phone and told John, "My husband thanks you for offering help but he'll be here shortly and said he'd take care of it."

Bosley had asked me if John was Dinky, to which I replied, "No, no, I'm okay." Now that the SWAT guys knew not to exit the van, I had to think of a way to get rid of John. I apologized for waking him up and suggested he resume his nap. *He wasn't biting.* Instead, he followed me, sporting the look of love, to within fifteen feet of the rear of the van. John decided he was going to wait until my "husband" arrived. *Can you have strike four on the same batter?*

Things were becoming positively insane. Knowing full well that no one was on the way to help me and unable to shake Romeo, my mind raced. I thought if I got closer to the van and attempted to drive away, he might follow me, thus exposing the SWAT guys. As I ran numerous scenarios through my mind while engaging John in distracting flattery by complimenting his non-existent bicep muscles and asking about his mechanical skills, a car pulled up. It turned out to be a friend of John's. He leaned into the passenger window to speak to the driver, while I slowly meandered back to the van. I put the key in the ignition and drove off, my heart pounding out of my chest. The guys in the back shouted, "Go! Go! Go!" Seconds later, with my adrenaline skyrocketing, I burst into a fit of uncontrollable laughter. Barely able to keep the van on the road, desperately gasping for air, I attempted to explain everything that had happened.

Back at the station we conducted a debriefing and realized we were basically back to square one. We still didn't know Dinky's whereabouts and—concerned for the safety of the children—we decided to wait until the following morning to execute the search warrant at the farmhouse.

The next morning, our team assembled for a new plan. Our goal was, once again, to get Dinky out of the residence as safely as possible. Our informant had told Boz and me that Dinky might still be employed. If this were the case, he remembered that Dinky left the house before eight a.m. With this information, we had an unmarked vehicle head out to the farmhouse to see if his car was there. Due to the obscure location of the house and the junk cars in the yard, the detective was unable to tell for sure. The new plan was set in motion. Two detectives would stand by on the east and west ends of the block, so that if he did leave for work, one of the unmarked cars could halt him on a traffic stop. The only missing link was trying to determine if Dinky was home.

At that point, I decided to make an undercover phone call to Dinky's house. Momma crustily answered, "Hello."

I asked, "Is Dinky home?"

"I'm not sure, he might be sleeping."

Here we go again. I replied boldly, figuring she was now accustomed to Scarfo women, "Could you check and tell him it's Cindy?"

She angrily replied, "Hold on." But I was forced to hang up because my portable radio transmitted a detective's voice advising that he was in position. I called back moments later and again asked for Dinky. He got on and immediately asked who I was. I had accomplished the goal of confirming that Dinky was home; now I needed to come up with a story as to how I knew him. Ill prepared, I pretended to have reception problems, repeating, "Can you hear me?" over and over, to which he kept replying, "Yes, I can hear you." He then said what we needed to seal his impending fate: "Could you call me back, I have to leave for work soon."

With that, I ended the call and hastily radioed the information to our surveillance detectives. As I drove the surveillance van toward Dinky's house I called him again, as promised. He asked, "Who is this again?"

I told him I'd met him at a party about six weeks ago, thought he was cute, and gotten his phone number from one of his friends. He laughed with embarrassment, obviously flattered, and asked me what I looked like to refresh his memory. I sheepishly replied, "Oh my God, you don't remember me, I'm so embarrassed."

He interjected, "No, no, I think I know, do you have blonde hair?"

I excitedly said, "Yes!" and further told him I was petite with double Ds—*okay, the double D thing was a stretch.*

"Oh yeah, Cindy! I remember you." *It's comical when a set of double Ds are thrown into the mix, details like whose party we were at, where it was, what friend gave out his phone number and most peculiar of all, why Cindy would be calling him at 7:30 a.m., all thankfully became irrelevant.* Not wanting to push my luck, I again feigned reception problems and ended the call, promising to call him back that night. He enthusiastically told me to call him when he got home from work after six. With all of the troops in position, we awaited Dinky's exodus. Ten minutes later, our surveillance guys picked him up driving eastbound toward the very same McDonalds where he had sold cocaine, ironically, to our undercover officer. Two vehicles blocked the front and rear of his car and pulled him over in the parking lot, where he was arrested for the controlled delivery to our undercover officer.

With Dinky out of the house and safely in police custody, it was time to execute the search warrant. Our team met at a nearby gas station and devised an entry plan. We would drive up to the residence in a convoy consisting of an unmarked lead car, followed by the van, the K-9 squad, and an additional fully marked squad.

We proceeded to drive down the gravel road adjacent to the residence. Cujo greeted our team with similar tenacity, but this time he was chained and choking himself like a wild stallion, attempting to make a meal of a team of armed and vested gunmen. We were prepared for Cujo—had he not been chained—with a couple of friendly fire extinguishers. Two lead detectives did a "soft knock" approach at the farmhouse; there was no reason to ram the door and forge through the residence. The element of surprise was not necessary with Dinky in custody. Momma answered the door in the same appealing, dingy smock. She was immediately given a copy of the search warrant and quickly whisked out of the door and handed off to another team member, where she was detained outside.

Although it wasn't necessary to ram the door, it was still imperative that our team rapidly searched the home and secured the remaining occupants; there was always the risk of someone attempting to flush any evidence of Narcotics. As the team and I entered the residence, we began clearing room after room, all the while shouting out, "Police, search warrant, get down on the ground!" and "Show me your hands!" A teenaged girl, two filthy, naked little girls, and my friend "Romeo," who was too surprised to recognize me (how quickly they forget) were all escorted outside.

Once everyone was safely removed from the house, our tunnel vision dissipated. Our only priority when rapidly entering a home is to get our hands on anything moving and secure it. When this is accomplished, a more systematic search is conducted to find contraband (anything illegal we could use against him).

We were now all able to fully appreciate the state of our environment. The farmhouse reeked of excrement. The garbage can, sink, counter and kitchen table were overflowing with soiled diapers, pots, pans and dishes encrusted with rotting food. Animal feces were randomly piled on the carpet; blankets used as makeshift beds were strewn about the living room floor, and meowing cats were under the sofas. Dog food kernels and cat litter trailed through every room on the main level. A thick layer of dust coated everything. Nicotine-saturated walls with shades and curtains resembling Momma's nightgown surrounded the dusky house.

Once all of the residents were out of the house, Boz and I, as the case agents, were responsible for searching Dinky's bedroom for cocaine. Minutes into our search, Sergeant O'Malley entered the room and whispered that he had just opened a small closet in the hallway and found an elderly woman sleeping on a skinny mattress under a clothes rack. Finding this unbelievable, I had to see for myself. I looked into the closet and saw a woman that looked like the Crypt Keeper's wife, fast asleep. At that moment, I decided to have fun with the Sergeant, who was obviously not pleased that our search team hadn't discovered her. With my most tragic look I said, "Sarge, I think she's dead. Her chest isn't moving."

"Nice try, I already checked."

He returned to the closet and tapped her shoulder to re-confirm she was alive, while I stood in the hallway plugging my nose, beside myself in laughter. After she woke up, he looked at me and said with a sigh of relief, "See?" As if I were the one who was worried.

After all was said and done, Romeo was reunited with Dinky when we discovered he was wanted on an outstanding warrant. To our dismay, Boz and I came up empty in the house. However, Dinky was charged with the initial felony delivery of a controlled substance to an undercover police officer. To our great fortune, he later pled guilty and was sentenced to six years in the State Penitentiary.

CHAPTER 23
MISSY & THE FAMILY MAN

For the month of October, I swore off men. The marathon was weeks away and with Boz and I tearing up the city and me trying to squeeze in my fifteen, eighteen and twenty-mile runs on the weekends, I needed to stay focused on my goals. Poor Boz had endured so much with me juggling men. He actually watched me evolve from a woman in a nearly five-year committed relationship to a female gigolo. If I had a dime for every time he said, "You're a man trapped in a woman's body," I'd be rich. I laughed off the comment mostly, until one day I thought long and hard about what he said. It seemed Boz wasn't teasing anymore. He would say it with more conviction and I felt insulted, mostly because I started to believe him. *Have I become a man? Bosley would know; he knew me the best.* Maybe a month of alone time would give me clarity; hence my decision to swear off men, at least until after the marathon.

Rattan continued pursuing his passion of hunting men on the Internet who were actively pursuing little girls and soliciting them for sex.

At the end of October a man named David contacted "Missy" in a chat room geared toward teens. The stranger's profile disclosed the following: 44 years old, 5'8, salt and pepper hair, beard, 200 lbs, from Chicago suburbs, seeking divorce, loves sex. Age is not an issue. *Of course not!*

Missy responded to David's greeting with a simple e-mail that read, Hi, where in chiocago u sound kewl, I'm 14, can u send me a picture of you.

As expected, David was undeterred by Missy's age and sent a photo of himself in a baseball uniform, then asked for one in return. Rattan sent my teenage picture with a message that read, "my hair is blonde now." He was already laying the foundation, providing my actual hair color, in the event that David bit and agreed to meet me.

David then initiated an instant message exchange with Missy.

David: so are you a very bad girl?

Missy: never done anything, looking for a boyfriend

David: do you want to be? Are you curious?

Missy: yes I am where are you, in Chicago?

David: by the airport

David: is that picture really you?

Missy: y don't you like me?

David: we need to talk, promise that picture is really you?

Missy: YES!!!!!!!silly

David: and you aren't a cop or with a cop?

Missy: if u don't beleve me bye!!!!

David: promise you won't say anything to anyone about us

Missy: I will I promise

David: what do you have on your mind?

Missy: ?????? Nothing I guess I'll let u go then

Rattan had to use caution, so as not to be guilty of soliciting David.

David: you are curious?

Missy: yes

David: about sex?

Missy: yes

David: what have you done so far?

Missy: just kissed a boy at school that's it

David: has a guy ever felt you up?

Missy: no never even seen a guy without cloths

David: do you have pubic hair?

Missy: little

David: do you have little boobs?

Missy: I guess

David: do you masturbate?

Missy: no never have don't really know how

David: do you want me to teach you?

David was wasting no time to make his intentions known.

Rattan tried to keep the initial conversation brief to see if David would participate in future correspondences. Like most pedophiles, David ignored Missy's desire to end the conversation and continued to desperately asked her what she was willing to do.

Needless to say, David bit, and future correspondences were all related to setting a place and time to meet. I told Rattan to do his best to keep this guy on the line; I *had* to go to New York City to run the marathon (as if it were an inconvenience). I was so invested in this case I actually felt a bit selfish taking three days off from work to run a marathon. My personal life had deteriorated so much that I painstakingly needed to remind myself that I was running for a great cause; it wasn't about me.

Thankfully on marathon day, I gained some insight. *How fortunate could I possibly be?* I was fit enough to run. I trained hard for this day and I deserved to enjoy it. Dr. Ferro managed to use his connections to suit up his team in New York City Police Department running shirts. To add to this honor, I was shuttled to the front of the race. The marathon committee tried something different this year, the women were permitted to run on the upper bridge and the men ran on the bottom deck. At the end of the Verrazano Narrows Bridge the two groups melded together. For reasons unknown to me, I was gifted with being in the front row on the top tier.

My eyes welled-up as the Star Spangled Banner played for opening ceremonies. Mayor Bloomberg asked us to bow our heads in silence in memory of our fallen heroes and victims of 9/11. Even though I didn't know a soul, it didn't matter; we were all one that day and I had the honor of wearing a NYPD shirt for the next twenty-six miles. I was never more proud to be a police officer.

Wearing that shirt made me feel like superwoman. Over a million onlookers cheered us along the entire stretch. They called out, "Go New York City Police, we love you, you can do it!" This was the exact thing I needed on my last leg through Central Park. After five hours and forty-five minutes of non-stop running I crossed the finish line. I did it! I was met by a smiling stranger who placed a ribbon lanyard holding a medallion around my neck, and walked off sobbing alone. I was in a surreal place, limping along some unknown street, freezing in the thirty-seven degree evening. I questioned, *Why am I alone? Am I meant to go through this life without a mate? I just achieved the greatest physical accomplishment of my life and I had no one to share it with. Is this God's plan? Surely I'm doing something wrong.*

I painfully hobbled up to a fire engine whose job was to shut down an intersection, and asked for directions. The engineer, recognizing my NYPD shirt, was dumbfounded that I didn't know where I was. I explained that I was a police detective from Chicago. He opened his rear cab door, turned on the heat, handed me a Gatorade and asked me to wait. Thirty-minutes later the entire fire crew boarded the vehicle and drove me to my destination. I took this as a sign: God was there watching over me.

Back in Chicago, Rattan continued to talk to David.

On 11/4/02 Missy signed on and immediately received an instant message from David.

David: is there a theatre close to you that your Mom
       could drop you off to see a movie at?

Missy: yes, then what will we do

David: that will give us a couple of hours at least, we can go
       to a movie hardly anyone is at, sit in the back row

Missy: why the back row I won't be able to see the movie

David: we aren't there to see the movie silly

Missy: can't tomorrow grammas birthday, what are we there for?

David: kiss and feel each other up, like a bf and gf do

David: Missy, will you dress like I want?

Missy: sure like how

David: skirt, short enough for me to get under, loose enough
       to get under and a top that I could get under,
       loose also and a ball cap so I can find you.

This information was crucial, as these would be the garments I'd wear as Missy.

After that contact, David vanished. Rattan could no longer find him online and he didn't return e-mails.

Life is so full of surprises. I received a phone call from Dieter, who was ready to make good on his visit to Chicago. Months had passed and frankly I hadn't given him another thought. Surely he expected to reconnect with me physically and until that moment I'd kept my promise of swearing off men. I couldn't bring myself to tell him the offer was off the table. He was so hospitable and charming during my visit, yet I didn't want to give him the wrong idea. As a deterrent, I explained that I wouldn't be available to tour him around as he did for me because of my lack of vacation time, which was true. He still wouldn't take no for an answer and before I knew it I was picking him up from the airport for an extended weekend. His maiden voyage to the United States was to visit me in Chicago.

Bosley was appalled. "How could you let this man fly all the way across the world and then tell me you don't plan on boinkin' him? Did you tell him there wouldn't be any horizontal mambo?"

I felt horrible. Boz thought I was joking. He thought that after I saw Dieter in person, the hormones would spark. He was wrong. Some divine epiphany consumed me after the marathon and I was not interested in a cheap fling.

When Dieter saw a blow-up air bed in the living room, he looked at me quizzically. I seated him at the kitchen table and explained the "new Lisa."

He said, "You're joking, right?"

I scrambled to find a rainbow hidden in the gloom.

"I'm glad you're here. The time in Vienna was amazing; I'm just in another place right now."

"You should have told me" was his sullen response.

He was right. I said, "The entire time we spoke on the phone, I racked my brain trying to figure out an elegant way to say, 'Just so you know when you get here we won't be having sex.'"

With that he stood with his shoulders drooping and literally threw himself face first onto the air mattress. It was like watching a child throw a tantrum for saying no to the ice-cream truck. I sat at the table stunned, until I actually heard him sniffling. *Now what?* I went to him, stroked the back of his head and said, "I'm soo sorry." I almost considered giving him pity sex to shut him up. Still lying on his stomach he reached his arms around my waist, placed his head on my lap and cried. *I swear I didn't know who this guy was. Was he that upset over not having sex or was he in love with me? God please help me. I really thought I was straightening out the relationship department by swearing off men until Mr. Right walked into my life. Now I've hurt this stranger. I didn't like who I'd become.*

Dieter forgave me and we managed to get through the weekend. He toured the city, spent time with me my friends for dinners downtown and enjoyed some of Chicago's nightlife. A day before his departure, he offered me what he does best, a massage. Feeling relaxed and later aroused, I gave in to my carnal desire. After all, I rationalized, this is exactly what men do. They have sex on a whim for the sake of sex without ever considering the other person. I had reached the bottom of the barrel. I was a man trapped in a woman's body. Dieter's departure felt amicable and he continued to write me regularly for some time until that, too, dissipated to nil.

One month after David's vanishing act, on 12/5/02 David went on line and located Missy via instant message under a new screen name. He re-contacted Missy and explained he had to lay low and change his e-mail address because of an alleged stalker.

On December 15th, Rattan was ready for my phone call debut. He excused himself from the office and no doubt had his ear glued to the door when the Missy phone-line rang.

"Hello Missy, is your Mom home?"

I answered in my sweet, shy Missy voice, "No she usually gets home from work around ten after six."

David asked me if that was really me in the picture I had sent him. "How come you keep asking me that? I told you it was me, do you think I'm ugly?" *I was trying to push his sympathy button.*

David bit. "No sweetie, I think you're beautiful, I told you that, it's just that I want to be safe for both of us." Then he asked me how tall I was, perhaps as a test to see if it matched with what Rattan had previously written.

I remembered that Rattan used my actual height and replied, "Five-foot-five." Then David asked my age and bra size. I was playing along with his game and answered his questions. Once he was satisfied with my responses, he was ready to become explicit.

"Missy, I want you to rub your nipples for me, pinch them a bit and make them hard."

"Hee...he...he...." I giggled as my body became warm.

I couldn't help but think incredulously, What a sick pig! In some ways I was getting used to this line of questioning and the demands of these creeps and in some ways I felt it stripped me of my power. I wanted to reach right through the phone line and execute a Lorena Bobbitt.

"C'mon Missy, I want you to touch your nipples and imagine me rubbing my cock on your ass."

I was livid. This disgusting man, who was married with children (as Rattan learned through his investigation), was speaking to what he thought was an innocent teenager in a manner more suited to a 900 number.

I giggled some more.

He wasn't satisfied with my response.

"Close your eyes, Missy, and imagine my tongue licking you, can you feel me? C'mon, tell me baby, tell me you're getting wet."

I remained silent through the duration of his self-stimulation, until he requested I put down the telephone and try to have an orgasm while screaming his name.

The pedophile was clueless! I put the phone off to the side for a few moments. I looked around Rattan's office and was tempted to open the door to see if Rattan was pressed to it as I suspected. Sure enough, he was standing with his back to it, so I whispered, "Don't say anything, he's still on the line, he wants me to try and have an orgasm for him."

It was a bit scary how easy it was becoming for me to speak so vulgarly to the men in my department. It was truly becoming second nature. It seemed that, the more I spoke that way, the more my colleagues liked me. They felt safe and comfortable around me. Often, when we were in a setting outside the department with other police personnel for training or joint operations, my colleagues would say, "Don't worry about offending Lisa, she's got a worse mouth than most of us." That was who I'd become. It took no effort to fit in anymore. It became my adopted identity. Rattan's eyes widened, his jaw dropped and he asked, "Are you serious?"

"Please Rattan, don't push it!"

Quietly closing the door, I picked up the phone again. David asked if I "did it." I told him I'd tried but was too nervous about Mom coming home.

Fortunately, he cooled down and started to make more concrete plans for our first meeting. He suggested we attend an unpopular movie, so fewer people would see us together. He also told me to bring a bag with a short skirt and a loose-fitting shirt so I could change in the bathroom without Mom getting suspicious. Then he instructed me to be ready for him to massage my nipples and put his finger into me. He asked me again if I was a virgin, and I told him I was. He assured me that if there was extra time after the show, I could go back to his truck and suck him. *I'd have preferred going back to his truck to run him over.*

"OK," I whispered shyly.

He asked, "Do you think you'd wanna try to have sex in the truck, my windows are tinted and it'll be dark?"

"I'm a little bit afraid to try that," I replied.

"Okay, we don't have to the first time…we'll take things slow and see what happens." *What a gentleman!*

Rattan and I were both thrilled at the prospect of arresting David on Monday and began to prepare a plan.

On December 18th, David sent Missy an e-mail suggesting they meet for the 5 p.m. showing of *Miss Congeniality*, and instructing Missy to sit in the back row. If you haven't seen *Miss Congeniality*, it's about an FBI agent working undercover as a beauty pageant contestant. The irony is that David actually chose the movie and would unwittingly be meeting an undercover detective posing as a fourteen- year-old girl.

When I arrived, I raced into the bathroom and changed into my short black mini-skirt, loose fitting shirt, and ball cap—just as David requested. I wore a pair of gym shoes and short white socks to complete the ensemble, and put my hair in pigtails, allowing them to rest on my chest. I felt like an idiot in the ladies room—like one of those women trying desperately to look young. It was twenty degrees outside and I had a miniskirt on! I received a few strange glares from ladies using the facilities, and a few double-takes from the men in the lobby. It didn't matter that I didn't quite look fourteen; all we really needed was for David to arrive and approach me. By picking a dark movie theater, he'd helped the police immensely.

We had one of our detectives scout the theater prior to my arrival to make sure David hadn't gotten there first. When the coast was clear, I came out of the ladies' room and pretended not to know Rattan, who was on lobby look-out. He discreetly mocked my exposed, winter-white legs, whispering out of the side of his mouth, "You look like a chicken," before giving me the green light to head into the theater. I took my place in the last row. Then Rattan and a female detective, posing as a couple, sat ten rows in front of me, while two additional detectives sat at the two entrances to the right and left. The crowd was definitely sparse, about forty moviegoers. I watched as Rattan and his "girlfriend" shared popcorn and pretended to antagonize each other.

The movie was halfway through, and I had become so consumed with it, I'd actually forgotten I was working until I saw Rattan rise from his seat and exit. He returned minutes later and signaled that we were closing shop.

Rattan and I were livid about David's no show. Rattan was especially pissed at having to explain to Selleck why David was not in custody after a three-month investigation. Rattan opted not to reach out to David via e-mail as punishment for his humiliation. But David sent an e-mail the following day apologizing for his absence and asking to reschedule the next day. Rattan decided to torture David; he ignored the e-mail and played the jilted girlfriend role. David bit. He sent Missy e-mails almost daily begging forgiveness and promising to show up next time. In early January, with detectives returning from holiday vacation in great spirits, Rattan gave David another chance to get arrested.

January 15th was the new D-Day. David chose the 4:50 p.m. showing of none other than *Family Man*. *This guy's got some interesting movie choices.* That went over well with the detective unit, who cracked jokes left and right. We went through the same drill as before, except now it was five below zero and I was wearing a miniskirt! I took my seat in the back row and watched the coming attractions as people trickled in. This time the theater actually filled to capacity. With perhaps 150 patrons, I began to feel uneasy, and scanned the crowd to see if anyone resembled the photo of David. I placed my jacket on the seat to my left and my bag of clothes to my right to reserve a spot for him. A young couple sat directly in front of me, stealing an occasional glance and whispering about the freak behind them. I couldn't wait for the lights to dim. Rattan and his "girlfriend" sat seven or eight rows in front of me, enjoying their popcorn. I could no longer locate the additional two detectives who were covering both entrances.

At approximately five p.m., Rattan spotted a man fitting the description of David. The man made a beeline for the top row of the theater, on the opposite side from which I sat. Then he must have noticed me because he proceeded to exit from the same entrance he'd come in, obviously looking for a more direct route. A detective followed the suspect as he made his way to the entrance on my side. Fortunately, David hadn't yet adapted to the darkness and made his way directly toward me. He literally had to step past me to get into the seat I prepared for him next to my bag of clothing. *Don't think I didn't feel like sticking a taser right between his legs and setting his balls aflame. I worried about who I was becoming from this job.* I placed my right elbow on the armrest, keeping my hand in a position that concealed a portion of my face. My heart was thudding through my chest. He was literally a seat away. David and I made eye contact and he smiled at me. I whispered a meek, "Hi."

He said, "Missy, I'm David."

With that I reached into my blouse and pulled out my necklace badge, then grabbed my cuffs from the back waist of my skirt and stood up. "Police, stand up, you're under arrest!"

I had the entire back row fixated on me. David stood up in horror, and I reached for him as he flung his arms out to his sides, bellowing "Noooooooo!" The cavalry arrived, desperately climbing over moviegoers to extract David from his seat. We managed to pull him into the aisle as he flailed and yelled, "I'm not going to jail, I'll lose my kids!" He locked his arms in front of him, resisting as if his life depended on it. There were five of us trying to pull his arms apart to get him cuffed. In the midst of the chaotic scuffle, one detective accidentally cuffed another detective's arms. Meanwhile, my miniskirt was climbing higher and higher up my butt as I tried to stabilize one of David's legs.

Movie patrons became irate, screaming, "Take it outside!" as if it were our goal to make a spectacle out of it all! Half the theater was watching us, and the other half was watching the movie as if it were nothing unusual to have a fight break out in the back row. One patron, watching the mayhem, actually came over and offered his assistance—it turned out he was an off-duty state trooper.

We finally got David into custody and escorted him outside. Cheers and applause erupted from the crowd. My adrenaline level was so high that I walked outside in the bitter cold—still scantily dressed—to watch as David was secured in a squad. I forgot what I looked like until I caught the responding patrolmen smiling at me. I laughed; I'd actually gotten to a point that I didn't care who saw me after the fiasco in the theater. Then Rattan told me I needed to go back into the theater and retrieve one of the portable radios that was *lost* in the shuffle. *He's got to be kidding?* He wasn't. Everyone else had already left, and he needed to get back to interview David. I could not have been more embarrassed. I walked back in and thought, "*Yes folks, the crazy pigtail lady with the miniskirt up her butt trying to arrest some warped pedophile is back!*"

I was spotted by a few fans, and did receive a few more cheers as I scurried past them, shrinking as low as I could, desperately searching for the radio. After a few minutes I discovered that Rattan was mistaken—one of the detectives had the radio in his pocket back at the station. It was no surprise that half of the theater complained to management looking for a reimbursement due to our interruption. Luckily, management was thankful for our efforts and gave everyone a free pass.

Back at police headquarters, David was extremely cooperative and gave a full written statement. He revealed that he had not had sex since 1998 and had *only* planned on having Missy suck his cock and to take nude pictures of her. Condoms and a camera were recovered from his car. He was charged with indecent solicitation of a child and three counts of resisting arrest.

Sadly, after a year-long trial of court continuances, David's reward for his efforts was a mere fine and six months probation. I wasn't sure how many more of these cases I could stomach. Don't get me wrong, I was ecstatic that we were catching these guys; it just takes so much time and effort and the punishment is never equivalent to the crime. It's positively insane!

CHAPTER 24
LESLIE FROM HOOTERS

After my failed Dieter experience, I wanted to make a concerted effort into attracting quality men into my life. I still thought abstinence was the key. Frankly, I was growing more and more disgusted; the pedophiles, Dean's ménage-a- trois requests—just the shallowness of it all. Maybe there was hope for me. I decided to continue keeping the easy men at bay. I'd abstained before with Tony. The last year with him was intercourse free. I felt this was the only way for me to truly evaluate men for who they are.

Boz was his usual supportive self: "Oh right, Lockwood, now you're going to become a nun."

I couldn't blame him for the comment. I spent more time with him than anyone in my life. We were practically handcuffed to each other for over two years. If anyone had an insight into the mind of Lockwood, it was him…and that was a hard pill to swallow. He was the last of the Mohicans in the "decent men" department. If Boz was saying he didn't believe me, I really needed to question what I was trying to do.

In the midst of the Missy operation, Boz and I had been working with Trevor, one of our more reliable informants. Trevor, originally from Tennessee, had a history as a traveling carnie. Tall and lanky with a scraggily goatee and a Southern accent, he loved to get drunk and fight with the police. He had a reputation within our department, having been arrested multiple times for petty theft and minor drug cases. He'd settled in the local area when he impregnated his teenage girlfriend, but was now unemployed, living with the girl and her mother in an unkempt shack of a house.

My first contact with Trevor originated one night when he sat in our lock-up for threatening his girlfriend and requested to speak to "the blonde nark." I had never met him but knew of his exploits. I arrived outside his cell and introduced myself. He said, "Just so you know, this arrest is bullshit! My girl didn't even wanna press charges."

I was certain that Trevor wanted me to help him get out of jail. I asked him why he'd requested me. He said he had heard about this "hot blonde nark" and wanted to meet me. I didn't have the authority or desire to get him out of jail for his alleged crime, but my goal was to extract as much information from him as possible by listening to his sob story, thus building the hottest commodity in law enforcement: "rapport." When he was finished, I expressed sympathy for his plight but explained, "You know it's outta my hands due to the *new* legal ramifications of Domestic Violence cases; besides, if your girl doesn't show up for court, you'll be released in the morning anyway." He believed me and began telling me about some of the local cocaine players.

Moments like these made me so thankful for studying psychology in college. I found human behavior profoundly fascinating and understood that Trevor, although intoxicated, was simply looking for someone to sympathize with his plight. I've found that the more sympathetic we are to criminals, the more willing they are to provide full disclosures of their crimes.

As I suspected, Trevor's girl never showed up to file charges. Several days later, I attempted to contact him but discovered that he'd gone to Tennessee to visit his family for a few weeks. I wrote him off as an informant.

But then, he resurfaced. A female Domestic Violence detective had contacted Trevor to follow-up on a new case against him. Trevor, allegedly, had been drunk and disorderly in the driveway of his girlfriend's residence the night before; when police arrived, he was gone. Trevor contacted me by telephone, assuming that I was the female detective who had left him a message. I didn't ask him anything about his case, but inquired instead about Tennessee and how far along his girlfriend was in her pregnancy. He was taken aback by my concern and volunteered to come into the station to resolve the domestic matter and get to work on drug cases.

In mid-November Trevor supplied Boz and I with information about a guy named Dog, a major supplier of Ecstasy. Trevor told us that Dog would get "boats of X" (1 boat equals1000 tablets) weekly and had three good soldiers to get rid of it for him on the street. Trevor was unable to buy directly from Dog but knew one of the soldiers, Ace, from whom he might be able to buy. Under our direction, Trevor made a series of phone calls to Ace attempting to set up a jar deal (1 jar equals 100 tablets). He told Ace that the "X" was for a chick that worked at Hooters. Ace finally agreed to meet Trevor for the transaction, but never showed. Hours later, after Ace supplied a weak excuse for his absence, we decided to give it one more try. But Ace again called Trevor at the last minute and said that Dog was sold out. Having set up two separate meetings between Ace and Trevor, Boz and I grew weary of Ace's antics. Each time, we had to conduct briefings with our team of detectives, assign vehicles and equipment, and utilize manpower for long hours in preparation for the bust. The fact that Ace stiffed us twice was not going over well with us or the troops.

On November 21, 2002, without Trevor's knowledge, Boz and I decided to have me place an undercover phone call to Ace. I was posing as Leslie, Trevor's waitress friend from Hooters.

Ace answered, "What up? What up?"

"Hi, is this Ace?"

"You got who you dialed."

"Oh [giggle], okay, this is Leslie, Trevor's friend."

"Yeah?"

"Huh…he was trying to buy some 'X' from you for me."

"Do you work at Hooters?"

"Yeah and I need to get a bunch for this weekend."

"How much?"

"A jar if you got it."

"I tried to set it up with Trevor but there's something wrong with that guy."

"Yeah, I know, he's a freak, that's why I wanted to call you. I figured he was trying to rip me off."

"How much did he tell you he could get a jar for?"

"He said $1450…he said they're real potent."

"Shit man, you kiddin' me? That's bogus…I sell my jars for $1300."

"Aw cool, could I get them from you then?"

"Yeah, when you need 'em?"

"You available tonight?"

"Yeah, I'll meet you in an hour."

I was hardly prepared for such rapid success, and repeated "one hour" for Boz to hear. He gave me the thumbs up and started rallying the troops to once again prepare for a buy/bust.

Occasionally dealers try to set up deals on their terms in an attempt to throw off the buyers, just in case they might be the police. They work under the assumption that the police need more time to set up a bust. Had I tried to vie for more time, this may have discouraged him from dealing with me; we had to negotiate on his terms if we wanted the deal to go. We decided we could pull it off.

"You want it or not?"

"Yeah, cool that'll be great. One thing though, I'm at work right now and get off at 4:30, and then I have to run to the cash station, so how 'bout we meet at five?

This bought us an extra thirty minutes.

"Yeah, meet me inside the pool hall on Halsted," he said.

Boz and I preferred to execute buy/busts in vehicles and parking lots in order to keep passersby out of harm's way and maintain optimum control of our surroundings. Quickly I responded: "No, I can't do that, my boyfriend's pals hang out there and I don't want anyone telling him that they saw me there. He's so jealous, he'll kill me if he finds out I'm talking to some guy and that I'm buying 'X'".

"Okay, how 'bout the White Hen on Hermitage?"

"Okay, I'll be there at five. Are you gonna be alone, 'cuz I'm a little nervous doin' this with someone I don't know?"

"Yeah, you come alone too."

Immediately after hanging up, I made a cover call to Trevor. I told him to call Ace in five minutes with the news that Leslie had found a new supplier. That way, Ace would be more trusting of Leslie, thinking that Trevor had been cut out as the middleman. Additionally, Ace would feel comfortable dealing with some silly Hooters waitress who didn't have a clue that Ace was taking her for well over three hundred dollars. Trevor bought my story, called Ace, and then phoned me back to say that Ace was cool about it.

I ran up the rear precinct stairs to the detective division, where a flurry of cops were racing from their desks and grabbing equipment as they headed to the conference room for yet another briefing. The guys were razzing Boz and me relentlessly: "Is this gonna go this time? You know, you're pulling us from more important police related investigations," and, "Why don't you guys give up on this guy already?"

Having had our share of drug deals that did not go according to plan, we were growing tired of this hopeless talk. We taped a banner on our office door that read, "It goes…when it goes," and pointed at it every time someone asked the fateful question.

In our experience, drug deals rarely took place on time, and we'd adapted to "dealer time." We also knew that the razzing was good-natured and even joined in. *Cops live for cut-downs and sarcasm.*

The troops headed out to the White Hen in our trusty beater panel van. The van took a parking spot on the far right side of the lot, while one detective, dressed like a construction worker, posted himself on a pay phone in front of the building. Another detective made his way inside the mini-mart and pretended to be a shopper.

I stayed in the driver's seat of a Jeep Wrangler and waited for Ace in front of the Hen. At ten minutes past five I phoned him, sounding, intentionally, nervous. He said he would be arriving in ten minutes with a friend. I told him I didn't want another person there and was afraid I was going to be ripped off. Ace assured me not to worry, that his friend was just doing him a favor because someone borrowed his car. When I phoned Sgt. Degnan and informed him of the additional criminal, he was not pleased. Degnan was extremely officer-safety conscious and very protective of me. He had been my mentor from the start of my career in law enforcement.

He asked me how I felt about my conversation with Ace. I told him that we should still let the deal go. We had eight police officers on hand—more than enough to deal with a couple of twenty-year-old punks, so Degnan agreed.

I sat in the Jeep with the radio tuned in to a dance music station and took off my jacket to disarm Ace with my cleavage-revealing shirt. I had become accustomed to using my femininity whenever possible as a means of distraction. It had kept me safe in numerous situations.

Moments later, a black Chevy Blazer backed into the parking slot on the driver's side of my vehicle. The driver rolled down his window, looked at me, and asked if I was Leslie. I nodded and confirmed he was Ace. The driver was young and didn't look like much of a threat. Ace was about the same age, thin with short black hair. He appeared nervous, glancing around the lot. I waved him over to my Jeep and pointed to the passenger seat. He jumped inside.

"I'm Ace, nice to meet you."

"You too," I replied.

"So you work at Hooters?" He struggled to keep his eyes from looking at my breasts.

"Yeah, for six months now."

"Trevor called me and said the deal is off, that you found a new supplier. Good job; he doesn't have a clue we cut him out."

"Oh cool, he took it pretty well when I called him."

"Yeah, sounded like it to me too. How did you meet Trevor?"

In order to protect the informant, I try to be as vague as possible when revealing how I met the bad guy.

"I don't really know him that good, he came into Hooters a couple of times and he looked like a burnout, so one day I just asked him if he could get stuff."

"I don't really know him that good either," he said.

There was an uncomfortable pause when he lost his battle against my breasts and saw that I noticed.

He blushed and distracted himself with an impromptu phone call to his buddy; he told him he needed a few more minutes. I was growing impatient; as I'm sure my surveillance guys also were. The "construction worker cop" had been on the pay phone for nearly thirty minutes, watching me occasionally.

I thought at one point that Ace caught him looking at us. He hung up and started to look through the lot again.

I couldn't take the suspense and finally said, "You got the pills?"

"No."

"What?" I asked incredulously.

"I wanted to make sure you were cool and had the money."

I fanned out the $1300. His eyes lit up. He got on the phone and told Dog, "I need the jar for that Hooters waitress…no man, she's straight, I'm with her right now."

When Ace completed the call he told me to meet him at a gas station on Broadway for the exchange in ten minutes. This told us that Dog lived close by. Boz called my undercover phone to check on me, pretending to be my jealous boyfriend. I looked at Ace and put my index finger over my lips.

"Hi babe," I said.

"Are you okay?"

"Yeah, sweetie, I'm at the cash station and I'll be at your house in twenty minutes."

"You got the pills?"

"No, because after the cash station I still have to get gas." I continued with the charade.

"Is this gonna happen, partner?"

"Yes, no later than twenty minutes, I promise."

"My boyfriend is freaking, he wants to know my every move. I have to get going soon," I said to Ace.

"Yeah, yeah, no problem, meet me at the gas station in ten minutes."

After Ace was out of the parking lot, I phoned Boz and gave him the new game plan. Degnan exclaimed, "I don't like this!" as he weighed whether or not he was willing to put me at risk. I told him I felt it would be a sure thing, considering Ace's conversation with Dog, as well as his non-threatening demeanor. With a heavy heart, Degnan permitted us to continue with the operation.

The troops once again rallied and settled into their new positions at the gas station. This time I couldn't see any of them. I assumed the undercover cars parked behind the business and may have been using the bushes next to the gas station for concealment. We couldn't put any of the vehicles in view, because Ace had scanned the last parking lot and surely would have recognized some cars.

I drove into the gas station and parked next to the pumps closest to the building. Ace pulled in moments later, next to the pumps nearest the street. This was a perfect spot for a takedown because it would allow me enough time to get out and give the signal (a stretch with my arms raised above my head), and also allow the team time to get him into custody before he had a chance to split.

Ace made his way toward me and hopped into the passenger seat. He dug into his pants pocket and pulled out a baggy containing a hundred Ecstasy tablets with a Superman logo stamped on them. I placed the baggy down the front of my shirt, smiled and handed him the cash. He counted the money and proudly said, "Let me know when you need more," before exiting my car.

I got out of the Jeep and stretched, all the while wondering where my team was hiding. Within seconds, two policemen came running from the side of the business with their guns drawn, shouting, "Police, get down on the ground!" as they neared Ace. The van and the unmarked vehicle simultaneously screeched up to a piercing halt at the exit and entrance to the gas station. The men scrambled out and ripped the driver of the Blazer from his seat, as two detectives mounted a ground-eating Ace, who was sprawled out on his stomach.

Occasionally, to protect the identity of the informant, I'd stay in character and continue my role-play. *This is where we got to have fun.* Two police officers ran up and shoved me into the hood of the Jeep, "roughing" me up as they cuffed me. I shouted obscenities and continued to be unruly for Ace's benefit. The cops played along: "Ma'am, calm down, you're under arrest—where are the drugs?"

"In my bra. You want 'em? Get 'em yourself!"

I knew they'd be at a loss, because they couldn't actually go through with my request. The job would normally have been given to a female police officer. The problem; *I* was the only female police officer on the scene. I eventually gave in and handed over the Ecstasy tablets. They walked over to Ace and showed him the tablets he'd just sold me. With that, Ace and his accomplice, Mikey, were transported to the police department, as I sat in the back seat of another squad waiting for them to be taken from the scene. Once they were out of sight, Boz uncuffed his partner. We traded knowing smiles and a quick high-five before heading back to the station.

After completing two counts of the Superman X tablets, I realized that Ace had shorted me by one pill. I told Boz before he went in to the interrogation room. As usual, Bosley would initiate the interrogation without me present. He would ask questions like, "How do you know the girl you sold the drugs to?" Most of the time they'd be honest and say she was a friend of a buddy's and they didn't really know her that well. Then Boz might ask if they knew her last name, where she lived, etc. When they said no, Boz would become indignant: "You mean to tell me you just sold a hundred tablets of Ecstasy to some girl you hardly even know? You committed a Class X Felony and you don't even know who she is? Do you think I'm an idiot? Only an idiot would believe a story like that."

They'd become emotionally beaten down trying to convince Boz of their own stupidity, and hence begin telling the truth. This was exactly what happened with Ace and Mikey. With their heads hung low, Mikey confessed to merely providing transportation for Ace, although he had known that Ace was selling drugs but uncertain as to the quantity. Ace laid out all of his cards, giving a full confession. He was more than willing to do anything to help with his case. After consulting with Boz, we decided that we wanted to have Ace go back to Dog and buy a boat of "X." Boz returned to Ace with our proposal.

Ace explained that Dog was very smart when it came to protecting his business and his crib—he had a system in place. As soon as a soldier completed a drug deal, he had to phone Dog immediately and coordinate a plan to provide Dog with his money. If Dog did not receive a call within a reasonable amount of time, he would assume that the cops busted the soldier. Due to the fact that Ace had been in our custody for over an hour, Dog had the advantage.

Boz once again updated me on the grim news. Our goal in Narcotics was to climb higher up the food chain. With Dog's protection plan in place, we needed to brainstorm. We thought that we could have Ace trump up an alibi to Dog for his absence and have Dog meet him, give him his $1300, and still stay in the game. Our risk was having Dog take Ace's cash, then refusing to give Ace any more X as punishment. Boz and I knew our superiors would frown on the loss of $1300. For them, it was too much of a gamble. *Bureaucracy.*

It was decided that Dog would have to be saved for another day and another informant. Boz went back to Ace and explained that wouldn't be able to go any further with Dog, then called me into the interrogation room.

Bosley provided a formal introduction: "Ace, I'd like you to meet my partner, Detective Lockwood." There is nothing comparable to this moment of truth, my only regret was not having a camera in the room. Ace gaped at me as I stood there in jeans, with my gun and badge woven through my belt loops. I said hello and thanked him for being so forthright with Bosley. All the while, Ace remained in shock, unable to respond. Boz smiled at me and said, "Okay, that's enough, get out of here. We still have work to do!" That was an understatement. We had about hours of paperwork to process for our two criminals.

Ace owned up to taking the missing X tablet for his personal use and hiding it in his jacket pocket. He gave a full confession, admitting to selling Narcotics for at least three years and making thousands of dollars as Dog's soldier.

Due to Ace's relatively clean criminal past, he was only sentenced to Cook County Boot Camp for six months.

CHAPTER 25
BOSLEY GETS NAKED

What makes police work so exciting is that it's not all about drugs, thugs and twisted pedophiles. There's nothing mundane about police work, especially undercover.

Boz and I frequented a local restaurant where I befriended the hostess, Bertha, who was extremely forthcoming with narcotics information. She had proven herself reliable six months prior, when she'd coerced Sanchez, one of her busboys, to speak to Boz and me. Sanchez ended up working a case that yielded a sizable amount of cocaine and a pistol. Bertha was more interested in the notoriety of working with the police than any monetary gain—although she wasn't shy when given cash for her drug tips.

On many occasions Bertha would phone me about suspicious patrons or vehicles. I loved that she wanted to get involved; it just seemed that she would call at the most inopportune times: in the middle of a drug bust, during a Narcotics briefing, or while we were in the middle of an interrogation. Most of the time there was some drama surrounding her reports and everything was made to seem exigent. We didn't want to lose her as an informant, so we would drop by her restaurant to listen...and listen and listen.

On my night off, I received a page from Bertha. Recognizing her number, I took a deep breath and debated whether to return her call. But guilt finally got the best of me, so I called.

She began to whisper, "Lisa, listen to this. I have to whisper because if my brother finds out I'm telling you this, he'll kill me. He told me to mind my own business. My brother was making a lunch delivery at this office building and he had to get buzzed into a basement door. He said the place looked really weird and dark and smelled like incense. He asked the big black guy behind the counter what kind of business it was and the guy told him it was modeling agency. Then when the guy paid his food bill, my brother saw some slut wearing high heels and a short silky robe walk out of one of the rooms with her butt hangin' out."

Bertha, single and overweight, was disgusted by this information and expected me to march right over and arrest everyone in the building. I have to admit I wasn't fully prepared for this, and asked her a few more questions before assuring her I would look into the matter.

As comical as I found Bertha's reaction, I knew the case needed to be investigated. The following afternoon, I requested a closed door meeting with Cmdr. Selleck and told him about the suspicious business. He abruptly picked up the telephone to summon Detective Blazer into the office. When Blazer arrived, Selleck said, "Lisa's got some information you might be interested in."

When I finished, Blazer revealed that he'd received an anonymous tip that the business was a massage parlor operating under the disguise of a modeling agency. *Bravo Bertha!*

Boz, Blazer and I took an exterior surveillance to ascertain the gender of patrons who were soliciting the business. After a few days, it was obvious that the business attracted a male clientele ranging from their mid-twenties to mid-fifties.

The next day, Boz and I watched as a woman carrying a white trash bag exited the business and discarded the bag on the top of a closed dumpster lid before driving off. We knew what we needed to do next. We retrieved the bag and brought it back to the department, where we prepared for the glorious job of sifting through its contents.

Not ecstatic about the job, I told Boz to wait for my return before starting. Minutes later, I returned with my sleeves rolled up, donning three pairs of latex gloves and a surgical mask. My hair was pulled tightly into a rubber band and stuffed down the back of my shirt. I even covered my body in a large black garbage bag with armholes punched out. Bosley, who wore only a single pair of gloves, was used to this display and called me a "Nimrod" before dumping the contents onto the floor of the evidence garage. Most of the contents were balled-up paper towels smelling of baby oil; it definitely seemed to be waste from a massage parlor. A few foam take-out boxes and cups, soda cans, cigarette wrappers, and baby wipes completed the inventory. Then my brilliant partner suggested we open the balled-up paper towels. To our repulsion—and elation—we found a used condom. *Pretty jazzy massage parlor!* Through mock gagging, I helped Boz open a few more paper towels and uncovered more of the same. I kept repeating, "I'm gonna Ralph!" until he'd had enough of my whining and barked, "Get out of there! I'll do the rest!" *I absolutely adored my partner!*

We packaged our disgusting evidence and began to brag to a few of the dicks about our discovery. Selleck was pleased and a plan was formulated. He received information that the business advertised in the *Chicago Sun-Times* as a sensual massage parlor with services performed by models for $45 per half hour. Selleck said we needed someone to go in undercover and pose as a client. I immediately raised my hand to volunteer, even though he obviously meant a male. Boz gave me his piercing *You're such a dumb ass* expression.

Not wanting to miss an opportunity to create discomfort for my colleagues I stood my ground and asked, "Why can't I go in? If I act like a lesbian, they may offer me a sexual favor."

Selleck blushed and shifted in his chair, trying to repress an uncomfortable smile before diplomatically replying, "Well you know Lisa…that could be true, it's just that there are different types of lesbians. Some are glamorous and some are more masculine."

Boz and I wondered where he could possibly be going with this. He continued: "You would fit the profile of a more glamorous lesbian and the likelihood of a glamorous lesbian soliciting a sexual massage parlor would be minimal."

I gave him a lot of credit for his quick thinking, but acted mildly disappointed as I told him I understood.

"Now Bosley, on the other hand, he looks like one of those seedy, peep-show-pedophiles."

Boz raised his eyebrows. "Wow boss, I really appreciate that, I'm glad to know you think of me that way."

Sarcasm and insults at their finest.

The solicitation of detectives to work undercover began; I expected a mob to storm Selleck's office for the job, but three declined right away, stating their wives would kill them. One said, "I don't want some skanky prostitute touching my body." That left two men available, Boz and Blazer.

A week later, Boz, who looks more like a construction worker than a cop, took on the "duty" as the first undercover client. He was given a wallet filled with fake credentials and a traffic ticket in lieu of a driver's license. A tactical officer picked up a bottle of whiskey for Boz to gargle with and spill on his flannel shirt as a cover. The gang ribbed him mercilessly about his pending massage: "Watch out for crabs!" and "Does your wife know you're doin' this?" and "Don't enjoy it too much!"

Boz was buzzed into the business and a man requested his driver's license. He handed over his undercover credentials. He then handed Boz a form to complete, including a list of rules regarding conduct with the "model" and a question at the bottom that asked if the client was a Law Enforcement Officer. *Talk about a red flag question. I don't know where these criminals are educated on how to fool the police.* Boz circled "No" and returned the form. The man reviewed the form, requested $45 from him and told Boz to have a seat in the lobby while the model was summoned.

A twenty-five-year-old woman, 5'1", about 125 pounds with dark brown hair appeared before Bosley. She wore a tight, short-sleeved shirt with a plunging neckline, a micro mini-skirt and black stiletto high heels. "Layla" led Boz to the massage room and closed the door, where she informed him that the $45 was just a cover charge. An additional $65 was required for her to perform the massage in lingerie. For $120, the massage would be performed topless, and finally, for $160, Layla would perform completely nude. Boz, being the gentleman that he is, requested the lingerie. (Actually he opted for that because he felt it would be less suspicious for his first massage.) As Layla left the room with Bosley's $65, she directed him to remove all of his clothing, lie on the table, and cover his genitals with a small white cloth. A few candles illuminated the room, incense burned, and numerous body oils lined the shelf. Erotic music played softly from a mini boom box on the floor.

Layla returned and immediately began undressing. She wore a black push-up bra and a leopard print g-string. Layla immediately began tracing Bosley's skin lightly with her fingers, as Boz asked her questions about her personal life. Layla revealed that she was an exotic dancer during the day and had just started giving massages in the evening. Upon the conclusion of the massage she told Boz that next time he might want to consider one of the other two massage options, because they got more erotic as more clothes came off. Boz gave her a $10 tip before departing. He was met back at the police station by a sea of starved vultures. Everyone wanted to know, "What happened?" The initial cheers quickly turned to hisses when Bosley admitted that he'd chosen the lingerie option. Still, we'd received great intel from his massage and were ready to send Blazer in.

A day later, Blazer went into the business and was met by the same formalities, except this time the man behind the desk summoned two women for him to choose from. Blazer recognized one of the females who had been arrested by our department and immediately chose the other. Heather was skinny, small-breasted, and had a severe case of acne. She led Blazer into the massage room, where he was given the options. He chose the topless massage for a hundred dollars—twenty less than the day before. Heather took Blazer's money and re-entered, wearing only a red thong. She lightly massaged his back and legs for a few minutes, then requested he turn over. Lying on his back, Blazer watched as Heather caressed his chest and legs. She asked, "Have you ever been to a massage parlor before?"

Blazer answered, "A few times."

"Do you remember how those sessions ended?"

"The normal way."

Heather reached for a bottle of baby oil and poured it into Blazer's hand, saying, "You can apply this anywhere you want."

Blazer put the baby oil onto his own chest and legs. Heather got onto the table, straddling Blazer's middle and continued to lightly massage him, at times using her hair to trace his body. After twenty minutes, she completed the massage and left the room.

Aside from indecent exposure, we were still at square one. We still needed probable cause to arrest for prostitution and shut down the business. Since Boz had built such great rapport with Layla, the only feasible solution was to send him back for an additional massage.

The following day, Boz "liquored up" again and headed back to the trenches, while Selleck, Detective O'Malley and I waited outside in a panel van, and Detective Burke and two other detectives remained in their unmarked car. We gave Boz a panic button that emitted a series of slow staggered beeps. If he was offered a sexual favor he would depress the alarm, which increases the pace of the staggered beeps, indicating that it was time for the troops to storm the place.

Boz entered the business and was buzzed in by a man. He read the rules of conduct, circled "No," and paid his $45. The man summoned two women for Bosley to choose from. The first one, Alexis, wore a see-through white button down shirt tied in a knot at the waist and a tight pair of black spandex pants with high heels. As the second female made her way down the hallway, Bosley immediately noticed a face full of acne and a head of ratty black hair.

Bosley panicked and, with a hint of urgency in his voice, said, "This one's good," referring to the first woman. The other woman shot Bosley an evil look before storming off. Alexis led Bosley into the massage room and made her offer. Bosley knew that he would request the fully nude massage because of the implications Layla had made previously. He handed Alexis the requested $125.

Alexis returned to the room wearing a robe, put on more erotic music, and allowed the robe to slip down to the floor. She stood naked before him, and then slowly walked to the massage table, where she began rubbing oil onto Bosley's back. She asked him to turn over and began to rub his calves. Seconds later, she jumped onto the table and attempted to grab his penis through the white cloth. Bosley held her wrist and asked, "How much is this going to cost?"

She replied, "It's included in your original fee."

"Great, let me run to the men's room first, I'll be right back."

Bosley leaped from the table, threw on his jeans, and scurried into the washroom, where he activated his panic pager. As soon as we heard the rapid beeps, we drove our van closer to the front door, relaying to the second undercover vehicle to move in. Seconds later, Bosley phoned from the bathroom and advised Selleck that Alexis had gone for the gusto. With that, the six of us rapidly exited our vehicles and ascended the stairs; Blazer peered through the window and was buzzed in. On Blazer's heels, we poured in, shouting, "Police, get down on the ground!" Blazer entered the massage room and discovered a naked Alexis sitting on the table waiting for Bosley's return. Boz stood barefoot and bare-chested outside the washroom, hands spread out above him against the wall. Still in character, he thought he was going for an Oscar: "Oh no! Please don't tell my wife, she'll kill me if she finds out!"

With that, Burke handed Bosley his gun and joked, "Why don't you just shoot yourself now, buddy," completely spoiling Bosley's cover.

We all had a good laugh as I retrieved my partner's shirt and told him to get dressed. The acne girl and Alexis were arrested for prostitution. The guy behind the counter was also arrested for running a place of prostitution.

After our suspects were transported to police headquarters, a man entered the massage parlor. Upon spotting a slew of police officers, he started to make his way out. Burke stopped him and said, "Were you looking for someone?"

"Uh, yeah, I was looking for Denny's restaurant."

Burke didn't miss a beat. "You thought Denny's was in the basement of a commercial office building?"

The man was speechless.

Burke said, "C'mon, man, we both know why you're here; listen, you're not in trouble, just tell us what you know about this business."

The man broke down and told Burke that he had been there once before and got a topless massage—a friend on his bowling team had referred him. Burke took his information and allowed him to leave. With that, Burke suggested to Selleck that he should sit behind the desk and pretend to be the manager, while I posed as a model, to see how many "Johns" we could arrest. The Chief arrived moments later and nixed Burke's idea, shooting him a piercing look of disbelief.

CHAPTER 26
DEA TRAINING

Soon after this, in December of 2002, I had the privilege of being sent to a two-week DEA multi-agency training course in Springfield, Illinois. It was similar to Basic SWAT school in that we were re-introduced to search warrant tactics and case law.

One training day, we were randomly divided into four teams of twelve for field exercises. The DEA managed to acquire the use of a dilapidated prison compound earmarked for destruction. We donned our SWAT gear and supplied ourselves with a full equipment load. As we assembled in the gymnasium, a team of cameramen and a reporter from NBC News arrived.

After a brief conversation between the reporter and DEA Agent Steele, I was approached by the duo. "Lisa, NBC News would like to interview you regarding your perspective on this DEA Course," Steele said. *How the heck did they decide to choose me for this?* I wondered as my heart pounded in my chest.

Wide-eyed, I responded, "Sure."

In my navy blue SWAT uniform, no make-up, and a black bandanna around my head, I answered the reporter's questions. "I felt privileged to be attending the course. The ability to train under a Federal Agency like the DEA was an honor..."

Afterward, we assembled on a stairwell in the prison to begin briefing for our first scenario. Steele explained that three prisoners responsible for killing a guard had last been seen on the third floor of the building. "You have exactly three minutes to devise a plan and capture the offenders," said Steele. A moment later the news crew appeared again. Steele added: "By the way, the news team will be wearing protective helmets and goggles and filming the operation. Who's your team leader?" Five men pointed to me at once. *What? Not again?* "Get your team briefed, Lockwood!" he commanded, before disappearing into corridor.

With the light of the news camera blinding my eyes and eleven men waiting for instructions, there was no time to ask, *How did this happen, again?* Instead I thought, *Of course they want me as a team leader; they witnessed me coolly respond to the reporter earlier and some of them were exposed to my running a successful operation in basic SWAT school. NOT! I was their sacrificial lamb and none of them wanted to be responsible for failing with the knowledge it could potentially be aired on television.* I must admit, I did share that fear, but I'd learned to turn fear into action. I assigned everyone to their positions, performed a radio headset check, and we "went live."

Our team stealthily scurried through the corridor and ducked down into an elevator foyer, where we regrouped. Leaving our hallway cover guards in position, I and six members of the team performed a dynamic entry into the room. Mattresses were strewn about, wall lockers doors nearly pulled from their hinges, as we bellowed, "Police, get down on the ground!" in order to dominate the area. One prisoner was rapidly swooped up by two of my men during the stampede; a moment later a gunshot pierced the musty prison air. The bullet ricocheted off of a metal locker and into the concrete cinder block wall as four of us dove for cover. I found myself squatting behind a concrete support post, watching as two of my men skidded on their bellies out into the corridor. The camera crew found themselves in the middle of our gun battle as I and a hallway cover officer unloaded our weapons into the corner from which the first bullet originated. During our reload, we noted no return fire from the prisoner. Our bunker/shield guy was summoned into the room to approach the corner and move an overturned desk—where we hoped our gunman lie dead.

After a swift sweep of the desk, lo and behold, prisoners number two and three had "expired." No member of my team was injured, and the threat was successfully extinguished. The camera crew and Steele applauded our efforts. A clip of my interview and our prisoner apprehension scenario highlighted the evening news.

I have no doubt I have an angel watching over me.

During my two-week stint in DEA school, I was mandated by the police department to return to town for the annual awards ceremony. At the time, I wasn't too excited about making the two-and-a-half-hour trip from Springfield, attending the two-hour ceremony, then driving back after a full day of training. Bosley and I heard rumors that we were nominated for several awards, and I understood the importance of being there to receive them; however, sleep was consuming logical thinking.

Members of my family and two of my best friends attended the ceremony, where they proudly witnessed Detective (Bosley) Leary and Detective Lisa Lockwood, receive the honor of Officer of the Year 2002. After two years as narks, Chief McCarthy announced to our families, superiors, and colleagues the following:

"These two superb investigators have worked long hours, regularly sacrificed personal interests and have endured difficult and physically dangerous assignments in order to successfully dismantle a number of organized Narcotics operations. These accomplishments were not attained without preeminent dedication and professional skill. Over a twenty-nine month period the Drug unit has made seventy-seven arrests, executed 23 Narcotic search warrants, recovered eight firearms including a Mac-10, seized in excess of $143,196 in United States currency, a Jeep Wrangler, a Chevy Convertible, Pontiac Bonneville and Lincoln Town Car, confiscated in excess of $82,500.00(street value) of illegal Narcotics, namely, cocaine, heroin, hashish, ecstasy, P.M.A. and cannabis and seized 297 counterfeit prescription forms. For their momentous accomplishments in the continuing fight against illegal Narcotics activity, these outstanding investigators are presented with the Officer of the Year Awards in the finest tradition of the police service."

This served as another defining moment in my police career and life. I had finally received what I thought was the most authentic recognition of respect and appreciation for my service to the city. But the drive back to

Springfield was far different than what I'd previously surmised. I replayed the event and pondered, "What more do I want from this career?"

CHAPTER 27
THE END?

Nuzzled fireside on my cocoon-like futon, writing my list of goals and dreams for 2003 was no different than past Januarys. I had asked myself repeatedly over the last year, if money were abundant, what would I love to do in this life? After attending a series of life-balancing seminars in 2001 and 2002, I was beginning to get a clearer picture of what I truly wanted from my life. I wanted to travel the world helping people. I felt so comfortable offering a kind ear, giving advice, and opening the eyes of family, friends and colleagues. People took notice of how I was able to form associations with people from all walks of life. I even had my share of arrestees and informants tracking me down, seeking a connection, and often trumping up some unlikely cover story speak with me. One man, whom Bosley and I put away for seven years said, "The first thing I'm gonna do when I get out of jail is marry Lockwood."

After seven years of law enforcement, I felt I had truly fulfilled all my police desires for excitement, challenge and growth. Many of my superiors and colleagues assumed that I would become a sergeant and even foresaw the chief's position in my distant future. One officer planted a copy of *The Police Chief* magazine in my mailbox and superimposed my head on the front cover. So many people could not understand why I wasn't interested in becoming a sergeant. I remember meeting Officer Hull for coffee on midnight shift before one of the sergeant's exams. At the time, I was a three-and-a-half year veteran and had the specialties of Juvenile Officer, Firearms Instructor, and member of SWAT.

Hull asked, "So, have you been studying for the police exam?"

"I'm not taking the exam."

"Bullshit! They have you pegged as the first female sergeant."

"Well, I'm not sure how that is going to happen if I don't take the test."

"You're so full of it Lockwood, you're gonna be like one of those sleepers that says they're not taking the test and is secretly studying every minute of the day."

"You'll see," I said, giggling.

"Okay. Maybe you don't plan on taking *this* test, but I guarantee you become sergeant on this department."

"Wanna bet?"

"Yeah, I get five hundred bucks the day you get promoted."

"And I get five hundred bucks if I retire or resign?"

"You're only taking the bet to camouflage your intentions; it's all part of your master plan to throw us off your trail. Besides, five hundred bucks ain't nothin' after you get your salary increase."

Again I laughed and offered my hand to shake on our deal.

It's peculiar to me even now that I knew I didn't want to become a sergeant. It was early in my career and like most rookies, I wanted the variety and excitement that patrol and tactical units offered. The duties of a sergeant—running the street, ensuring officers remained in their beats, proofreading officer's reports and disciplining the wayward boys for various infractions—did not seem enticing. I also figured that I had plenty of time to think about that decision later in my career, after I've had years of experience on SWAT and in the detective unit.

Time had flown since my meeting with Hull. I was in flux. Bosley and I were finishing the last leg of our three-year assignment as Narcotic Detectives. My choices were: leave Narcotic Detective and be promoted to sergeant (provided I aced the exams and interviews), go back to patrol, or go for a lateral transfer as a general case detective. But none of those options were compelling. Becoming a general case detective translated to paper and financial crimes. It was the complete opposite of what I was currently doing, and I couldn't imagine spending long hours at a desk or processing crime scenes. Returning to the street as a uniformed patrol officer offered variety and challenge, but I perceived the uniform and the restrictions of assigned beats as a loss of freedom.

Without knowing exactly how I was going to generate income commensurate with my lifestyle, I secretly set my resignation date for December 31st, 2003. That gave me one year to find my dream career. I went through the motions of preparing for the sergeant's exam. I thought I owed it to everyone who had helped my career to at least take the test. Hours passed as I continued writing my 2003 goals. Then I was paged—I was to report immediately to assist the detective unit serving an arrest warrant on an armed robber. I jolted from my cozy nook and bundled up to prepare for surveillance on the frigid winter evening. *One more year, I lamented. Could I really leave law enforcement?*

* * * * *

As I sat in front of the five interviewing members of the Police and Fire Commission, I felt confident. I was congratulated for scoring well on the written exam, and for my new Officer of the Year title. I sailed through the interview, sharing innovative ideas I had for motivating the patrol force, recapping the highlights of my career, and recently receiving my Master of Science degree. I had put so much effort into preparing for the exam for a position I had no interest in obtaining that I needed to question my integrity. I didn't want to let my superiors down, yet I was letting myself down by behaving incongruent.

I started a part-time gig in multi-level marketing in the little personal time I had outside of police work and went into it full steam ahead. Before I knew it, I had hired five cops to work for me. Even though I knew I wasn't passionate about that career either, it would at least give me the freedom to work for myself. So, I concentrated all of my spare time on the new job as a temporary means to leave law enforcement.

During that time I took a trip to Miami to volunteer at another life balancing seminar. On the first day of the event I was approached by this ripped, six-foot hunk named Rock. I soon discovered that not only was he strikingly handsome but he was charming, intelligent, successful, humorous. But, I also learned that the single father of three was from Montreal.

After returning to Chicago, we continued corresponding. Less than two weeks later, he sent a dozen roses to the office for my birthday, which began prompting my colleague's interest.

"Now who's sending you flowers, Lockwood? Another guy lookin' to get dumped or what?"

The guys knew that I broke up with men for what they thought were ridiculous reasons. I broke up with one man for leaving a mark in my toilet. Another guy was dumped for repeatedly knocking on my bathroom door while I primped. Then there was the guy I broke up with for making the most ridiculous faces while we were intimate.

Needless to say, Bosley was always skeptical about the new men in my life and fired off his interrogation: "Is it so hard to find a nice guy to settle down with? Why are you starting something with someone in Montreal? You can't have a future with someone living in another country. Ever heard of 'geographically undesirable?' And he has three kids! C'mon partner, you told me yourself you'd never date a guy with kids. Or is that your intention, another long-distance love affair to keep your single status?"

I couldn't blame Boz for his remarks. In many ways he was right, but this one felt special. Rock was different. He wasn't anything like the other men in my life. He was strong and confident. He listened to me intently and provoked some of the most insightful dialogues about the results I was getting in my life. I had never met a man so well rounded. From what I could see, he was successful in nearly all areas of his life. That's what I wanted: a man who was like a locomotive; powerful, focused, directed and unstoppable. Someone who I couldn't walk on. Until then, although he didn't know it, I thought Bosley was the closest thing to that kind of guy. Bosley would never take my shit, would often put me in my place and call me out if he felt I was being manipulative. He had zero tolerance for *girlie* behavior.

After three weeks of spending countless hours on the telephone, Rock made me an offer I couldn't refuse. "Are you up for something spontaneous?"

"Sure."

"I'm headed to Vegas for a business convention next weekend and would love for you to be my guest. I realize that this will be our first date and don't want to pressure you. I'll get double beds so as not to pre-suppose anything. I really think this would be fun."

I needed all of a millisecond to say, "Absolutely, I'd love to!"

"Great, I'll have my personal assistant phone you later with your flight itinerary." *Gulp.*

Not only was this guy gorgeous and intelligent, he was generous too. "See, Boz?" I said to my partner after receiving this news. "He's the real deal."

"Lockwood, are you crazy?" he shouted. "You hardly know this guy; he could be a fuckin' axe murderer. Have you even checked him out?"

He spoke to me as if he'd forgotten I was a cop and didn't take precautions when assessing men with whom I chose to spend my personal time.

Boz practically wanted me to run his fingerprints before I jetted off to Vegas. When I told Rock what Boz said, Rock gallantly asked to speak to him. I couldn't believe it. Boz reluctantly grabbed the phone from me and abrasively said, "Hello." Rock must've been charming, because as I listened to the one-sided conversation, Boz began to lighten up. He recanted the axe murderer bit by saying, "You can appreciate where I'm comin' from; she's like the sister I never wanted."

Boz winced from the punch I gave him in the arm, knowing he deserved a harder one than he got for that comment.

I, of course, phoned my woman tribe to fill them in on Rock's spontaneous idea for a first date. Not since Dean had they seen me get excited about a man.

Sitting at the gate in O'Hare airport, anxiously waiting to board, three men struck up a conversation with the solo blonde dressed to the nines. They learned that I was flying to Vegas and would be meeting a man for my first date at the Bellagio Hotel. Impressed, they continued to look for ways to poke holes in their perceived competition. "So is he flying you first class?" one of them men asked.

All I had was a faxed flight itinerary and it didn't indicate the seat. I assumed it wasn't and said, "I don't think so."

"Aaaww man, what a cheapskate. If you were my woman you'd be flying first class."

Yeah, right! I boarded the plane without giving it another thought and was astonished when the flight attendant led me to the first class cabin.

Arriving at the Bellagio, I was stunned by the lobby's extravagant décor. I knew that I would have time to check in and freshen up before Rock was due back from his afternoon conference and looked forward to a little downtime to settle my nervous stomach. As I rode up the posh elevator, I became even more excited. I wondered: *Will I be as attracted to him as I was when we first met? Do I kiss him on the cheek to say hello? Does he have sexual expectations? What if the attraction is gone? How do I handle it? Do I fly home early? Yuck. I didn't want to think about that stuff, it made me nauseous.*

I slid my key card into the panel and couldn't believe my eyes. I was speechless. The room was exquisite. In the middle of the king bed (I know, what happened to the double beds for my comfort?) lay a plush stuffed bear, a bottle of Chanel perfume and a note written on Bellagio stationery. It read, *Spontaneous! Get ready for the most extraordinary weekend of your life. I couldn't wait to see you. I'm poolside awaiting your arrival. Find me.*

Is this for man real? I stood stunned, not knowing what to do first. Should I change? No! What was I thinking? I can't have him see me for the first time in a skimpy bathing suit. I wasn't ashamed of my body, but wouldn't feel comfortable waltzing up to him half naked for our first encounter. I decided to wear what I already had on; heck, it was good enough for the guys on the trip here.

After twenty minutes I made my way to the outdoor pool. Like a child stepping foot in Disneyland for the first time I felt as if I needed to rub my eyes to believe what I was seeing. The pool landscape was impeccable. Every quadrant was lined with perfectly manicured bushes and shrubs that lay as a backdrop to Romanesque columns, pillars and water fountains. There were two enormous pools. I wondered, *Where could he be?* I elegantly walked passed the sun gods and goddesses, trying to appear calm and sophisticated. I was in act-as-if mode. *Today I'm a snooty Hollywood starlet who can't be bothered by the goings-on around me. I am directed and focused on doing nothing more than walking around the pool.*

Halfway around the pool, I saw "the Rock" approaching. Shirtless and tanned, he hurried to me smiling, exposing some of the most ripped abs I'd ever seen. If I thought I'd lost my mind before, it was now obliterated. He embraced me tightly, lifting me from the ground, and sighed, "I am so glad you're finally here."

"Me too," I whispered. I felt lightheaded as he took me by the hand and escorted me to a lounge chair, where we sat face to face. He held both of my hands for most of our conversation. We studied each other's face intently as we shared our thoughts. There were no more questions. My insecurity vanished and I was smitten.

Rock played out the weekend as he'd promised: like a fantasy. We shared the first of many kisses on the dance floor as Glenn Frey's band played in the background. We dined at some of the top restaurants Vegas had to offer. We were mesmerized by Cirque de Soleil's performance of "O," rocked to *Mama Mia* scored by ABBA, split our guts through a Rita Rudner comedy act, took a romantic helicopter ride over the Grand Canyon at sunset, exercised at an exclusive fitness center and spent an afternoon indulging in pampered spa treatments.

As our weekend came to a close, Rock escorted me to the taxi stand outside the Bellagio. Every time my turn came up, Rock let two or three people jump ahead of me. We held on, kissing and squeezing with our eyes locked on to each other, as if it were a final goodbye. Finally he asked, "When can I see you again? You cannot enter that taxi until we've set our next date."

It was a no-brainer. "As soon as you can make it to Chicago," I answered. *This was a real invitation.*

I drove off in the taxi, stealing my last glance at Rock as he offered a final wave. I took a deep breath and thought, *he's the one.*

* * * * *

Rock and I commuted between Montreal and Chicago nearly every weekend. I knew from the start that he was *different*. He was passionate, goal oriented, selfless, generous, and consumed by the desire to grow. I'd designed this man in an exercise a year earlier, and literally attracted him into my life.

Assuming Rock was getting used to my police work, I phoned him one evening and nonchalantly explained that Boz and I were spending the night in some family's home because they'd received a Mafia death threat. "Are you serious?" was his response. Jobs of that nature were a piece of cake to me, and I really hadn't thought much of it until I heard Rock's response. *Ooops, I did it again.* I forgot I was a woman, and men (real men, that is) have an inherent desire to protect their women. He continued: "So, the Mafia can actually show up and try to kill them?"

"Um, yeah," I replied.

Still shocked, he asked, "So if they do come, you have to shoot them?"

Biting my lower lip, I thought, well, it's either us or them, but chose to word it differently. "If they do show up, which I doubt, Boz and I will assess the situation and handle it accordingly."

I sounded like I was reading from a police report, but forgot what it was like to downplay my masculinity for a guy. He said, "Where are you now?"

"Watching a video with Boz in their living room and having some popcorn."

Although that was true, I was intentionally trying to downplay the assignment to prove that we weren't in any danger.

"You lead an interesting life," was his closing remark before saying goodnight.

I thought that if a man can tolerate that part of me, without being scared off, he could be *a keeper.*

Within two months we knew that we were soul mates. In April, as I sat in my hotel bed at a Narcotic Conference, he said over the phone, "So you tell me you want to leave law enforcement by the end of the year, you have no desire to become a sergeant and you're attending a police conference of which you have no interest. What is preventing you from resigning right now?"

I loved the way he put things right out there. I explained that I wasn't generating enough income with my part-time job to cover my mortgage and car payments.

"You've also told me that you wanted to write a book about your police experiences…when do you foresee making time to accomplish that with everything on your plate?"

"Great question," I responded.

Then, Rock gallantly proposed the following: "How would you like to live with me in Montreal for six months—kind of like a sabbatical—and write your book? You planned on selling your house anyway and moving downtown, so it's like your plans have been moved up. After six months, we could see where we are and at the very least your book will be finished."

I now sat upright in bed with my sweaty hand locked in a death grip on the telephone and my heart thumping rapidly. I knew I already loved this guy…but, *was he serious? Is this man really offering to take care of me for six months while I disappear into his home office and write a book?* I thought I was dreaming and realized I had *him*. "Oh my God," was my response, "that sounds like a dream." After an eternal silence, I closed my eyes and listened to my heart: "I would love to!"

I gave my thirty days resignation notice to the department. The Chief summoned me into his office to explain my unexpected departure. After listening to my incessant gushing for fifteen minutes about meeting my soul mate, moving to Montreal and writing a book, he said, "Well I can't compete with that." He thanked me for my years of service and dedication to the department and told me I would be greatly missed. Word had spread about my resignation and I was approached by everyone from the custodian (Corey, my special friend) to judges, bailiffs and clerks from the courthouse, all wishing me well.

On May 7, 2003, one day after my seven-year anniversary as a police officer, I left behind SWAT member, Narcotic Detective and Officer of the Year. I handed in my gun and badge and turned the page from one of the most rewarding, exciting, challenging—and dangerous—chapters of my life.

I bid a personal farewell to Boz, who often remarked, "Partner, the day you leave I might cry, but you'll never know if they're tears of sadness or tears of joy."

Bosley's eyes did well-up that day. But I left him knowing ultimately that he wanted me to be happy, even if it meant losing his partner, so I surmised his tears were for both, as were mine.

On June 27, 2003 I moved to Montreal to begin my dream relationship with Rock and his three children. It was time to write the story that I hoped would inspire people by showing them a unique transformation: from a welfare kid into a beauty pageant contestant, a soldier to victim of domestic violence, Swat cop to a man-eater and finally back into the skin in which I was meant to live. A loving, adventurous, nurturing, driven and passionate lady…who just happens to know how to storm a drug house at a moment's notice.

EPILOGUE

Since my law enforcement resignation in 2003, the next chapter of my life has brought me into yet another unfamiliar realm. The contrast from independent Top-Cop/SWAT officer into the role of cherished wife and step-mom has been my most rewarding and challenging role to date. Learning to juggle family life and career ambitions is a book in itself, and I've developed a new respect for working mothers.

As fulfilling as family life is, switching gears so radically has caused me to create new outlets for the adrenaline-pumping addiction I found in police work. In my free time, I've engaged in activities such as NASCAR driving, marathon running, scuba diving, skydiving, hang gliding and snowboarding. *The infamous need for speed.*

In 2004 I became certified in Neuro-Linguistic Programming, Time Line Therapy and Hypnosis. Because of my desire to teach people how to break through their fears and personal limitations, I've directed most of my career focus in the area of personal life coaching and speaking.

Four years into the most gratifying love relationship of our lives, my husband Rock and I have created and co-host a seminar called *Relationship Secrets.* Using an array of tools, our goal is to teach secret techniques that offer insight into having whole, healthy and passionate love relationships.

As for the future, my goals are to enjoy the balance of spirituality, wedded bliss, child rearing, physical conditioning and to continue sharing the lessons I've accumulated from my unique life experiences.

9 781434 302779